THEIR LIVES WERE IN HIS HANDS

"Haul this stuff out into the park," ordered Gudenian, "and then you can go back—if you're anxious to commit suicide."

"We did nothing wrong, we've got nothing to be afraid of. I say we go back now!" cried Dr. Nadine Boden.

"With eight packs gone, eight complete survival kits and eight people missing, you'll have a nice time convincing them it wasn't a planned breakout," said Gudenian.

"That means we can never go back!"

Gudenian grimaced ruefully. "Sorry, Doctor. I didn't have time to ask for volunteers. Cooperate and I'll give you a signed letter saying I forced you into it. My word on it. That goes for all of you, okay?"

But there was no going back. Gudenian, tall and blond and murderously determined, would see to that . . .

Bantam Books by Gordon Williams

THE MICROCOLONY
THE MICRONAUTS

The Microcolony

Gordon Williams

THE MICROCOLONY
A Bantam Book / May 1979

ISBN 0-553-12103-0

Published simultaneously in the United States and Canada

Bantam Books are published by Bantam Books, Inc. Its trademark, consisting of the words "Bantam Books" and the portrayal of a bantam, is Registered in U.S. Patent and Trademark Office and in other countries. Marca Registrada. Bantam Books, Inc., 666 Fifth Avenue, New York, New York 10019.

PRINTED IN THE UNITED STATES OF AMERICA

The Microcolony

THE GREAT PARK

Vulpes Vulpes—The Intruder

All through the night of high winds his tireless legs loped mile after mile under the concrete escarpments of the silent city.

It was two days since he had eaten and now he was in a race against his own death.

When he came to an open space he froze, his wet nose analyzing the wind that buffeted through Man's dying city. A brilliant Moon emerging from scudding white clouds turned his night-hunter's eyes a brilliant green.

He crossed the huge square in a slouching walk, instinct commanding him to travel into the wind, nose and eyes and ears sweeping and scanning the blustering darkness.

Eyes that could register the twitch of a rabbit's ears halfway across a meadow . . .

Ears that could locate the vibration of a human footstep at a hundred yards, or pinpoint the rustle of a vole in a field of hay . . .

A nose that could detect and identify scent-molecules from a chicken-run two miles upwind . . .

In the three days since gale-driven flood waters

had drowned his old hunting ground, he had covered at least fifty miles, moving westward in search of high ground, finding no other prey than a savagely gulped litter of half-drowned rats.

On the edge of a ghostly motorway he froze again. His scent organs picked up lingering traces of Man's poisonous traffic but hearing nothing he crossed the endless ribbon of gray concrete.

At the top of the overgrown verge on the other side he stopped again but the wind carried no messages.

Once again he was back among Man's sterile buildings. Here and there a bird dropping triggered the saliva glands among his thin, steel-trap teeth but the pigeons and starlings and sparrows were safe in their night roosts high in the huge tower blocks.

Coming on rough ground strewn with bricks and rusting metal, he was driven by a sudden upsurge of acrid, fetid odors into a ferocious attack, tearing at stones and bricks with teeth and paws, crunching slugs and snails and beetles until through the gale his ears caught the faint barking of a dog pack . . .

It was almost dawn when he came slinking up out of the muddy water of the flood-swollen river. He tested the air again, then shook his thick red coat and haunched himself down to lick his fur dry.

The wind had died down. In an early dawn light he saw a brick wall surmounted by barbed wire. Instinct warned him that Man was near—experience told him that wherever Man built walls Man had something to protect.

His eyes passed over twelve-inch red capitals on a slowly rusting metal sign:

DANGER—KEEP OUT!
BIOLOGICAL RESEARCH TEST SITE,
POISONED GROUND.
CONTACT IS FATAL.
YOU HAVE BEEN WARNED!

He crossed a riverside path buried under weeds and nosed along under the wall, skirting clumps of bramble, assessing every inch of high red brick for a possible entry point.

Through the still, damp air he heard the yelping of dogs.

His pace quickened.

And then he found his way in. A dead poplar had toppled over where floods had eaten into the muddy bank. The crown of the dead tree was crushing down on the barbed-wire strands on top of the wall. He sniffed round the mass of exposed roots, then jumped onto the sloping trunk and picked his way up to the top of the wall.

He crouched, letting his senses explore the great park. His head cocked this way and that. *Man!*

Man meant danger but Man also meant food, the twin inseparables of his life. He heard loud barking from the opposite bank but went on sniffing, refusing to panic even when he saw the pursuing dog pack.

Scent-traces triggered a variety of reactions, some chemical, the inherited imperatives of his hunter's genes . . . some from specific memories of his own fight for survival, for he was more than a genetically programmed robot. Pictures were his thoughts and from the trees and shrubs and overgrown lawns and decaying buildings of the park came visions of birds and mammals . . . and Man.

A flash of red fur and he was rolling quickly to his feet on a spongy layer of pine needles and heading into the secret hunting ground behind the high wall . . .

Book One

"There is no psychology practiced in this dark hole in the ground, no subtle breaking down of the will. I am simply going to kick the truth out of you. Think about that."

1

Gudenian's torch missed the pale fungus growing round a crack in the floor of the sloping iron tunnel. Magda felt her boots skating on slime. He grabbed her before she fell, his gloved hand stifling her scream.

"Noise carries a long way in these pipes," he hissed. He took his hand away from her mouth. "Not far to go now."

"I'm scared to death," she whispered, clinging to him. His nose touched her cheek. Even through a silk-lined OD suit of rubberized canvas his body tingled at the contact.

A pale gray light brought them to the outlet of the old overflow pipe. The tunnel levelled out in a crunching rubble of dust and dry insect shells. Through fine veils of cobweb she saw a moving glint of greenery.

He took her hand. Realizing he wanted her to push through the spider's web, she pulled back, shuddering in revulsion.

"We're too big for the menu," he said cheerfully, pointing at the roof of the tunnel.

In the half-light filtering through cobweb, Magda made out a large yellow globe. It took her a second or two to distinguish the rest of the spider, a female Segestria, close enough to reach up and touch.

She started to back away, eyes wide with fear. "No . . . no . . ."

He grabbed her round the waist and hoisted her over his shoulder and charged head down through clinging curtains of fine silk.

Warm air bathed her face as they crashed into the pale green stalks of dandelions growing at the base of a great white wall. Gudenian fell to his knees, letting her roll off his shoulder onto a cushion of flat leaves. Shattered dewdrops spattered on her face like fine rain. He stood up, pulling sticky hanks of silk off his head and shoulders.

She blinked.

Rainbows.

Wherever she looked, rainbows, dazzling myriads of them from every drop of dew on every moist leaf, diffusing the glaring sunlight in a kaleidoscopic infinity of color.

He pulled her to her feet and they pushed among the big cool leaves. There was a fetid stench of decaying humus and a great buzzing in her ears . . . and wherever she looked—rainbows.

Then they were gazing out over a vast slope of gray concrete toward the hazy greens and yellows and browns of a jungle that she knew only from rumor . . . *Beyond.*

She tried to pull him back into the shelter of the dandelions.

He patted the mesh-nozzle of his spray gun. "Don't be frightened—the cat is the biggest thing out here and even it runs from the acid-gas."

Again she pulled back. "What if they have a spot-check and find I'm missing?" She looked at him pleadingly. "*Please,* David—"

His fingers tightened on her arm. "Start running—and don't stop for anything!"

The thick soles of their OD boots squeaked on damp concrete as they sprinted across the vast gray slope, hand in hand, two tiny black and red figures on a landscape so huge and empty and exposed she felt giddy, as if they were falling out into endless Space . . .

In sunlight diffused green by huge vegetable leaves the tall, gaunt man strode so quickly along the narrow catwalk the rest of the inspection party was forced into an undignified scramble to keep pace.

The catwalk, suspended on wire hawsers under the mesh canopy of the Net that stretched over Colony One's outfields, began to sway. The tall, gaunt man strode on, the Net's thin lines of shadow flicking across his battered safety helmet and pale, drawn features.

Seeing the single white star on the tall man's helmet, a black-uniformed Security Guard stepped down from his surveillance platform and came to attention.

"Give me your transceiver, son," snapped the tall, gaunt man. The guard's eyes flicked nervously to the oncoming party.

"Give the Controller your radio, Suarez," said Area-Captain Steane, a burly young SG officer. The guard hurriedly unclipped the black casing from his shoulder strap.

"Get on with the briefing, Schwab," growled the Controller, "you don't have too long before they cut that monster down."

"Of course, Controller," said the pink-faced Schwab, Director of Organic Research. He gestured for the inspection party of administrators and agronomists to line up at the handrail. They looked down at a huge swell of waxy leaves thrusting up toward the Net. "That's it, gentlemen, the star of our operation—*Brassica capitata*, otherwise known as head cabbage . . ."

The distorted voice of a Surveillance Ops radio girl told the Controller to stand by for linkup with his office. Below he saw lines of field workers crossing black earth toward the shadow of the towering cabbage. From that height they looked neat and predictable, like ants . . . programmed.

". . . but we estimate a net weight of two kilos," Schwab was saying with obvious pride, "enough to give the whole Colony a fresh vegetable ration for maybe a week. Vegetables are an important source of vitamins and minerals . . ."

The Controller turned away, speaking quietly into the transceiver. The white-tagged administrators joined in a collective shrug. "Yes, it's a nice big cabbage," said a dark, sour man called Wisnovsky, head of the Allocations Office, "but we've grown cabbages before, haven't we?"

Schwab frowned at this grudging reaction. He gestured toward a young man with a hooked nose. "Doctor Ternan is the project leader—explain the significance of this nice big cabbage, Ternan . . ."

Steane, the SG officer, edged closer to the Controller but before he could eavesdrop the tall, gaunt man shoved the radio unit at the guard and turned away, face muscles bunching in anger.

Schwab muttered urgently at the hesitant Ternan, who began reluctantly, showing the customary scientist's dislike of the crude simplifications necessary for a lay audience. "We grew this particular plant from seed to maturity without chemical fertilizer . . . what we did was incorporate a nitrifying enzyme in the cabbage's cell structure—"

"A tremendous feat of biological engineering," Schwab enthused, cutting off Ternan's baffling flow of jargon about macro-nutrients and nitrogen compounds.

Controller Bruce joined them at the handrail, his face even bleaker than usual. He looked down at the massive leaves, heavily curled and veined, blue and gray on the outside, a pale green toward the huge curve of the heart, waxy leaves on which each separate dewdrop stood apart in a silvery shimmer. But for the lacy shadow of the Net there would have been rainbows, he thought grimly.

"Are you saying we can implant this enzyme in all our crops?"

Ternan reacted aggressively to Engineer Grouchy's question. "I never make exaggerated claims! We have a lot of work before—"

"Of course we can," Schwab exclaimed, giving Ternan a warning look. "We can now start to phase out artificial nitrogen fertilizers—another step toward self-sufficiency, another—"

"Another step toward total slavery," Bruce growled, "but what's that compared to a self-fertilizing cabbage?"

The Controller was well-known for his eccentric sense of humor. Only Area-Captain Steane did not join in a general exchange of uneasy, smirking smiles.

At first she was breathless from their climb up the massive honeycomb of half-broken drainpipes and giant shards. Then, when they stood in a shallow curve of red terra cotta near the summit, she found herself shaking. He held his glucose flask to her lips. Some of the warm concentrate ran down her chin and neck. "What's that awful buzzing?" she whispered.

He gestured at the vastness of the purple-blue sky and the hazy greens of the grass and weed jungle. "Bugs."

She shivered. On the few occasions she had been out of Glasshouse the overhead Net had given her some feeling of security. Now, under the open sky, she felt utterly defenseless. He helped her sit down in the curve of the broken pipe and took her hand, drawing it over the rough red clay.

"Warm, isn't it? Soaks up heat, this stuff. I'm telling you, Magda, those bastards tell everybody lies about what it's like out here." He loosened the press-seam collar of his black and red OD tunic, calmly stripping to the waist.

Almost paralyzed with dread of the enormous open spaces above and around them, *knowing* an SG squad had to be searching for them, she did not resist as his strong hand pulled off the close-fitting hood of her warm-suit. He stroked her shiny black hair and kissed her neck. She saw the brilliant haze of green below and the gray expanse of concrete which formed a neutral zone between the teeming life of *Beyond* and Glasshouse. His hands were insistent, opening the press-seam which ran down over the heavy contours of her breasts, peeling off her black and red jacket. At that distance her eyes could make only a glinting blur of the skyscraper which housed Colony One . . . *Glasshouse*.

Terrified of the hugeness of the sky, of the heat and the smells and the incessant buzzing, she pushed him away.

"What's wrong?"

"I think you're mad!"

"You didn't think I was mad those other times in the storeroom." She shrugged. He stood up, a blond giant looming against a sky of purples and blues and gold. "You'll get used to it." He reached for his webbing harness and brought out a flat tin from a belt pouch. "Rub this all over—it's insect repellent."

"It won't repel you, will it?"

He squatted beside her, rubbing her bare shoulder with gray ointment. "You don't seriously think I risked Section Six for a bit of animal lust, do you?" he said gently.

"Don't tell me it's *love*."

"Is that so hard to believe?"

"Everybody knows what the guards are like—you're just bored of dragging female field workers behind a pile of dirt!"

"Yeah, I've done that." His hand moved down her firm white arm. "What do you expect? We're still men—nobody told us we were signing up for a goddamn monastery. I wish I'd stayed at fullsize and taken my chances in the Outlands—my brother did, he deserted from the Central American Zone army and headed up north toward Hudson Bay . . . I don't know if he made it or not but he—"

"Why don't you apply for reversal if you hate it so much?"

He snorted bitterly. "*Reversal?* You still believe that crap, do you?"

"I know two people who—"

"You think they got enough cryogenic labs to keep five thousand fullsize bodies in suspension? You think they'd risk anybody going back Up Top to tell people what the Colony is really like? Anybody who applies for Reversal goes automatically to the Diggings!"

She lay motionless, staring up into the blinding shimmer of the sky, sensing rather than seeing the trajectories of dark creatures beyond her range of vision. He tried to stroke her hair but she pushed his arm away.

His brown eyes stared down at her. "Are you saying you only made love those other times because you were *scared* of me?"

"Everybody's scared of the guards. You said you'd plant Chalk Circle leaflets in my locker—"

"All right," he said coldly, "get dressed."

"Are we going back?"

"I can indulge my animal lust without risking Section Six. As a matter of fact I was stupid enough to think we—"

The ear-shattering drone and the downward blast of warm air came simultaneously with the shadow cast by a huge red and yellow body. For a moment she thought it was an SG helicopter, then she saw the glinting arcs of transparent wings fanning up a storm of small dust-stones that smacked against her face. She stared up in disbelief at a monstrous hairy face with honeycomb eyes and flicking antennae. She started screaming, trying to scramble away on all fours.

He pushed her flat, grabbing for the spray gun. The yellow armor-plating of the hideous face and the huge striped body loomed closer.

Flat on his back, he aimed the mesh-nozzle of

the HASG. A fine mist of foul-smelling hydrocyanic acid caught the giant hornet full in the face.

It turned in midair and zoomed off in a lumbering flight that took it up over the bank of drainpipes and high into the limitless blue sky.

"Only a curious wasp," he said, holding his nose against the stench of repellent acid, "a short blast of this stuff is all you need—"

"It was going to sting us to death!"

He let her cling to him, stroking her lustrous black hair. "It was looking for nectar, not blood," he said gently. "Don't believe the propaganda—most creatures out here will leave you alone if you leave them alone. Bruce and the Arcadia party survived more than a year in the wilds without a Net so why—"

"Hold me," she begged, trembling uncontrollably, "hold me tight!"

A small bell tinkled and the white cat erupted among chattering sparrows, her needle-fine claws impaling a downy youngster whose reflexes were a fraction slower than those of the rest of his family, now screaming indignantly in the safety of a great yew hedge.

The cat playfully mauled the young sparrow but the shock had stopped his heart. She gripped the warm body in her mouth, walking head-high as if proud of her skill.

The official reason for freeing a cat in the great park was to keep down pests. The planners of Colony One, however, had known that while she roamed free in the jungles of Beyond few people would be tempted to leave Glasshouse—even at the theoretical stage it had been obvious the Colony could only be maintained under a regime of maximum strictness. The cat had quickly learned to associate the Net with instant blasts of hydrocyanic acid from the guards' spray guns and now avoided the Colony's outfields.

In a nest beaten down in long grass she delicately shredded feathers and skin, cutting bloody flesh from thin bone with precise, chomping bites of the cutting teeth at the side of her mouth.

A few yards away the sparrow family returned to its feast of grass seeds, chattering happily, danger and death forgotten.

Vulpes Vulpes the red intruder skirted the reedy bank of the park lake, the ammonic scent of Man's cat stronger at every yard . . .

In defiance of field regulations, the Controller had taken off his safety helmet. His gray hair was cropped close to his skull. "Look down there," he said, leaning on the handrail, "what do you see?"

Schwab frowned. On the black earth below, field workers were forming into two lines, spacing themselves along the parallel strands of the steel cutting wire.

"They're looping the wire into the groove made by their axes," he grumbled. "I don't see anything wrong."

Bruce nodded. "And what about the ones in black uniforms?"

"They're guards," Wisnovsky protested, "they're guarding—what else should they be doing?"

Steane edged closer to the Controller. He looked down at field workers forming up like two tug-of-war teams facing in the same direction, taking up the wire and leaning back on their heels. The glinting lines of steel went taut. The shouts of group leaders rose up to the catwalk.

"Is there something we're missing, Controller?" Steane asked, sounding genuinely concerned.

"Yes, you're missing the whole point." Bruce straightened up, easing his stiff shoulders. "I keep wondering—who actually decided to turn Colony One into a forced-labor camp? Was it me—I don't remember signing the order. Or did it just happen organically?"

This time the nervous glances showed no sign of amusement. "We'll see better from this side," Schwab said quickly, crossing the catwalk, carefully avoiding the Controller's eye. Bruce looked down at two piston-lines of field workers pulling alternately on the wire. Warm air fanned their faces as giant leaves began to sway.

Steane kept his voice down. "Are you serious, sir, you really think it's a forced-labor camp?"

Bruce scratched his neck, knowing he had said too much. "I just heard on the radio that Geneva has confirmed those death sentences, Captain. I was upset, that's all."

Steane nodded sympathetically. Bruce turned away abruptly, disgusted by his own moral cowardice, angrily telling himself that he had no choice . . .

Vulpes Vulpes the red fox stood fifteen inches at the shoulder. Before the long trek from the floods he had weighed almost twenty pounds but now he was beginning to show signs of emaciation. Weakened by hunger, his clumsy rush into the flock of sparrows succeeded only in scattering them back up into the yew hedge.

He chewed at some grass stalks. He was hungry enough to wolf down a big black slug. Then he picked up the cat's scent again. In lean times he had eaten cat before, the flesh was of a fellow carnivore, rank and foul but still eatable if the alternative was starvation. The one part of him now dull with fatigue was his hunter's brain. He came from countless generations of ruthless survivors—caught in one of Man's iron traps his mother had gnawed through her own foreleg, silently enduring the self-inflicted agony, then learning to survive on three legs, eating frogs and worms and beetles and the carcasses of birds decaying under electrified fences.

He heard the cat before he saw it. His head moved this way and that, taking bearings on the deep purr, moving forward through long grass one slow step at a time.

The cat's small, pink tongue rhythmically sandpapered a wet-smooth path across the white fur of her haunch.

Vulpes Vulpes made no noise, not even of breathing. In strong sunlight the vertical ellipses of his pupils narrowed to hairline slits.

Through swaying grass he caught a glimpse of white fur.

The cat stretched luxuriously. With a lazy, voluptuous precision, she dragged her forepaws down the jagged cornerpost of an old summer house now disappearing under green creeper. A small silver bell attached to a thin leather collar round her neck tinkled softly as she padded at scarred, splintering wood with her extended foreclaws, balancing gracefully on her hind legs, a sensuous killer-queen relaxed and secure in her private domain.

Red fur exploded from the greenery in a ferocious, snarling rush.

2

The giant cabbage hit the ground in a crunching of big leaves and then the crump of the cannonball heart. High on the catwalk under the Net the inspection party heard workers cheering.

"It's only a question of proper motivation," Schwab said with pompous satisfaction, "I insisted that they were made to feel part of the project and not just labor units."

With a straight face Steane said, "A guard was spattered with mud, sir."

Schwab waved irritably at the party to make for the descent landing. Field workers were already clambering over the huge leaves. Steane kept close to the Controller, speaking in a murmur.

"You don't think the Chalk Circle ringleaders should be executed, sir?"

Bruce gave him a curious glance. "You must be pretty naive, son."

"There's a lot of us would follow where you lead, sir."

Bruce quickened his step. "Well don't tread on my heels!"

They were on the ladder scaffolding when the

cat's first tortured scream broke over the outfields like a cry from the damned in hell.

His naked body stretched limply beside her on the warm red clay. She kissed his shoulder. "I'm glad we risked it."

He smiled. "Let's stay out here forever . . . can't you see me as a savage hunter?"

The tip of her nose traced a feathery path across his skin. "I thought you were just a typical Security bully—"

"You were right."

"I'm serious. I hardly know anything about you. Why did you volunteer for the Colony?"

He grunted bitterly. "They made it sound like an adventure—saving humanity on full rations." He kissed her hand.

"They promised to train me as a nurse. I always wanted to work in a hospital for children . . . David —will we be able to come out here again?"

His powerful right arm held her against his chest. "If those bastards think they can stop us they—"

It came from a bank of greenery only a few feet away from the stacked drainpipes, a horrendous scream exploding across their naked bodies in a battering gale of sound . . .

The white cat weighed nine pounds. In her year behind the high wall she had lived well on birds and rabbits and mice and cavies, growing fat and lazy, learning she had nothing to fear in the great park.

Vulpes Vulpes knew how she would fight. In his first savage rush his jaws aimed for a point behind her head, where one brutal jerk would snap the cat's neck before it could use its foreclaws to blind him and its steel-spring hind legs to disembowel him.

Instead his teeth clamped into ribs and soft belly. Their interlocked bodies rolled through weeds and creeper, lashing up a storm of leaves and dust and insects.

But for the weakness of hunger the fox would

have opened his jaws for another murderous lunge—instead he held on, knowing his strength was failing, crunching into white fur, denying the cat any chance to escape.

Bowled over and carried two yards by the first impact, the tortured cat ripped and tore at the thick red coat, desperately contorting in electric convulsions, trying to get her claws at the fox's eyes and nose.

High above in the shallow curve of the broken drainpipe, Magda was paralyzed with the shock of that first awful scream. Gudenian shouted at her but she had no strength in her legs. He snatched at their scattered clothing and the HASG, trying to drag her into the shadowy tunnel of the unbroken section of the pipe.

The fox shook his head violently, trying to crack the cat's neck like a whip. Red bubbles burst in a spume of blood where his curled lips and nose were buried in white fur. He started jumping round in circles, flailing the cat through the air, giving it no leverage for the savage upward kicks of its powerful hind legs.

Then his teeth met through the cat's belly.

Her scream sent every bird in earshot flying up into the trees.

The fox sensed a weakening. He momentarily released the grip of his jaws, feeling for the spine.

In that moment the cat's hind legs lashed across his face, steel-spring claws raking through his left eyeball.

Their threshing bodies smashed into the bank of drainpipes. Magda was thrown to one side. The pipe moved with a lurch, tilting out from the stack. She started to slide. The pipe lurched again.

Looking down she saw red fur and white fur joined in a giant dance of death.

With his full weight smothering the cat's convulsive jerks, the fox's teeth met with a crunch through the thin, hard neck. Life went out of the cat in a last orgasmic shudder.

Magda's fingers clawed on tilting clay. The pipe lurched again with her weight as she slid back toward the outer edge.

Then she felt his hand snatching at her ankle. Flat on his stomach, trying to keep his weight in the middle section of the pipe, he tried to drag her back from the sloping edge.

She was yelling incoherently, twisting round to clutch at his arm. He moved back slowly, sensing the sway of the loosened pipe. Her fingers clawed red weals on his bare shoulder.

Vulpes Vulpes listened. Through the chattering of birds he heard a small voice of Man. He seized the dead cat with a gulping toss of his head and started to trail the carcass between his forelegs. The little silver bell tinkled dully. His bloodied, torn nose rapped against something hard.

He dropped the cat, baring his teeth, puzzled by a strange sensation of blindness. Again he heard a distant voice of Man. He moved his head this way and that. He saw the stack of drainpipes into which he had bumped. It took him a few seconds to understand that his left eye was in darkness.

Raising his nose he detected a warm and close scent of Man.

Teeth clamping on white fur stained red, he slunk quickly into the shadowy heart of a massive rhododendron bush.

Two field workers began to pump the buggy-car lever. Wooden wheels lurched and then rolled forward on tram lines which ran in a long curve across black soil and through the towering vegetable crops that fed Colony One.

Steane stood beside Bruce at the rear of the open buggy-car. They had their backs to the rest of the party. "Surveillance Ops located the cat's screams as coming from somewhere to the north of Glasshouse, sir. There are no entrances on that side—I'm sure it's nothing to worry us."

"When we were in the wilds we learned never to

be sure of anything," Bruce said drily. He raised his voice. "Anybody care to guess what was attacking the cat?"

"They like to yowl," Wisnovsky said dismissively. "It's probably in heat."

"Let's hope tomcats can't get over twelve-foot walls," joked a young agronomist.

Bruce shook his head but said nothing. They passed a plantation of tree-sized carrots where a team of field workers and a caterpillar-tractor were wrestling to haul a partially exposed root out of black earth. As the tractor moved forward its vulcanized rubber belt tautened round the red shoulder—and the carrot gave a sudden jerk.

The broad belt slipped its hold and slashed through the sawn-off stalks, flailing into scattering field workers. The sudden release shot the tractor forward in a lurch which threw the driver clean over the tractor's yellow engine casing.

Bruce saw workers picking themselves off the ground, watched idly by the lounging figure of a black-uniformed guard, with his spray gun for repelling insects and his long-barrelled pistol for controlling the workers.

The two grunting field workers pumped the lever and the buggy-car ran under one of the criss-cross stanchions supporting the Net. He saw men and women carrying soil in baskets, digging holes for seeds, tunneling into the bank of a potato furrow. For a moment he felt a sense of humility—the ever-present black silhouettes of the guards might annoy his ego, for he had always nurtured a secret image of himself as a benevolent patriarch, but there was no denying the visible energy and ingenuity that the Colony had inspired. Ego, that was his trouble, the same self-willed obstinacy that had led him into voluntary exile in the Outlands rather than face the hurly-burly of collective human society. For years he had deluded himself that it was the stupidity and brutality of his fellow men that had isolated him but . . .

Looking round he caught Schwab's eye. His rueful smile was intended as an oblique apology for the sour note he had brought to Schwab's moment of triumph but the pink-faced head of Organic Research quickly looked away.

Bruce felt his temper rising again partly at Schwab's prim disapproval, partly at his own moment of weakness. The hell with it, people *were* stupid!

At the first line of electrified fencing they passed into the shadow cast by the towering mass of Glasshouse. Guards checked them through the sentinel point and they closed their eyes through a fine spray of disinfectant from an overhead gantry. The buggy-car creaked across a barren landscape of gray concrete, the neutral strip where any invader, insect or mammal, became an open target for poison sprays or bullets. High above, on a ledge jutting out from the glass escarpment of the old Victorian hothouse, he saw the rotating windmill vanes that supplied most of the Colony's electricity, while technicians and scientists worked on solar energy projects involving amorphous silicon barrier cells so that the conspicuous windmills could be replaced by flat panels which would draw less attention to the micro-colony's existence.

The tram lines ended at the foot of the white brick base wall. Only Bruce bothered to thank the two field workers on the crank handle. Their sweating faces responded with sullen nods.

The inspection party filed past a guard and entered a steeply sloping tunnel with narrow concrete steps. They climbed in single line toward a bright electric light over a steel door.

"That's the question, gentlemen," Bruce said in a loud, mocking voice. "Was the cat screaming in agony or ecstasy?"

Schwab looked over his shoulder at Wisnovsky. Bruce's removal was now a matter of urgency.

Running hand in hand across the flat expanse of concrete she almost tripped, trying to look back for the giant red fox. Gudenian yelled at her to run faster and they crashed into the narrow strip of dandelions. This time she did not hesitate. Lowering her head and closing her eyes, she burst behind him through the newly repaired web. She did not get her breath back until they were far into the cold darkness of the iron tunnel.

She was shaking.

"If you hadn't caught me . . . ! I was looking right down on them! Monsters!"

He took her hand and started up the iron slope. "They'll have to know," he said ruefully.

"Know what?"

"The Net won't stop a goddamn fox!"

"But . . . tell them we've been outside? They'll put us in Detention!"

"You want to risk the life of everybody in the Colony? They don't have to know you were with me —I'll think up some kind of story for that bastard Lindsay. He might even give me a commendation."

Vulpes Vulpes crunched and cracked through fur and bone, gulping down rank flesh and white fur alike, gnawing at the sightless eyes. The pain from the gory socket of his left eye throbbed through his head but he did not whimper.

Soon only a bloody skull and a few bones and a small silver bell on a thin collar were left to prove that the white cat had ever existed.

3

TO: CHIEF OF STAFF, WORLD FOOD CONTROL,
GENEVA.
FROM: BRIGCOM, LONDON.
REF: CS/53/11/4/91.
MESSAGE: LONDON GARRISON NOW STATUS TOE-HOLD. EVACUATION OF NONESSENTIAL PERSONNEL NOW COMPLETE. ACTIVE GARRISON STRENGTH FIVE HUNDRED AND FORTY-THREE. METERIOLOGICAL PROJECTION COLD/WET THROUGH APRIL. FLOOD LEVEL CONSTANT. FOOD SUPPLIES ADEQUATE TWENTY-FIVE DAYS, PETROL THIRTEEN DAYS, WATER SIX DAYS. CIVIL POPULATION HOSTILE, MAJOR RIOTING. SENIOR MEDICAL OFFICER ESTI-MATES TYPHOID LOSSES SERIOUS AND INCREASING.
FAIRFAX.

Chief of Staff Voigt had to wait twenty minutes before the Commissioner's secretary led him into the big conference room.

Commissioner Canetti read the signal twice then sighed despairingly. "I'm reluctant to abandon London, Dieter."

Voigt was well-practiced in the art of pushing the philosophically inclined Canetti toward the correct decision. "In that case, sir, we can deploy reinforcements from France. I'll check on tanker capacity—petrol and water are the obvious priorities—"

"On the other hand, is London worth it?"

Canetti adopted one of his favorite poses, that of the great man wrestling with insuperable problems, elbows resting on the green marble table, splayed fingertips pressing on his forehead.

"Policy has always been to keep a strong military presence in London for strategic reasons—"

"You're wrong, Dieter. We've held onto a lot of these major cities purely for psychological reasons. Agrarian dispersal—when I was in New York last month that's all their zonal heads could talk about. It makes sense—it reduces the strain on security forces, it produces a self-reliant and self-supporting population." Canetti licked the tip of his middle finger and drew wet lines on marble. What significance this was meant to have Voigt could only guess at. "They're even claiming a slight population increase in their Middle West zone—"

"These floods haven't given us time for a phased dispersal of the London population, Commissioner . . . that's if typhoid leaves any civilians to disperse."

Canetti took on an air of tragic contemplation. Voigt watched him impassively, knowing the ritual could not be rushed. The man was all posturings and hot air, a kind of human smoke circle, but his very lack of substance meant that he could be manipulated. Many people wondered why Voigt showed no signs of wanting the top job for himself. Voigt knew the answer to that. To all intents and purposes he *was* the Commissioner. He took the decisions, Canetti carried the unpopularity.

"That's where our future lies," Canetti was saying, "not in vast new programs for oceanic cultivation but in thinly spread peasant societies . . ."

Voigt let him ramble on until he was repeating himself. "There are difficulties—if you're considering a withdrawal from London," he broke in. "The civilian population won't like it—and with the amount of transportation involved it couldn't be done in secret."

Canetti stood up, easing his shoulders, sighing dramatically. "That old bastard Towne had it easy—people were starving in millions, decisions were simple. You did it his way or you died. We're in a gray phase, Dieter, we've stopped the mass deaths, we've sensibly limited our responsibilities to viable scheduled areas—we're holding the line. But where do we go from here? Coastal communities living off the sea? A static society of medieval villages? The grain blight seems as virulent as ever—even when it's been dormant for twenty years!" He closed his eyes and stood with his head bowed. "Europe, Dieter, the place where modern civilization was created—*my* responsibility . . . do we struggle to keep the flame of thousands of years of culture alight? Or do we . . ."

As always, Voigt kept an attentive face, nodding where required, all the time thinking of the poor bastards fighting off the London mobs. He had served the three commissioners, each of them suffering from delusions of historical significance. The truth was that people accepted the authority of World Food Control because it could send food from one place to another. When their bellies were full they occasionally showed signs of wanting to revive the old nation-states; when their bellies were empty they would crawl to *anybody* who could give them a loaf of synthetic bread.

"I'm glad I don't have your awesome burden of responsibility, Commissioner," he said when he decided Canetti had been indulged enough. "As you say, whatever we do with London has important psychological implications—"

"You don't know how true that is!"

"To withdraw might be taken as an admission that WFC can't control one of Europe's greatest cities—"

"That's a defeatist interpretation. The media will call it part of our farsighted policy of encouraging self-help—"

"It might encourage an upsurge of national separatism."

Canetti became petulant. "The British have been nothing but trouble ever since the famine started! They're only interested in cooperation when it means taking. I'd like to teach them a lesson. No, I've made up my mind—we withdraw." He hesitated. "Can it be done?"

"The best way might be to hand over to the civilian government infrastructure the moment we're ready to pull out—our troops can be withdrawn while they're making whoopee in the food stores."

Canetti made a fist and punched his palm. "That's the way! In two or three months they'll be begging us to go back in—and they'll be the most docile population in Zonal Europe!" He frowned. "What about the cloning project—have you thought of that?"

Voigt nodded seriously. "Yes, that is a problem, Commissioner. We could leave a small detachment of Rangers—"

"If Colony One can't survive on its own for a couple of months then Special Research has been conning us. I'm surprised you'd even suggest risking soldiers' lives for that damned project—I inherited it and frankly I would've abandoned it but I can't afford to antagonize the scientific establishment. They're projecting a budget of *millions*—fifty thousand crossovers in the next twelve months! Well, this is a good chance to put it on trial."

"It's useful, of course."

Canetti snorted. "So far it looks like a dead end—we're not in the business of saving individuals, we've got to find new dimensions for the future. Until they prove to me those micro-cloned people can produce babies I'll maintain the project at a minimum budgetary level for one reason only."

He looked pointedly at Voigt. The Chief of Staff had heard it all before, indeed had instigated the policy. But Canetti's ego had to be fed its full ration of tidbits.

"Siphoning off excess population?"

"Siphoning off troublemakers!" Canetti's grin was childishly triumphant. "Am I glad *we* decided to keep control of the selection process! Our little secret, eh Dieter? Colony One—the biggest concentration of careerists and misfits and criminal adventurers since the California gold rush! All in the name of science."

Voigt gathered his papers together. "Perhaps it's just as well they can't reproduce . . ."

"They'd be a threat, even at that size. Like a marching column of soldier ants—the first hundred you can squash flat, the next hundred thousand will be picking your skeleton clean!"

As always, Canetti put his arm round Voigt's shoulders to steer him to the door, a clammy intimacy which the Chief of Staff endured as part of the price that had to be paid to keep the performing dog jumping through the correct hoop.

TO: BRIGCOM, LONDON.
FROM: CHIEF OF STAFF, WFC HQ.
REF: DV/109/ 12/4/91.
MESSAGE: TOP SECRET. TOTAL WITHDRAWAL LONDON GARRISON TO COMMENCE 0600 HOURS 16/4/91. INSTRUCTIONS REGARDS PUBLIC ANNOUNCEMENT, HANDOVER OF AUTHORITY AND MOVEMENT SCHEDULES FOLLOW. VOIGT.

4

"Eighteen hundred hours in the Table Room," growled the deep voice, "and it isn't a request, it's an order!"

Against a golden flood of sunshine from the plate-glass window that formed one wall of the long, bare room, Annette Rosa saw the Controller only as a dark silhouette.

Bruce slammed down the phone and glared at Sasso and the tall black girl. "Annette Rosa from the Information Office, Controller," said Sasso, a small jumping-bean of a man. "She's taking over your eagerly awaited masterpiece from Haskins."

Bruce reached for the phone again. "It will have to wait."

Sasso smiled apologetically but she stepped up to the rough trestle table. "Director of Information Bello asked me to see you urgently, sir, there have been so many holdups . . ."

Sasso winced, expecting his master to wither the poor girl. "The holdups were caused by Bello," Bruce said irritably. "What happened to Haskins anyway?"

"I'm not really sure, sir."

"I smell censorship." Then he shrugged. "You're certainly prettier than Haskins—okay, I'll give you half an hour. Sasso—make sure all members of the ICC know this meeting is compulsory."

"What about the Commandant of Security?" asked the stocky little Argentinian. Bruce gestured at the black girl to sit.

"I wouldn't use the word compulsory in his case —just say I'd appreciate his presence."

When Sasso closed the door he leaned back, marvelling at the girl's vibrant, athletic youth. But then, all the colonists looked young to him—young and innocent and deadly serious.

"They didn't like the way Haskins handled the Arcadia stuff, that it?"

"Not exactly, sir—everyone thinks you handled the original illegality with considerable tact."

He smiled ironically. He remembered Commissioner Towne threatening him with certain death in a permafrost labor camp if he did not cooperate in locating the secret project set up illegally by George Richards . . . he remembered Khomich slaughtering four shaggy men on a long, empty road in faraway Finland . . . was it tact to suppress these things—or was it cowardice?

Her first minor questions prepared gave him the drift of the censorship. Arcadia had been a bid for power by George Richards, yet his megalomania had given birth to the whole concept of micro-cloning as a possible escape route from a starving world. But for Richards there would be no Colony, no mass cloning program now being prepared at WFC HQ in Geneva; Colony One was the pioneering test bed and soon they would be crossing over in their thousands, opening up the strangest frontier Man had ever faced.

Old Commissioner Towne had destroyed the original garden known as Arcadia with a murderous but politically correct brutality; he could not be criticized overtly for there was another commissioner in Geneva now, like all powerful rulers exquisitely sensitive to the slightest nuance of criticism, however oblique.

The trick was to give Colony One historical legitimacy. And if history had to be rewritten . . .

"How old are you, Annette Rosa?" he asked, interrupting a question about Arcadia's system of safety shelters.

"Twenty-two, sir. I crossed over nine months ago."

"Twenty-two? You know you haven't smiled once since you came through that door?"

She looked at him steadily. "What do you suggest I should be smiling about, sir?"

"You're a living miracle—isn't that a good enough reason?"

"As you don't have much time shall we try to cover as much ground as possible, sir?" she said briskly. "According to the stuff you gave Haskins five of you escaped from the burning garden—but only three survived. The two who died were . . ." she scanned her pages of notes . . . "Corporal Fitzroy Carr and . . . Doctor Anne Richards."

"Your generation should flourish if there is a new Ice Age on the way."

"Pardon?"

He tilted his chair back until he was almost horizontal, swinging his feet onto the desk. "Anne died of blood-poisoning—tetanus, otherwise known as lockjaw. She probably picked up the bacillus from a scratch—you live pretty close to the soil out there. Poor Anne . . ."

"And Carr?"

He grunted. "I suppose it's policy to pile on the horrors—make people so terrified of the wilds they'll cling to this Colony like social insects. Okay, let's pile it on. Carr was one of these impetuous macho types you've probably only read about—plunge in first and ask questions later. He found a bumble bees' nest and thought we would all like some honey." He glanced over his sandals. For the first time she was looking uncomfortable. "Aren't you writing it down? Carr was stung half a dozen times—once would've been enough but insects don't think like us. You could call it a quick death . . ."

She started writing quickly. "It's not a case of distorting things to suit a propaganda line," she said defensively, "it's very dangerous out there in Beyond and people ought to know. Don't you think that's right, sir?"

He grimaced. "Three of us survived for more than a year."

"You had weapons, of course—"

"Common sense, that's what kept us alive. Everybody imagines the wilds are full of bloodthirsty predators just waiting to snap up anything that moves. The number of times people have asked me about goddamn weasels!" She shivered audibly. "What most people don't realize is that most of these predators hunt by smell—as long as they didn't see us we were pretty safe. Small as we are, we still have the good old human stink." He glanced up at her again. "Aren't you writing that down?"

"I don't think we want to stress anything that makes Beyond seem attractive, sir."

"Things may be grim but it's absolute hell out there so don't complain." He yawned. "I don't suppose it matters, I don't see many people with the guts to break out of this place."

She hesitated. "Speaking off the record, sir . . . I don't agree."

"Oh?"

"If it was my decision I'd make everyone read it exactly the way it was."

"Be careful—heresy isn't normally considered a plus-factor in a bureaucratic career."

"If you don't mind me saying so, sir—if I'm a bureaucrat you're top of the heap."

He looked at her in mock astonishment. "An emotion? Congratulations!"

"It's your system that's made it dangerous to show emotions!"

He sat up abruptly. "*My* system? My dear girl

—this Colony is run on strictly scientific lines laid down by the best brains in the Research Division!"

"You're Controller-in-Chief."

He was puzzled by the sudden change in her attitude. Did everybody in the Colony have this instant aggression just looking for a priming-charge? "Well?" he demanded. "What's the complaint? We eat a nutritionally adequate diet while millions Up There are still at risk. Did you know there's bubonic plague in Greece? We have almost quarter an acre under the Net, making five thousand of us damned near self-supporting. You know how many millions starved to death when grain blight first hit us?"

She was not abashed. "Is the philosophy of a full belly all we have to look forward to?"

"What the hell do people want?" he growled. "We're a test-bed society—five thousand human miracles, identical cloned-twins of the bodies we used to inhabit but thirty-five times smaller. How many achievements do you expect all at once? We're not just laboratory freaks either—we've got our own solar heating, windmill generators, micro-forges, micro-lasers, electronics will be next, textiles . . ." He stood up and turned to look out of the big window at the endless mesh of the Net below . . . "And today we harvested our first self-fertilizing cabbage . . ."

A moment's silence left him feeling almost nervous.

"That will be good news for the three condemned machinists." The hostility had gone from her voice but that only angered him. What right did a 22-year-old girl have to call the psychological shots?

"I've called a special ICC meeting about the death sentences. I'm proposing we commute them. What the hell's this got to do with—"

"And if the Coordinating Committee refuses to commute them?"

"It's out of my hands then, isn't it?"

She stared at him. He experienced a wave of guilt and then anger of an intensity he had not felt in years. Before he could think of something to say that would remind her of their respective positions she produced a sheet of yellow paper from inside her coarse gray blouse. "This might interest you, sir."

He let her put the yellow sheet on his desk. Appearing only half-interested he turned it without picking it up. It was a hand-printed pamphlet headlined BETRAYAL! On each corner was a neat red circle.

He stared at her in disbelief. "This is a Chalk Circle leaflet!"

She nodded. For a moment she looked very young and vulnerable. "Yes, sir."

He raised his hand to silence her. "Whatever you're going to say I don't want to hear it! You could be slammed in Detention just for carrying it—why give it to me?"

"Maybe I believed all that crap about humanity in your book, sir," she said bitterly.

No sound from the outfields far below reached Tier Five of the inner wooden structure known as Control. The red-haired man who sat with his back to the outer wall of glass took a slow sip of water from a beaker. Through the big window the late afternoon sun was a holocaust of golden fire.

Deputy-Commandant Lindsay, number two in the Security Division, looked up slowly at the big blond guard standing to attention in front of his shining metal desk.

"Why didn't you report this drainage pipe when you first found it, Gudenian?"

"I've heard there're apples in Beyond, sir."

"Apples?"

"We don't get much fruit, sir."

"Nobody does—in April. Who else knows about this tunnel?"

"Only me, sir."

"Are you a member of the so-called Chalk Circle movement?"

"Of course not, sir."

"We have a twelve-foot wall regularly patrolled

by WFC Rangers. How do you suggest a fox got into the park?"

"I don't know, sir."

"Did somebody instruct you to spread this alarmist rumor to panic the field workers and disrupt production?"

Gudenian flushed. "You think I'd voluntarily admit to breaking Section Six if I hadn't seen a fox . . . sir?"

Lindsay emptied the last drops of water in the fired-clay beaker onto a big cactus growing in a pot on his windowsill. "I don't like submitting my own men to Interrogation, Section-Leader, but I just don't believe you. Apples in April?"

"Interrogation?" Gudenian frowned incredulously. "I report the biggest menace the Colony's ever faced and you're sending me to *Interrogation*?" He took a step toward the desk. "I want to see the Commandant—"

"Guard!"

Gudenian looked round as three white-strapped SD guards came through the door from the outer office.

"You can discuss this with Captain Jimenez," Lindsay snapped, "or you can tell me the truth."

"I'm telling you the goddamn truth! There's a fox out there—"

"Take him down to Detention."

The three white-straps caught hold of Gudenian. When he struggled one of them rammed a heavy wooden baton into his stomach. His toecaps trailed noisily on wooden planks as they dragged his retching body into the corridor.

Lindsay closed the door behind them, crossing the long window-room to the door of a small cubicle where Area-Captain Steane was writing at a trestle table.

"Almost finished, sir."

Lindsay picked up one of the handwritten pages. He raised his eyebrows. "Did Schwab and the others hear him say these things?"

"Some of them, sir." Steane shifted uneasily on a shaky stool. "You don't think Gudenian was telling the truth, sir? Something had to be attacking the cat."

"Captain Jimenez will find out if it's true or not. Either way I don't want a mass panic on my hands."

"I know Gudenian, sir, he's wild but—"

"He concealed the existence of an unguarded way in and out of Glasshouse. Finish your report and then get me the names of all Chalk Circle suspects Gudenian had contact with."

Steane was still uneasy about his new involvement with the widely feared Deputy-Commandant. "You don't think Controller Bruce is having some kind of nervous breakdown, sir?"

Lindsay put his hand on the burly young captain's shoulder, for him a gesture of surprising intimacy. "The Controller is a maverick and always has been. You must never forget he's one of only three people who ever survived out there unaided—as if his ego needed any boosting. Well, he must learn like everyone else there's no room for destructive individualism at this stage in our historical development."

"He's very popular, sir."

"Since when were we in a popularity contest? Our duty is to the long-term security of this Colony. Of course, people complain—they always do. But they're still alive. I hope you agree with me that is the important consideration."

"I think I know where my duty lies, sir."

Lindsay patted his back. "I'm having you transferred to my staff, Steane."

"Thank you very much, sir."

Lindsay went to the door, then hesitated. "I have great respect for Bruce's past achievements, naturally. You may be right about mental strain . . . but can we afford a Controller-in-Chief who isn't functioning properly?"

Whistles blew as the first shadows of twilight fell across the Net. Long lines of field workers filed past armed guards into the tunnel entrances to Glasshouse. Steel doors closed, sealing off Colony One from the quickly advancing night.

An unfamiliar mammal scent brought Vulpes Vulpes to the disintegrating wire mesh of a long, open-fronted shed which had once been the park's ornamental aviary. In darkness the loss of an eye was no handicap.

Night had brought the smooth-haired cavies together in the dark warmth of a communal nest among moldering jute sacks, three adult males, five adult females and eleven youngsters, descendants of pet guinea pigs once kept by a parkkeeper's children.

Vulpes Vulpes did not kill for amusement, but when his first savage rush scattered the cavies in blind runs against brick walls his killer's instincts drove him wild, slaughtering everything that moved in an orgy of squeals and blood.

Betrayal!

WORKERS OF COLONY ONE . . .
DENIED ALL DEMOCRATIC RIGHTS, FORCED TO SPEND OUR LIVES UNDER ARMED GUARD, FORBIDDEN ELEMENTARY HUMAN FREEDOMS, WE DEMAND THE FOLLOWING:

- Immediate release of the three strikers under sentence of death.
- Amnesty for all colonists undergoing punishment.
- Democratic elections.
- An end to Security Guard brutality and abolition of the Rehabilitation Compound.
- The right of men and women to cohabit freely.

WE CAME HERE TO BUILD A NEW WORLD—WE REFUSE TO BE SLAVES. LET US FIGHT TOGETHER IN THE BROTHERHOOD OF THE CHALK CIRCLE!

5

Lindstrom bent over the microscope, adjusting the magnification. What looked like whip-tailed tadpoles swam energetically through an opaque, motile fluid. "How the hell did she manage it?" he muttered. "You realize the whole program is now at risk?"

The two white-coated doctors stared through the observation window at a dark-haired girl asleep on a clinical examination table. Freedland cursed under his breath.

"The moment we report it we'll have whole platoons of Security thugs crashing through this clinic."

"Do we have to report it?"

Freedland's brow furrowed. "She doesn't know she's part of the program . . ."

"None of them know."

"So she's not to expect that we've discovered . . ."

Lindstrom snapped his fingers. "That's it—we pretend we didn't discover it!"

"Trouble is—if she's done it once she'll do it again. We'll have to get rid of her—quickly."

"Kill her?" Lindstrom whispered.

"Don't be stupid. We'll say she's failed her practical tests and have her reclassified as a field worker."

"Brilliant! She'll find the guards more than willing to cater to her sexual inclinations!"

"Stupid bitch has ruined seven months' work," Freedland said vindictively. "I hope she enjoys digging holes in mud!"

Bruce put down the yellow pamphlet and looked at the faces of the eight people facing him across the Colony's table of government. "I called this meeting to discuss the death sentences but I think this pamphlet throws open the whole question of where Colony One is headed."

"Geneva has confirmed the death sentences," said Chief-Administrator Bogaert. "I don't see what we have to discuss."

Bruce shrugged. "I'm proposing we tell Geneva we're not in business to hang people."

"We can't defy World Food Control," Wisnovsky protested.

"They might be glad to hear we're ready to make our own decisions."

Bogaert shook his head. "Under the legal framework—"

"Legal framework?" Bruce slapped the heavy cross-section of oak. "A secret trial? The accused allowed no representation? Judged by the very people who imposed these wonderful work schedules? Legal frameup you mean. Those machinists went on strike because our system gives them no other way to make a protest."

"Why have you changed your mind, Controller?" asked Engineer Grouchy.

"It isn't solely my delicate conscience—could be we're facing organized disruption and I don't see Geneva being too happy about that."

"I have every confidence in the Security Division's ability to maintain discipline," Schwab said emphatically, glancing at Lindsay. "The workforce has to understand—individuals count for nothing compared to the long-term strength of the Colony."

Bello, Director of Information, nodded wisely.

"History shows that revolutions come when previously strict regimes lose confidence and try to placate agitators with so-called liberal measures. But once the dam has been burst—"

"I could not disagree more," exclaimed Engineer Grouchy, who prided himself on a superior endowment of common sense and logic. "I come in daily contact with hundreds of workers and I can tell you —there is general discontent. Creating martyrs will play only into the hands of subversive elements."

Lena Davidson looked pointedly at Lindsay. "One thing we don't want is a reign of terror. And I want to know why the Commandant of the Security Division isn't here."

"The Commandant is probably justified in treating these social evenings with contempt," Bruce drawled, glad of Lena's support while noting how little weight she carried with the others. He let his eyes move slowly until they rested on the red-haired Lindsay. "May I ask the Deputy-Commandant if his silence means anything in particular?"

Lindsay sat back, folding his arms. "I'll answer with another question. Do I understand the Controller to suggest he has some sympathy with the attitudes represented in that illegal document?"

Lena gave Bruce a warning look. He leaned forward on his elbows. In the soft light of oil lamps it was difficult to see subtle changes of facial expression but he sensed an increase in tension. He held up the yellow pamphlet.

"I didn't read this out to entertain you. I read it out because I agree with every damn word in it." A gasp went round the big table. He went on quickly, knowing he had to keep the initiative. "I feel ashamed of myself for helping to trick five thousand people into something not far short of slavery—"

"They weren't *tricked*," Schwab protested. "They volunteered to escape starvation, they knew the risks—"

"Did they know their full-sized bodies would be destroyed?" Bruce retorted.

"We're building a new society," Bello snapped. "They are lucky to be alive."

"That's how I rationalized it—until today." Bruce sensed the general mood turning against him and tried to keep a placatory note in his voice. "I'm as guilty as anybody else but this Colony has started on the wrong lines. We should be learning to live *with* Nature, not sealing ourselves up in a sterilized fortress. We've put productivity and technology before human dignity—the very priorities that turned Earth into a deathtrap. We ask for volunteers to open up a new frontier—and then we treat them like criminals. We can miniaturize tractors and telephones but we don't allow men and women to live together. Everything is for the future, the next generation of Colonists—exactly how every totalitarian regime in history justified brutal repression. Is that what we want—conspiracies, a neverending campaign of dehumanization, more alienation, more repression? Is that going to give us strength and efficiency?" He was tapping his clenched fist on the oak table, looking from face to face for some sign of comprehension. "If we don't remember that we're dealing with human beings then this Colony will blow up in our faces!"

In the clamor that followed only Lindsay kept silent. He waited for a lull and then held up some sheets of paper. "I, too, have a document," he said with quiet authority. "This is a verbatim account of statements made in public by the Controller—some as recently as this afternoon. I will pass it round the table and you will see that Bruce's sympathies with these Chalk Circle gangsters leave us no alternative but to suspend him from office."

Captain of Detention Jimenez rammed his toecap into the shin of the big blond man whose wrists and ankles were roped to a heavy wooden chair. Captain of Detention Jimenez did not enjoy his work but he was willing to endure the pain of others for the greater good of the Colony. Captain of Detention Jimenez always maintained that he found the work degrading and got no perverted pleasure from it and he used the most brutal methods because they were mercifully quick.

He kicked the prisoner on the other leg. He gestured at the bare earth walls of the small cell, a solitary oil lamp making a huge shadow of his arm. "There is no psychology practiced in this dark hole in the ground, no subtle breaking down of the will. I am simply going to kick the truth out of you. Think about that."

He picked up the prisoner's dossier. Gudenian, still in his black uniform, bit on his lower lip . . .

David Gudenian, aged tweny-six, born Atlanta, US West Zone; mother a biochemist, father a research coordiantor who disappeared during an administrative purge before his second son was born; childhood spent mainly in premilitary training schools, inducted into the WFC army at sixteen; two years' front-line service with WFC infantry battalions in the Brazilian rebellion, eighteen months garrison duty, West Europe Zone, rising to rank of Captain; reduced to ranks following court martial on charges of striking a fellow officer, resisting arrest, refusal to obey the orders of a superior officer; thirty-one months field service with the WFC army of occupation in Saudia Arabia; faced with participation in reprisal executions of suspected Islamic terrorists, he put his name down for Colony One, about which he knew very little except that it was a secret scientific project involving security duties.

Due to the nature of the micro-cloning project, it was run in total secrecy; by the time volunteers realized it meant genetical replication and extreme miniaturization they knew too much to be allowed to withdraw.

The psychoprofile in his dossier said he had strong leadership potential coupled with an almost reckless sense of independence. The report recommended assignment to duties where the issues, like those of front-line combat, were simple and clear-cut. Only then could his loyalty be guaranteed.

Jimenez indicated where the next blow would fall by tapping Gudenian on the bridge of his nose. A white-strap guard, bored by a performance he had witnessed many times before, leaned nonchalantly against the door.

"You have been a brave soldier, Gudenian," Jimenez said, putting down the file. "You have been foolish, that's all. However, I have to get the truth out of you and I don't have time to make allowances. Do I really have to reduce you to a broken wreck?"

Gudenian twisted his head to escape the hard knuckles that tapped harder and harder on the bridge of his nose. "All right," he said quickly, "I'll tell you, Jimenez. It was a nurse from the Clinic on Tier Four, she's in the Chalk Circle, she showed me the tunnel. They wanted my help to get the three strikers out of Detention . . ."

When he could manage a painful limp, Jimenez and the white-strap escorted him to the Detention Area checkpoint and then into the narrow box of an elevator which ran from the lower Sub-Tier level up through the six administrative tiers of the inner wooden building known as Control. Once the quiet whine of the electric motor told Gudenian the box was rising he turned ingratiatingly to Jimenez.

"What'll I get, sir? I mean, I'm willing to cooperate—and I didn't give you any trouble . . ."

Jimenez patted him on the back. "Once you identify this girl we can root out the whole Chalk Circle gang. That should count in your favor with Lindsay. And what's a couple of months in the Compound to a tough big fellow like you? They don't kick as hard as I do!"

Jimenez and the white-strap enjoyed the joke. Gudenian looked at them pleadingly.

The elevator stopped at the ground-level checkpoint. Only authorized personnel were allowed unrestrained movement inside Control—one look at

Jimenez was authorization enough for the duty guard. The doors closed again. Jimenez nudged Gudenian.

"You risked Section Six to screw a girl? She must be . . . well, was she worth it?"

Novak the white-strap winked. "Those nurses know the score."

Gudenian smirked. "You'll enjoy questioning her, sir."

"I will not *enjoy* it," said Captain of Detention Jimenez pompously. "I will do what has to be done."

"You can go back to your quarters now," Freedland told Magda Hoessner when she was dressed again in her regulation blouse and trousers. "Don't check in for duty till midday."

"Thank you, Doctor." Magda bent down to tie the laces of her soft indoor mocassins. "What is it you keep testing us for?"

"Strange as it may seem, our main worry is ensuring a *high* enough ratio of bacteria in the body," Freedland explained, ignoring Lindstrom's furtive smiles. "When you were cloned they took the nucleus of one of your body cells and used it to fertilize one of your own egg cells—the ovum. This was then grown in a simulated womb. The human digestive system operates only with the help of symbiotic bacteria but as the cloned individual has been produced in sterile laboratory conditions the normal donation of bacteria by mother to child cannot take place. Therefore, the bacteria must be introduced artifically—and we have to make sure the levels have been maintained. Does that make sense to you, Hoessner?"

She smiled. "Well, sir, I think—"

Loud voices were raised in the outer reception area. Magda turned in time to see two black-uniformed Security men escorting David Gudenian into the clinic.

"What is the meaning of this?" Freedland demanded.

Gudenian pointed at Magda.

"That's the one, sir."

"What is this girl's name?" Jimenez demanded.

Freedland's face went red. "Who gave you permission to enter this Clinic?"

Jimenez loomed toward Magda. "What is your name?" he snapped.

"Magda Hoessner." She looked helplessly at Gudenian. Jimenez nodded and Novak caught hold of her sleeve. Jimenez turned to Freedland. "The guard outside will let no one leave or enter this clinic until further notice. There will be no communication with any other part of the building."

"What the hell is all this about?"

Jimenez grimaced indifferently. "This girl is a member of the Chalk Circle." He pointed at Gudenian. "She will be accused of attempting to corrupt this Section-Leader, going outside without permission, concealing the existence on an unscheduled entrance to Glasshouse. You can expect a rigorous enquiry into the general discipline of your clinic, Doctor. Thank you."

Magda stared incredulously at Gudenian. "He's lying!"

At a signal from Jimenez, Novak gripped her arm and steered her toward the door. Freedland moved as if to intercede but Lindstrom stepped quickly between him and the guard. "What our nurses do off-duty is hardly our responsibility," he said, "but naturally we are shocked and will cooperate fully with your colleagues. I should also say that Doctor Freedland and myself have already processed a reclassification for Hoessner—her work has been very poor."

They took the stairs to Tier Five, Jimenez leading the way, Novak holding Magda's arm, Gudenian limping painfully to keep pace.

The outer office was in darkness. "He's still at the ICC meeting," Jimenez said, feeling for the switch that gave the Colony's elite the privilege of electric light.

Novak shoved Magda into the Deputy-Commandant's suite, silencing her with a laconic threat to break her arm. He pushed her onto a chair. Jimenez tried the handle of the inner office, which was vaguely illuminated by moonlight.

Novak leaned over Magda, hands on the arms of her chair. "Now then, beautiful—"

Gudenian moved quickly, his limp disappearing. He snatched the pistol from Novak's belt holster. The white-strap swung round. Gudenian pushed him in the chest. Novak shouted something and jumped at him.

There was a muffled explosion and the white-strap's jackknifing body crashed against a desk in a welter of blood.

Captain of Detention Jimenez, who spent his working life within arm's reach of desperate men, was too sensible to carry a weapon. When Gudenian pointed the dull-alloy automatic at his chest he raised his hands. "Why did you do that?" he asked coolly.

"Get your harness off, Jimenez."

"You can't go anywhere. Why are you making things worse for yourself?"

"Get the goddamn harness off!" Jimenez unbuckled his white belt and eased the cross-strap off his shoulder. "Drop it on the floor," Gudenian snapped. "Take off your jacket."

Jimenez dropped the white harness and fumbled with his buttons. He dropped the black tunic on the floor and stood back with his hands raised, looking almost womanly in his bulging white undervest. His eyes flicked from Gudenian to the terrified face of the girl. He realized she was as surprised as himself. Novak was twitching slightly on the floor, with blood bubbling from his gaping wound. Jimenez looked at Magda. "He betrayed you—now he's dragged you into a murder." He was already savoring the satisfaction it would give him to break Gudenian's fingers.

Magda stared at Novak and then at Gudenian, blinking stupidly.

"What are you going to do now?" Jimenez asked.

"I'm going to see how you kick your way into the next world, Jimenez!"

The second bullet exploded into a full belly that had only just begun to enjoy freedom from the tight belt of the Discipline Section.

Jimenez hurtled backward, smashing through the door into Lindsay's room. His boots jerked in the light from the outer office, then he was still.

Magda stared up at Gudenian in a daze. "You've killed them . . ."

"Pity that bastard Lindsay wasn't here as well!" He started pulling on the tunic with the captain's insignia. "I warned them about the fox and they sent me down to Interrogation for that pig to cripple me.

She stared unbelievingly at the dead Novak. Gudenian buckled on the white harness, shoving the pistol into the belt-holster. She stared at the black boots of Captain Jimenez jutting from the silvery shadows of the inner office.

Gudenian shook her. "You're a nurse, you've seen plenty of dead ones! Come on—if anybody stops us I'm taking you to Interrogation."

"*Interrogation?*"

"For Christ's sake—we're *escaping*. First we make for Field Patrol stores on the ground level—"

"How can we hide there?"

He opened the door a few inches, checking the corridor. "We're not going to hide, we're going to grab all we need to stay alive and we're going to crash out of this hellhole."

"*Beyond?*" She tried to pull back, shaking her head.

"You want to stay here and wait for them to put a rope round your neck?"

6

Bruce's mouth and throat were dry but it was his own rule—no drinks, snacks or refreshments of any kind at ICC meetings, the idea being to keep them short. He felt tired and uncomfortable but decided to make one last effort.

"You don't have to push it to a vote—I can see how things are. But . . . you get rid of me. What does that change? This Colony is near to open revolt—you think cracking skulls will solve all problems? You think productivity will be boosted in the Detention cells?"

Wisnovsky seemed to be in competition with Schwab and Bello for Lindsay's approval. "It is soft leadership which brought us to this crisis. Regretfully—in view of Bruce's past services—I must agree with Deputy-Commandant Lindsay's analysis of—"

The door was thrown open. A black-uniformed white-strap took two steps into the big, shadowy room and came to attention.

"The Commandant."

As if caught in some mischievous prank, guilty faces turned toward the doorway.

Andrei Ilyanovich Khomich, Commandant of the

Security Division, Colony One, strode to his vacant seat at the oak table.

"I was delayed."

It might have been an apology. It sounded like a threat.

Bruce felt the same ambivalence of emotion that always swept through him with the man once known throughout all European Zones as "The Butcher." He had known Khomich as a murderous brute, in the old days of the famine riots, and then had come to recognize another side to him, in the garden of Arcadia, on that first journey into the unknown terrors of life at micro-level. Three years had passed since their first meeting in the Outlands of Finland —Khomich had cropped his blond hair to the very skull to disguise the fact that it was going gray and his broad, peasant face was still boyishly pink, but there was no hiding the lines under his eyes. *We're both getting older, Khomich,* he thought, *maybe they're right to want us out, maybe Lindsay's ambition is a healthy force for progress . . .*

"There are two motions before the Committee," he said to Khomich. "I have proposed we commute these death sentences—and also that we discuss various reforms. Deputy-Commandant Lindsay has accused me of subversion and wants a vote on my removal from office."

Khomich's broad face remained impassive. Lindsay put Steane's report in front of him. "This is a verbatim account of inflammatory statements made in public by Bruce."

Khomich made no attempt to pick up the report. "Bruce has been a subversive since the first day I had to arrest him," he growled.

Lindsay's eyes crinkled in triumph. Schwab and Bello exchanged relieved glances—they had chosen the right side after all.

"Without Bob Bruce there would be no Colony," Lena stormed. "The idea that he's trying to destroy it is ridiculous!"

A quick survey of faces told Bruce he had lost.

The whole debate had been a put-up job, he knew that now; Lindsay wanted control of the Colony, Schwab and Bello and Wisnovsky and probably Bogaert were his caucus. He understood now why the young SG officer had been trying to lead him into open sedition.

"Can we take the vote now?" Lindsay said calmly.

Bruce looked at Lena. They both knew the truth —he would lose the vote, next step would be a rigged trial—

"No more childish games," Khomich barked. "I was speaking to Zonal Command. The London garrison is withdrawing because of typhoid. We will be on our own for an estimated three months."

"How will they supply us?" Wisnovsky demanded.

"The nearest WFC troops will be at the French port of Le Havre—"

"They can fly in food and fuel on the patrol helicopter," interjected Bogaert.

Khomich gave an exasperated grunt. "The patrol was suspended six days ago! They are not going to supply us!"

"All the more reason for getting the leadership of this Colony settled," Lindsay snapped. "I believe we are ready to—"

"You are a fool!"

For a long moment there was silence in the softly lit room.

Lindsay recovered first. "You said yourself Bruce is a subversive—how can we—"

"Bruce is a damned scientist but he would not have suppressed information vital to our safety!"

Bogaert looked at Schwab and Schwab looked at Bello. Khomich had always been the main obstacle to their plans and already they felt the first twinges of panic.

Khomich's small blue eyes fixed on Lindsay. "Did a Security Guard called Gudenian report a fox in the park this afternoon?"

Lindsay grimaced disparagingly. "Gudenian had

concealed a secret way in and out of Glasshouse. I'm dealing with the matter—"

"Dealing with it? Have you increased Surveillance? Put the field guard on alert? Sent out patrols?"

"The man is being questioned now—when we have confirmation—"

Khomich thumped the table. "We will have confirmation if a damned fox breaks through the Net!"

"The man's in the Chalk Circle—they're trying to panic the Colony with wild rumors! How could a fox get over a twelve-foot wall? Wait till Jimenez has finished with him!"

"Jimenez?" Lena gasped.

Khomich looked at the others in turn. "A guard came voluntarily to warn us—risking severe punishment for being outside without permission—and this imbecile handed him over to Interrogation. This is the man who should be responsible for our lives?"

Lindsay jumped to his feet. "We will put that to a vote! Now!"

Nobody moved.

Bruce saw Wisnovsky nervously licking his knuckles.

"All right," Lindsay said icily, striding to the door, "you leave me no option."

Throwing open the door he was faced by Area-Captain Steane, flanked by two white-straps.

"*You?*" he snarled at Steane. "You went behind my back!" He made to shove past the burly young SG officer. Steane did not give way.

"Acting under orders from Commandant Khomich I cannot allow anyone to leave the committee room, sir."

Lindsay still tried to get past but the two guards blocked him, closing the door in his face.

"Why don't you sit down, Lindsay?" Bruce drawled. "We'll have the policy discussion later."

Lindsay hesitated. His former supporters took care not to catch his eye. With an unmistakable petulance he came back to the table and sat down. Bruce turned to Khomich.

"It could be a false alarm but we'll have to issue an alert. The Net's strong enough to keep out birds and small mammals, not a fox—"

"This is the army's responsibility," Schwab protested, "they have no right to leave us unprotected. I say we tell Geneva—"

"*No!*" Khomich slapped the table. "This is for you all to understand. I have been given certain orders. The safety of the Colony is my responsibility —in an emergency I have powers to suspend this Committee. If there is the slightest threat to security that is what I will do. No more games!"

The door opened again and Steane approached the table. "Sir?" he said to Khomich. He leaned beside Khomich's chair, murmuring urgently. Bruce knew he had to reassert his authority before Khomich steamrollered them into accepting a *fait accompli*. The trouble was—he felt tired. In a way Lindsay had been right—he had allowed things to drift. Maybe—

Khomich's savage snarl made everyone jump.

Fists clenched, eyes narrowed to glinting pinpoints, barrel-chest swelling with anger, he seemed momentarily paralyzed by rage.

"Search the building!"

Steane saluted and turned on his heels.

Khomich stood up, glaring at Lindsay. His voice was like the rumble of a wakening volcano. "Gudenian has killed Captain Jimenez and a guard. He warned you of a fox and you rewarded him with torture. Now he is a murderer. We will have to shoot him—because you—"

Before Lindsay could move Khomich grabbed at his epaulettes and dragged Lindsay off his chair onto the floor, where Khomich started to kick him, screaming words that blurred unintelligibly into raw sound.

Magda gaped in astonishment when Gudenian strode into the low-ceilinged field-patrol storeroom on the ground level of Control. Behind him came six prisoners in the shapeless blue fatigues of the Rehabilitation Compound, four men and two women, followed by a white-strap guard with drawn pistol.

Gudenian gave her a warning frown.

"This is the equipment," he snapped, pointing at eight large field packs he and Magda had filled after bluffing their way past the ground level checkpoint and then forcing the door of the storeroom.

"I should have written authority to let prisoners out of the Compound," grumbled the guard.

Gudenian snorted. "Should I interrupt the ICC meeting—tell Lindsay you're complaining about his procedure? That equipment's got to be ready waiting for the patrol or you'll be in the Diggings before your feet touch the ground, Markstein!"

The guard turned on his prisoners. "Hurry it up!" He noticed Magda for the first time but before he could ask who she was, Gudenian shouted at her to pick up one of the packs.

"Stupid bitch was distributing Chalk Circle leaflets," he told Markstein. "I'm signing her into the Compound as soon as we've hauled these packs to the tunnel."

Magda struggled with one of the big packs, afraid to look at Gudenian. Surely the guard would see that his uniform didn't fit!

Gudenian patted the pistol in the white belt that had so recently girthed the big belly of Captain Jimenez. "For Christ's sake, Markstein—I thought you had these Compound rats jumping to orders."

Straining under the weight of enough equipment and supplies to maintain an eight-man patrol for five days, cowed faces anticipating a blow from the guard, the six prisoners and Magda filed through the narrow door.

"I'll lock up," Gudenian told Markstein.

As soon as he was alone he found a heavy angle iron and smashed at the padlock which secured a thin chain running through the trigger guards of stacked repeater rifles.

Nobody had ever broken out of Colony One before but he was not deluding himself—killing Jimenez and Novak and getting this far in a dead man's uniform was the easy part.

7

Crossing a vast cement floor under a mountainous cathedral of glass, Magda heard a ghostly sighing noise, as of a distant ocean.

She knew it was only wind blowing against Glasshouse but she kept her eyes down, frightened to be reminded of the vast, unimaginable night beyond the glass.

"Pick your feet up," snarled Markstein the Compound guard, striding up and down the trudging line of prisoners, trying to conquer his own fear of the gloomy canyon across whose floor they moved like little dots.

Magda glanced over her shoulder at the receding lights of Control, the prefabricated wooden building which housed the Colony. Back there people would be crowded in sweaty dormitories, arguing and complaining, seething with resentment at a system which left them too tired for rebellion. Prisoners yes—but safely locked away from the unknown terrors of the night.

They passed the Compound, a single-story wooden shed built round a quadrangle. Gudenian switched on his torch, flicking it to wide-beam to light a way through the thickening gloom.

By then he had identified the six prisoners he had tricked Markstein into releasing from the Compound and was trying to guess their reactions to the shock he was about to administer. Hand-picking people would have been a lot better but he hadn't done too badly.

Three of the male prisoners he knew as former guards, each facing long sentences in the Diggings, an underground expansion being cut into hard clay beneath the subtiers of Control to house industrial plant and give the Colony an impenetrable bunker retreat. Nobody really knew what conditions were like down there except the white-strap Discipline Section guards but he didn't know of any prisoner who'd ever made it back—it was a safe bet these three would think they'd nothing much to lose.

The fourth man was a stocky field worker whose prisoner's name tag said Manuel Gento. One of the women was some kind of scientist, Peta Sandor on her name tag, a neurotic-looking blond who'd been put away for Chalk Circle activities, probably one of these politically intense intellectuals he could have done without. The other woman he remembered well, Nadine Boden, until very recently the senior psychologist in the Personnel Section; he'd been surprised to find her in the Compound, having associated her with the Colony's hierarchy. Obviously a political—probably trouble.

Markstein was the main problem.

The cement flooring gave way to hard-packed soil as they approached the northern section of the old botanical hot-house which formed the Colony's outer shelter, a shadowy region normally penetrated only by safety patrols. He took care to flash the torch-beam well ahead, frightening off any beetles and spiders.

When they reached the brick wall he flashed the torch in both directions until he located the bank of rusting pipes that had once been part of a steam-heat system.

"That's the place," he told Markstein, who barked at the prisoners to quicken it up. The torch-beam found a bolted inspection plate in a right-angled bend of four-inch pipe.

The blond woman, Sandor, let her pack fall heavily on hard, dry earth. "Be careful," Gudenian snapped, "you want to smash the equipment?"

"Stupid bitch!" Markstein raised his right hand as if to strike her with his pistol. She raised her hands to shield her face and Markstein punched her in the stomach. Sandor doubled over, making choking noises.

Gudenian slid the three rifles off his shoulder and propped them against the bottom pipe. "You really know how to handle these scum."

Markstein spat. "I don't know why we waste food on them!"

Gudenian had been undecided about Markstein—he knew all too well how the system forced guards, especially white-straps, to behave like sadists—but the decision had been made for him by the casual brutality of the punch. Lowering the torch-beam he saw a glint of smooth brown stone.

Markstein gave one of the male prisoners a push in the chest. "Move it, Delmer, I'm losing sleep here."

Delmer, a big man with prominent front teeth, made some kind of grunting noise Markstein took for insolence. "Watch it, Delmer—I hate renegade guards worst of all."

Gudenian brought the heavy pebble down on Markstein's green beret.

The white-strap guard collapsed to his knees, trying to cover his head with his arms.

Gudenian swung the stone down again . . . and again . . .

When he stood up he had drawn his pistol. His chest was heaving. He flicked the torch-beam across stunned faces.

"My name's Gudenian, I've just escaped from

Detention." He swung the beam on Magda. "Nurse Hoessner and I were arrested for being outside without permission. We're getting out of this goddamn prison." He shone the beam on the inspection plate. "That pipe leads through the brick wall. That's where we're going."

"Outside?" gasped the blond woman. "What can you do out there?"

"If I stay here I'm going to be hung."

He handed the torch to Magda and reached up to pull at the loose bolt that held the rusty oval plate in position. "I found this bolt-hole on a patrol—Magda and I used it."

He pulled the bolt free and jumped clear as the heavy plate thudded into hard earth. "Start lifting the packs into the pipe, I'll hide Markstein's body."

"What did you kill him for?" demanded Boden, the female psychologist. He swung the beam on her, remembering the first time he had seen her distinctively slanting eyes.

"You think he'd have helped us escape?"

"*Escape?*"

"Nobody can live out there," said the big ex-guard, Delmer.

Gudenian shrugged. "Been on patrols, haven't you?"

They were still too shocked to take it in—except the woman Boden. "I'm due to be released tomorrow—I'm having nothing to do with this!"

Gudenian let them all see the pistol. "Sorry, Doctor, I need you. Once you've hauled these packs down that tunnel you can go back. But just get one thing clear, all of you—try to hold me up and I'll blow a hole in you!"

"Well done, Khomich," Bruce drawled, "you saved my neck—thanks. It's probable you've broken every rib in Lindsay's body but you never were too hot on the rules of debate."

They were alone in the conference room, facing

each other across the table. Bruce had his hands rammed in his pockets so that Khomich would not see them shaking. Khomich seemed unperturbed. "I will promote Steane. Lindsay was a mistake for which I take full blame."

"What are you planning now—get him fit enough to be hung?"

Khomich hissed impatiently. "He will be useful for outside patrols—"

"Suicide missions?" Khomich blinked impassively. Bruce shrugged. "My heart isn't bleeding for Lindsay but I'm telling you one thing, Khomich—I'm still Controller-in-Chief and as of now I'm making it an order—no hangings!" He waited for a reaction. "You understand what I'm saying—we're not going to hang the three strikers."

Khomich's small blue eyes narrowed imperceptibly. "I understand what you are saying."

"We're agreed then?"

"There is nothing to agree about. I had them shot."

Bruce stared open-mouthed. "You did *what?*"

"Geneva confirmed the sentences and I had them executed. Delay would have given time for negative reaction. These things are best done quickly."

"Negative reaction . . . ?" Bruce put his elbows on the table and bowed his head. "You cold-blooded bastard . . ."

Khomich tapped the table with a thick forefinger. "I did not save you to become a popular hero. I saved you to prevent further unrest. Anybody who endangers our security will be summarily dealt with—that applies to you as to—"

"You didn't save me—you saved yourself! You want to run this prison camp singlehanded and Lindsay's power play gave you the excuse. Listen to me—"

"No, you listen." Khomich stood up so violently his chair crashed to the floor. "You are a sentimentalist, Bruce, I am a soldier. You would give the people holidays and they would cheer you—until they realized you had led them to their deaths! You can stay as Controller provided you leave all security and disciplinary matters to me."

He turned abruptly and strode toward the door.

"I'm not helping you become a dictator," Bruce shouted.

Khomich did not look back. "Inform me of your decision in the morning." The door slammed behind him.

Bruce closed his eyes, sagging forward until his forehead was touching the table. He saw a sparkling lake and a man floating on his back. That was the day Khomich had first come for him with young Robinson . . . there was a buzzard wheeling high above the lake in a sky so blue it still made his heart ache to see it in his mind's eye.

He could have killed Khomich that day . . .

He raised his head, as if in response to a nearby voice.

You could still kill him—just walk up to him and pull a trigger . . .

No!

Murder proves only one thing—that you are a murderer.

He stood up slowly. He looked round the empty chairs. He felt insubstantial, only temporarily occupying a space that would soon be as empty as the chairs.

He had been a fool—Khomich was right, a sentimentalist.

He had deluded himself that micro-cloning would give people more than a new physical life—a new outlook, free them of the murderous instincts that had cursed men from barely upright hominids of evolutionary Africa to scientific gods who had projected twentieth-century man into space.

Delusions.

Here they were, each of them a test-tube miracle, each of them given a chance to escape Man's hereditary flaw—*and still murdering each other.*

He left the conference room and made his

way through empty corridors, feeling like a trapped alien.

Escape?

Where to?

Did it matter? To stay was to accept membership of a species that built its own prisons because freedom was too dangerous for murderers.

In the end all a man could grasp was his own, lonely struggle through the dream that preshadowed death.

Escape!

They followed Magda's torch down the iron tunnel until the beam hit the silvery-gray web. The yellow spider immediately scuttled out of sight but the prisoners panicked, trying to turn back, tramping on each other's feet.

"It's harmless," Gudenian snapped from the rear. "Put the packs down—we wait here till dawn."

Reluctantly, with nervous eyes on the web and the black hole of the night, they squatted down. Gudenian rested the three rifles against the curved side of the tunnel. "If anybody comes after us we'll hear the noise a long way off."

"You want us to carry this stuff into *Beyond*?" demanded one of the ex-guards, John Lindop, a young Englishman with curly brown hair.

"I don't think you people have grasped the situation here," Gudenian said calmly. "Markstein wasn't the first—I also killed Jimenez and a guard called Novak—"

You killed Captain Jimenez?" Abram Chernitz, another of the imprisoned guards, blew a silent whistle. "How the hell did you manage that, Gudenian?"

"He interrogated me," said the stocky field worker, Gento. Gudenian recognized him now, a small bull of a man who'd hammered a field guard unconscious. "You deserve our thanks."

Nadine Boden turned on him angrily. "Our thanks? For killing three guards? The man's mad!"

Gudenian pulled his pistol from its holster and let

them see him taking a new clip from his belt pouch. "Nylon bullets with steel tips designed for hard-shell insects—they issue them for field patrols. Make a helluva mess inside, the nylon bounces around and tears 'em up. I don't know what they'd do to our kind of bodies."

"Are you threatening us?" demanded Nadine Boden.

"Haul this stuff out into the park and then you can all go back—if you're anxious to commit suicide."

"What d'you mean, suicide?" asked the big man, Delmer.

"If they don't hang you they'll stick you in the Diggings till the day you drop."

He rammed the new clip into the pistol, then squinted at each face in turn. They were still too shocked to grasp the fact that they had escaped from the Compound. Or else they were so scared by propaganda about Beyond they were already thinking the Compound wasn't so bad after all. He'd expected that kind of reaction—he hadn't bargained for Nadine Boden.

"Markstein ordered us to carry this equipment," she said to the others, "we did nothing wrong, we've got nothing to be afraid of. I say we go back—*now*."

Chernitz snorted. "Markstein won't be there to tell them what happened. All they'll know is we stood around and watched Gudenian smash his brains in."

"They'll know more than that," Gudenian drawled. "What'll they find in that storeroom? Eight packs gone, eight complete survival kits—and eight people missing. You'll have a nice time convincing them it wasn't a planned breakout."

"That means we can never go back!" exclaimed the blond woman, Peta Sandor.

Gudenian shrugged. "I thought I was doing you a favor."

Chernitz peered past the spider's web at the blackness beyond. "You *really* think people could survive out there, Gudenian? I mean, bully for you, knocking off Jimenez and those other two but . . . it's *dangerous* out there!"

He looked at Magda. "Tell them why we went outside in the first place."

Magda hesitated. There was no going back for her, not now, she was prepared to go wherever he took her. But she felt guilty about the others. She lowered her face to hide her embarrassment. "To make love . . ."

Chernitz frowned.

Gudenian grinned at him. "When was the last time any of you Compound rats made love to another human being?" He pointed at the hostile face of Nadine Boden. "How come you ended up in the Compound, Doctor?"

"I faked rest and recuperation authorizations for a few field workers—"

"It's true," said Gento. "She saved a lot of lives."

"Well you can thank me by letting me go back," she said firmly, "I get out of the Compound tomorrow, I don't want to *escape,* not now."

Gudenian grimaced ruefully. "Sorry, Doctor, I didn't have time to ask for volunteers. Carry this stuff till I find a safe place for Magda and me and I'll give you a signed letter saying I forced you into it. My word on it. That goes for you all. Okay?"

None of them was enthusiastic but there was no argument, not with the pistol still in his hand. He dragged over the nearest pack. "Now . . . I'm going to show you what's in these things . . . This is what you'll wear, they call it a warm-suit, black and red are warning colors in Nature, you'll be conspicuous but most people will assume you're poisonous . . . Try it on, Chernitz, you're one of the most poisonous guys I know . . ."

At the first gray glimmer in the eastern sky, five men and three women emerged from the pipe into a world that was cold and wet and scaled for giants.

But there was no going back. Gudenian, tall and blond and murderously determined, saw to that.

Book Two

"Don't you understand? This makes Magda Hoessner just about the most valuable woman on earth!"

8

The first raindrops spattered harmlessly on nylon mesh but before the guards got radio instructions to assemble the field workers big drops were hurtling down like bombs, smashing into the black earth, spewing up cascades of soil and water.

A ball of spinning water exploded round a woman field worker, knocking her to the ground. When her workmates reached her she was unconscious. Soon the hurtling drops ran together in sheer walls of water. Even the guards ran in panic.

Under the relentless battering of the downpour the Net began to sag. A pylon shuddered violently and toppled sideways, throwing a black-uniformed guard off his Surveillance platform high above the outfields. He plummeted down into black soil that was rapidly being churned into mud, breaking both legs.

He tried to crawl through the churning spray but the next direct hit hammered him face-down into the quagmire.

Another pylon collapsed, dragging down a section of the Net. Confused field workers huddled for shelter under giant cabbages, scrambling for safety among the streaming leaves as waterlogged fissures overflowed and ran together in a rising lake.

Reaching the concrete strip, scores of men and women struggled to stay upright against surging ripples pouring off the huge walls of Glasshouse, clinging desperately to each other, floundering waist-deep, their shouts unheard through the thunderous roar of the deluge.

"Are you going to open these doors, you imbecile?"

Section-Leader Linkhorn shook his head stubbornly. "Once we hear the alert siren our orders are to seal off all entrances. I'm sorry, sir, but—"

"*Sorry!*" Bruce fought back an urge to grab the idiot by the throat. He saw Engineer Grouchy hurrying toward them through crowds of half-drenched field workers and guards. He took a deep breath. "Listen to me, Linkhorn. There are four or five hundred people caught out there. If we lose one—I repeat, *one*—because you panicked I will make it my business to see you hung. Do you understand? *Hung!* By the heels! Above the Net so the crows can pick you to pieces you—"

"What is wrong, Controller?"

"You'll be my witness at the court-martial, Grouchy. This fool won't open the doors—"

"Don't be stupid," Grouchy snapped at the guard, "get the doors opened immediately!"

For some reason Bruce did not understand, Section Leader Linkhorn was prepared to take the Chief Engineer's order without question. Guards pulled on chains and the heavy steel doors at the foot of the concrete steps rolled apart. Half-drowned figures immediately fought each other to scramble through the opening.

"Get inside and change your clothing before you catch pneumonia," he shouted down the concrete steps. Already, where the doors had opened, he saw an unbroken curtain of running water.

"There's nothing we can do for those still out in the fields," Grouchy murmured at his shoulder. Bruce turned on him.

"So let's do what we can for these people. I want the temperature in this building raised ten degrees, higher in the dormitories—"

"The windmills aren't giving us any power—"

"Shut down the machine shops! What the hell—" He grabbed Grouchy by the arm and pulled him close to the wall. "What the hell's wrong with you, Armand? A few hours production compared to losing all these people through hypothermia? These people are almost chilled to death!"

Grouchy almost ran to the stairs down to the sub-tier levels. For the first time in his life, Bruce felt the savage pleasure of power. Next time he would not rely on somebody like Grouchy, he would—

He caught the eye of a broad-shouldered field worker who had stripped to the waist to dry his hair with his undervest, a dark-haired man with a broken nose, slightly older than the others.

"Get to your dormitories," he said loudly, "change your clothes, if you're shivering go to bed."

"What is being done for the people still caught out there?" demanded the field worker.

"You know some way to get through a cloud-burst?"

The burly man pointed at a mark under his eye. "The last time I gave an opinion on anything Captain Jimenez strapped me to the big chair."

Bruce turned away quickly, striding toward the elevator door. The contempt in the man's eyes had been totally justified. He was Controller-in-Chief of a system that closed the doors on drowning people, that tortured them for free speech in underground chambers . . . if he stayed here much longer he would either become a victim or he would start wearing a pistol to make sure they obeyed him.

The moment of decision had come.

Annette Rosa—she was his only contact with the Chalk Circle!

There was no sound of wind or rain in the sterilized whiteness of the Clinic.

Lindstrom tried to sound optimistic. "They won't survive out there—nobody will ever know."

"*Never know?*" Freedland winced at his colleague's stupidity. "Don't you realize what it means?"

Lindstrom waited until a nurse had passed the door. "Of course I realize what it means! It means you and I might as well go out in that downpour and drown ourselves! We let them take her away. We didn't bother to do the radioreptorassay on her blood sample." He made sure nobody was watching them through the observation window. "I say we drop that specimen down the waste chute!"

Freedland shook his head vehemently. "She might not be dead. This makes Magda Hoessner just about the most valuable woman on earth! We have to tell them."

"Tell Khomich? Have you any idea what—"

A nurse came to the recess. "Excuse me, Doctor, they're bringing the first field workers up now but I don't think we have enough blankets."

Freedland gestured impatiently. "All they need is a warm drink—wrap the worst cases in uniforms, sheets, anything you've got. Doctor Lindstrom will be with you in a minute."

"Very good, Doctor."

He stood up. "I'll tell Bruce," he said, "he can decide."

Lindstrom tried to stop him, pulling him aside at the door as they met the first flood victims being carried in on stretchers. "Bruce isn't on our side, he's bound to run to Khomich. Think of the program—"

"The program?" Freedland shook his head. "The program has nothing to do with it. We're talking about the one thing everybody said was impossible!"

Bruce waited till they were alone on the stairs. "Just a moment," he said, stopping to lean on the metal rail. "The book was only an excuse to get you out of Bello's office. There's something I want you to do for me."

His face had always been gaunt and pale but there was something new in his expression, something Annetta Rosa mistook for self-pity. She gave him no help, enjoying the sight of his discomfiture.

He saw the contempt in her face. Once again there was the instinctive desire for a gun in his hand. People had stopped listening to him.

"I want to meet the people who run the Chalk Circle," he drawled. "You know who they are, don't you?"

Her face broke into a smile of disbelief. "What gave you that idea, Controller?"

"For Christ's sake, girl! I went to that ICC meeting and proposed we carry out every demand in your goddamn pamphlet! You know how near I was to being voted into a cell?"

"The rumor is that Commandant Khomich saved you."

In his frustration he put his forehead against the rough wooden wall. "Did you know the London garrison is no longer supplying us or patrolling the outer wall? Did you know there could be a wild fox out in the park?"

"How could I know? Nobody tells the rank and file."

"I'm telling you!" He tried to grab hold of her but she moved down the stairs. Her youthful athleticism seemed like an open sneer. His face hardened. "We're in serious danger and that means emergency powers for Khomich. Your little band of happy conspirators can go on playing stupid games while he's turning this place into a prison fortress run by the guards. Knowing him, he isn't planning to give power back to the ICC let alone kids like you—"

"So that's it," she smiled sarcastically, "you're losing out in the power struggle and you're desperate enough to grab at—"

"I'm not interested in what you think." He pointed at her face, a technique he'd seen Khomich use so often. "I'll meet them anywhere they like under any conditions. If I don't hear from somebody by tomorrow at the latest I'll name you as a conspirator."

Before she could protest he turned away, knowing she was still watching him, forcing his legs to take the stairs two at a time . . .

When he reached his office Freedland, senior medical officer, almost pounced on him. "I have to speak to you urgently, Controller!"

Sasso caught his eye over Freedland's shoulder. "Sir? Doctor Schwab wants to contact you and—"

"Come in, Freedland."

It was still raining in sheets, so much water flowing down the big window it was impossible to see the Net or the outfields. A stormy wind buffeted the glass, blowing the cascading rivulets sideways.

"You could almost think Nature's decided to terminate our blasphemous existence," he drawled. "You think that's superstitious bunk, Freedland?"

"I have something to tell you—"

"I've known scientists all my life—rationalists, atheists almost to a man. Oh yes, it's all superstitious bunk—until the day death ceases to be an abstract concept. Then they're down on their knees like any illiterate peasant. Christians as well—spend all their lives singing hymns about heavenly glory and the first intimation of death they're sobbing their hearts out. People are dying out there, Freedland, I hope this isn't some gripe about *another* administrative foulup."

"It's about the AID program," Freedland said hesitantly, wondering if Bruce's ramblings were a sign of mental disturbance. "Well, that's not exactly correct—"

"Tell me later, Freedland."

"No—it can't wait!"

"Okay, tell me on the way downstairs."

Passing Sasso's desk he gestured dismissively at another reminder of Schwab's request. He strode quickly along the corridor, noting with satisfaction that the stiffness had gone from his legs. Maybe he'd underestimated himself, maybe all he'd needed was something to fight against.

Freedland caught hold of his shoulder as he started down the stairs. "I want to talk to you, Bruce!"

"Talk then, man."

"The girl who ran away with Gudenian—Magda Hoessner? She was one of our AID subjects."

"No wonder she ran away!"

"She didn't know she was part of the program, we use anesthetic—"

A black-uniformed guard passed them going up. Bruce perfunctorily returned his salute, promising himself to stop wearing his Controller's insignia as a first step in proving he was no puppet of the Security Division. Turning the corner at the next landing, Freedland complained they were going too fast.

"You obviously need exercise," Bruce said, enjoying the urgent squeaking of his rubber soles on wood.

"We were actually in the middle of her bimonthly checks when they arrested her. There was something we didn't report . . ." Freedland caught hold of the rail and stopped, shaking his head. "I'm sorry, Controller, this is complicated. Please stop and listen."

"No."

Freedland groaned and then tried to catch him, raising his voice to a shout. "We found traces of semen!"

"Why else would a healthy Security thug take a female out there?"

In his exasperation Freedland found new energy, taking two steps down at a time to grab hold of Bruce's elbow. "We've just put here blood sample through radioreptorassay and we've found a hormone called HCG!"

Bruce shook off his arm, hurrying onto the big open space on ground level. In front of the elevator doors stretched a line of bedraggled field workers, some of them full-length on the floor. "What the hell's the meaning of this?" Bruce shouted, striding toward a group of lounging guards. "Why are these people still down here?"

"They're waiting for the elevator, sir," said a fresh-faced young section leader.

"What are you people supposed to be doing?"

"We're on standby, sir."

Bruce peered at the section-leader's name tag. "I'm putting you in charge here, O'Donnell. Detail two men to each stretcher case and get them up to the Clinic—immediately!"

"That's too awkward, sir, carrying stretchers up the stairs."

Bruce remembered another of Khomich's psychological tricks. He put his hands behind his back and looked down at O'Donnell's boots. "I just want to get this right, O'Donnell. I've given you an order and you're refusing it?"

The young section-leader stiffened. "I'll have them moved now, sir."

Ignoring the hostile faces of the guards, Bruce strode to the head of the steeply angled entrance tunnel. Far below, at the bottom of the concrete steps, he saw wo figures in black SG uniforms. From the mouth of the tunnel came a dull hiss of running water. He started down the steps.

Freedland was still behind him. "Aren't you interested in what I'm telling you, Controller?"

"If you think it's more important than people drowning—"

"We found HCG in her blood sample—human chorionic gonadotropin!"

"I'd be impressed if I knew what the hell you were talking about."

"That hormone is only found in the blood of pregnant women!"

They huddled together for warmth at the middle of the drainpipe. Whichever way they looked they saw a curtain of beaded raindrops. Occasionally a gust of wind gave them a glance of blurred greenery through slanting tracer lines of hurtling water bombs.

"One thing's for sure," said Chernitz, "we're not going to die of thirst! Jesus Christ, Gudenian, how the hell are we going to get out of here?"

"We could be stuck here for days," said Nadine Boden. "It was only by luck we were able to get back to these pipes. What happens when the pack-rations run out?"

Gudenian stretched and yawned. "It's only an April shower—for every little bomb that falls a flower grows!"

"You are just a little bit mad," said the blond Peta Sandor.

He smiled at her. "Magda and I were out here in brilliant sunshine only two days ago." He reached for Magda's hand. "All we know is it beats that big glass prison back there. That right, Magda?"

She nodded shyly.

A few yards away, slinking quickly with his head down, Vulpes Vulpes the red intruder nosed into thick greenery, looking for shelter from the torrent, tongue lolling between the sharkfin canines at the end of his long, lower jaw.

9

"Pregnant?"

Freedland nodded. Bruce came back up the concrete steps. "Are you sure?"

"HCG appears in the blood of pregnant women approximately seven days after conception. Of course, without examining the girl we can't be a hundred percent sure."

Bruce rubbed his unshaven chin. He had an eerie premonition that this untidy moment, a muttered conversation against a confused hubbub of jostling guards and half-drowned field workers, was a turning point in his life.

"So . . . you think you finally achieved the impossible?" he said casually.

Freedland shifted uneasily. "It wasn't the AID program, we know that much."

"What?"

"She hadn't conceived when we checked on her last impregnation. Jimenez took her away before we completed her interphase tests . . . we were afraid to report that we'd discovered semen and—"

"Are you saying she got pregnant the old-fashioned way?"

Freedland shrugged ruefully. "There's no other explanation."

"But you had a natural-method program and none of those women conceived."

"Choosing her own partner was probably crucial. Psychological stress inhibits conception—in rats as well as humans. Those other women had recently come through the trauma of micro-cloning—they also knew they were clinical subjects. That's why we've used anesthetic in this AID series—as far as Hoessner knew we were only doing bacteria counts."

They heard a shout from the bottom of the tunnel. Khomich was coming up the steps, a distant figure in black with somebody else behind him.

"We must get her back," Freedland said nervously.

Bruce gave him a warning look. "You'll be blamed for letting her go. If you want to save your own neck you'd better leave this to me."

"The rain has stopped," Khomich announced as he climbed toward them, closely followed by the new Deputy-Commandant of Security, Andrew Steane. "We can start the rescue operation—" he frowned—"where are the guards?"

"Taking stretcher cases up to the Clinic," Bruce said offhandedly. "Listen, Khomich, that girl who escaped with Gudenian—"

"I had the guards standing by for rescue work!"

"I'll round them up, sir," Steane snapped, hurrying across the concourse toward the elevator. Bruce smiled. "Your humanitarianism does you credit, Khomich, but—"

"And don't use the word *escaped*," Khomich growled, "they are renegades and deserters and criminal murderers."

"Freedland needs that girl, Magda Hoessner," Bruce said patiently, "she's an integral part of the AID program—they can't have gone too far in this weather."

Khomich's small blue eyes travelled slowly from Freedland's nervous face to Bruce. He blinked slowly.

"We have approximately one hundred field workers and guards to locate in the floods," he said, his voice ominously controlled. "We have the Net to repair. We have to check Glasshouse for structural damage. We have to reconnoiter the outer wall. Are you asking me to divert men for a search patrol because of some games with test tubes?"

"I don't think that's how Geneva would see it," Bruce drawled.

"Geneva isn't up to its neck in mud!" Khomich strode off across the concourse. Freedland frowned at Bruce.

"Why didn't you tell him?"

"You think a few drops of blood in a test tube would cut a lot of ice with Khomich?"

"Let's get on the radio to Geneva and—"

"And tell them you've accidentally mislaid our first pregnant woman?" Guards were hurrying back into the concourse. Bruce tapped the white-coated doctor on the chest. "You wouldn't win a gold medal, Freedland—your next medical assignment would be mopping up blood in the Compound!"

Freedland swallowed. There was a furtiveness about him Bruce had never liked, which made it easier to rationalize his own calculated trickery. Freedland spoke in an anxious mutter. "We can't just let her disappear . . . can we?"

"I know how important she is. Let me handle it. I'll find a way to save your skin."

It did not stop raining until dark, too late for them to leave the shelter of the terra cotta drainpipe. Curtains of falling water gave way to a silvery light. From all round came the sound of drips and gurgles, with a faint breeze rustling on leaves.

"This whole park will be like a swamp," Peta Sandor protested when he told them they'd be moving on at dawn.

"There's plenty of high ground," he said. "Anyway, we haven't had rain for weeks, it'll soon soak away. Had enough to eat?"

"This stuff is revolting," Nadine Boden said, grimacing at the dry-pack protein cake that was standard rations for field patrols. She shuddered. "You must be mad—how could you possibly hope to exist out here?"

Gudenian gave her a smile. "You might as well get into your sleeping bag, Doctor, it's going to be cold in here."

"You will let us go back tomorrow, won't you?" she pleaded. "I'm due to be released—"

"I'm not due to be released," snarled Lindop, the ex-guard. "If Gudenian says we can make it out here I'm game."

"I'll go back on my own if necessary," she said eagerly.

The American, Chernitz, snorted. "In or out the Compound, that place stinks. You know something—ever since I crossed over I've had a funny feeling in my head—as if the whole thing wasn't *real* . . . you know, like fuzzy."

"There's a bromide they put in the food," explained Peta Sandor.

Chernitz and Lindop laughed at each other. Lindop pointed at Chernitz. "You think he'd be doing time for rape if he was swallowing that bromide crap?" he asked the blond woman.

"But it's compulsory for everybody."

"Us guards had a quiet word with the cooks, ma'am," Chernitz drawled. "We need some privileges to make up for loss of popularity."

Peta Sandor was genuinely shocked when Gudenian confirmed that the guards had found a way round one of the Colony's strictest policies. Until her arrest she had belonged to the administrative elite—and like most intellectual radicals she was just as contemptuous of the anonymous masses as the reactionaries she was trying to overthrow.

"That's disgusting," she said shrilly.

"I need to save the battery," Gudenian explained, switching off the torch. There was just enough silvery light to see Magda's profile. He felt for her hand.

After a few moments silence, Nadine Boden said, ingratiatingly, "You will let me go back, won't you, Gudenian? I only had another twelve hours to do in the Compound."

"We'll talk about it in the morning. Go to sleep."

He twisted in his sleeping bag, moving closer to Magda. When she whispered her breath was warm on his ear.

"You haven't told them about the fox!"

His hand moved up to her face. He pressed his fingers on her lips.

Darkness fell and still he stood at the big window, staring out at moonlight on jigsaw patches of water. Even now, out there in the bitter cold of the night, shivering men and women were clutching desperately at each other for warmth, praying for daylight and rescue.

The phone rang.

But if Freedland was right, the fertilized egg now growing in Magda Hoessner's womb was more important than a hundred lives. For the first time they would have a genuine future . . .

The phone went on ringing.

It was vital that he kept control of the situation—he had never wanted power for its own sake but simply to make sure the thugs did not take over entirely. And there was no doubt at all in his mind that Magda Hoessner was the key to power. She changed everything. When Geneva heard—

Impatiently he picked up the jangling phone.

"Controller Bruce?"

"Who is that?"

The man's voice was cool and guarded. "I am told you want to make contact with the Chalk Circle, Controller."

He felt his way onto his chair. "Who are you?"

"It's a long time since you inspected the machine shops, Controller. You might be impressed by what we're doing with lasers. You might also test your popularity with the workers."

"The machine shops? Now?"

"The guards aren't so energetic at night. If I'm satisfied you're alone I may introduce myself."

"But—"

The phone went dead.

He sat for a moment in darkness. It could be a trap but he needed their help—and now he had something to bargain with. What did he have to lose?

He made up his mind and strode quickly through the outer office into the deserted corridor . . .

Sullen faces.

He had always assumed that resentment in the Colony was aimed at Khomich's guards, even sneakingly believed that he was personally popular and looked forward to the moment when he could let the people see that he had gone along with brutality and repression as a purely temporary, inavoidable stage in the Colony's development.

In each harshly lit chamber, men looked up from industrial lasers and lathes and ultrasonic stress-detectors—but nobody smiled. Outright hostility would have been less frightening. When he asked questions about their work and conditions the overpowering noise of the machines gave them an excuse to shake their heads and pretend they could not hear his words.

He made a point of ignoring the guards but it made no difference. He went from one vaulted chamber to another through shored-up passageways, pretending to examine timber walls for water seepage, visiting every inch of the Sub-Tier industrial area, stopping only when he came to the floodlit entrance to a descending tunnel; over the head of a suspicious white-strap he saw half-naked men digging into hard clay.

He turned back then, feeling a new urgency; *something must be done.*

Not one of the sullen faces tried to speak to him.

Coming back to the main Sub-Tier guardpoint he gestured impatiently to the Area-Captain. His name tag said Empie. He looked about eighteen, with ridiculous jug ears, yet there was an air of condescension about him.

"I must be told immediately at the slightest sign of flood-seepage," he said. Empie nodded. "Tell me, son, how come all these people look so miserable?"

"Possibly they don't like twelve-hour shifts, sir."

"Do you like standing over them with a stick?"

"I do whatever job I'm allocated to, sir."

Bruce turned away, disgusted at himself for being part of the whole system. Empie summoned the elevator.

This time he switched on all lights as soon as he reached his office, fighting off a growing fear that he might be showing signs of instability.

The phone rang. It was the same cool voice.

"Did you enjoy your tour, Controller?"

"Why didn't you make contact?" he growled angrily.

"At least you saw conditions for yourself."

"Yes, and I intend to make drastic changes—"

"Is that why you want the help of the Chalk Circle?"

"I'll tell you one thing, friend, without me you'll get nowhere. There's a lot of things you don't know—"

"I'm afraid that's the trouble, Controller," said the cool voice. "You show liberal sympathies but your ego is paramount and unshakable. We don't need you, Controller."

"Will you damn well listen? I'm—"

The phone went dead.

In the whole Colony there was only one person he had known long enough to trust.

Lena Davidson was fully dressed in her executive quarters on Tier-Three—catching up on administrative papers she said unconvincingly. She drew warm water from the solar-heating tap and boiled it on a battery-ring for coffee, one of the privileges of her status. He remembered the first time he had seen her, on that first trip into the garden known as Arcadia. He hesitated, remembering the Lena of Arcadia, tough and tricky and perfectly willing to let them all die out of loyalty to the megalomaniac George Richards.

"Of all the people here I'm the only one who was forced into it," he began cautiously. "When they let my wife die I took off into the Outlands hoping never to *see* another human being. But Towne dragged me back—I never had a choice. Maybe . . . well, maybe I still resent the system because of that."

She shrugged. "I would have rather have died with George in the fire than drag out a meaningless life in this hole."

He took the tin mug and let it warm his hands. "They wanted me to set up an experimental colony and I thought it would give me a purpose—even if I'd had anywhere else to go . . . but it's all gone wrong, Lena."

She sat on the edge of her divan-bed, her hand restlessly smoothing her wrinkled blanket. "I don't care any more. Lindsay made me angry but . . . good old 'Butcher' Khomich saved the day. Ironic, I thought."

"The system will throw up more Lindsays! I want to change it, Lena. Will you help me?"

"Help you?"

"We're living like goddamn ants! We have workers and sentries and underground chambers, nobody is allowed to make a single move that isn't programmed. I want to see us living like free human beings again. Is that wrong?"

Her hand went on stroking the blanket. "It was free human beings who destroyed civilization. Sure, the system stinks but they're all eating, aren't they? Face up to it, Bob—we're test-tube creations and we're lucky to be alive at all."

"I didn't expect nihilism from you, Lena."

She grunted. "We're a biological dead-end and you're talking about the future? Now—if you don't mind—there's somebody coming to see me . . ."

He stood up slowly. "Another young guard?"

"It doesn't cure insomnia but it gets me through the night. I'm only twenty-nine, you know." She stared up defiantly, challenging him to say it, that she looked ten years older and sounded more.

"Lena . . . suppose I told you we could have a future . . . something worth fighting for . . ."

"The Chalk Circle? They sound like a bunch of puritans to me. At least I get real coffee and I don't have to sleep in a dormitory—all right, I admit it, I'm doing okay so why should I want to change things?"

"Suppose I told you it was possible for us to have children . . ."

Her shoulders shook with a wry laughter that failed to reach her face. "Go to bed, Bob, you're beginning to sound irrational . . ."

Going back through the empty building his initial sense of betrayal gave way to a grim elation. To have no friends was another kind of freedom.

The freedom to be utterly, totally ruthless . . .

10

Peta Sandor and Magda stood silently on a high ledge, scanning a vast gray sky. Halfway up the stack of old red drainpipes, they were at treetop level of a green jungle from which came a mysterious cacophany of clickings and rustlings and buzzings. Peta Sandor, who had lived all her life in cities, looked longingly over the topmost leaves at the distant bulk of Glasshouse, its towering walls already glinting as blue patches opened in the dull sky.

Hearing voices, they craned to look up the stacked pipes but Gudenian and the three renegade guards had climbed out of sight.

Nadine Boden emerged from the drainpipe cave. She looked up at Magda.

"You know it's madness—talk to him!"

Magda remembered the doctor well from her first days in the Colony. Like most members of the Colony's administrative class, Nadine Boden had treated her like a stupid peasant girl, far beneath her notice in the social hierarchy. "David knows what he's doing," she said coldly.

Nadine Boden turned on the stocky Gento.

"You knocked out a guard because he was bullying your friend—are you going to let Gudenian bully you so far into that jungle we'll *never* find our way back?"

Gento pointed at the mountainous shimmer of Glasshouse. "We were treated worse than dogs in that place—we should be grateful to him—"

"*Grateful?*"

"They were sending me to the Diggings for two years."

"You know it's not fair, Peta, help me, *please* . . ."

She was standing nearest to the edge of the red pipe when two shiny black stalks emerged into the daylight, gently probing the air . . .

Standing on broken shards which littered the top layer of pipes, looking at a distant horizon of gigantic blurs which might have been trees or buildings or storm clouds, Gudenian pointed east.

"There's a house beyond the lake—I reckon two days should get us there." He looked at Chernitz and Lindop and Delmer in turn. "You've all been on field patrols so you know it won't be any nature ramble. I can't go back now but you guys *might* get away with it—"

"The hell with going back," said Lindop. "I'll take my chances out here."

"Me, too," said Chernitz. "I'd be lucky to get life in the Diggings."

Delmer was the most doubtful. "You think they'll come after us?"

Gudenian shrugged. "They might. More likely they'll believe their own propaganda and assume we've been eaten up."

The big man folded his arms, eyeing Gudenian warily. "You really planned this thing? What happens when the field stores run out?"

"We kill things," Chernitz said eagerly.

"I mean ammunition, batteries—"

"We can raid them!" Chernitz dropped into a crouch, hauling out his pistol. "Hit 'em at night—lightning attacks—in and out before—"

"I did think of that," Gudenian said patiently, "but we find a safe hide-out first. We might even get more people to come with us—"

"More women," Lindop said pointedly. "Five into three does not go."

Gudenian held up his fingers. "Two into four, Lindop—Magda and me stay together no matter what. Okay?"

"What about Boden?" Chernitz asked. "You intending to let her go back, Gudenian?"

"What do you think?"

Delmer looked at them suspiciously. "Why are you smiling?"

A small black fly landed near Chernitz's boots. "We'll just have to let the lady choose, Raoul." He spat a gobbet of saliva at the fly. It folded back its wing cases, turning into a narrow-bodied beetle. He flicked at it with his rubber-soled boot. Its black wing cases opened again and it flew off. He grinned at Gudenian. "Not that I'm kind to dumb insects—I used to flatten 'em all the time but they make a helluva stink."

"We can't drag her along at the end of a rope," Lindop pointed out.

"We'll have to trick her—"

They heard a woman scream and moved quickly to the edge of the stack.

"Shoot it, for God's sake shoot it!"

Peta Sandor was pressed against a curved pipe, face contorted with fear. The black slug was sliding toward her, its eye-stalks probing forward as if in preparation for an embrace.

Gudenian unhooked his prod from his belt as he dropped down beside her. Showing her the grooved press-handle, he made her stand beside him as he touched the tips of the slug's tentacles, which immediately retracted. The black body changed direction, slithering away from them on a trail of glistening slime.

Gudenian gestured for the others to come out of the pipe. "There's one of these prods with each pack

—fix it to your belt. We don't have bullets to waste. It's time we got moving."

Before they climbed down he gave Chernitz and Delmer a rifle each. Delmer shouldered his without comment but Chernitz put the perforated alloy-butt to his shoulder, aiming at the distant shimmer of Glasshouse. "Feels as if it could do some damage," he said enthusiastically. "I always hoped I'd get a chance to use one against the cat but—"

"The cat!" Peta Sandor glared at Gudenian in horror. "You forgot all about—"

"No I didn't." Gudenian swung his legs over the outer rim of the drainpipe. "The cat's as big as a house and it's whiter than snow and it's also got a bell round its neck. We'll see it long before it gets anywhere near us." He caught Magda's eye and gave her an imperceptible wink. He dropped down onto the next pipe.

"Don't worry, Peta," Chernitz said cheerfully, taking hold of her elbow, "you got three trained marksmen here, we won't let that feline monster play pussyfoot with you."

She shook his arm off. Chernitz looked hurt.

They went down one at a time, lowering the packs from ledge to ledge, descending into the thick greenery that soon blotted out the sky. Gudenian reached the bottom first, finding a jagged shard which formed a dry platform in a sea of wet weeds and swampy earth.

One by one they jumped to meet his outstretched hands and started pulling on their packs again. All except Nadine Boden, who sat down on the curved roof of a pipe and glared at them.

"I'm not going any farther," she said stubbornly.

"Okay." Gudenian pointed vaguely through the green jungle of Beyond. "You'll hit the concrete perimeter strip that way—the tunnel is at the western end of the brick wall. Hope you make it." He turned to the others. "Travel in a tight group—the moment you look like you're falling behind give a shout. Use your prods and—"

Something dark skimmed over their heads in a feathery swoop that fanned cool air against their upturned faces. They stared up into the beady eye of a bird with its head cocked, sitting on a jutting pipe a few feet above Nadine Boden. It inspected them for a moment, giving them time to see the bright red feathers on its chest, then it snapped at something moving on the pipe and it flew off with a rustling beat of wings, the big black slug in its beak.

John Lindop let out a sigh. "It was only a robin redbreast—they bring you luck, don't they?"

"Particularly if you get to shoot one for roasting," Chernitz growled. "The quicker I get the taste of that dry-pack crap out of my mouth the better!"

Gudenian asked Gento to take first turn of the extra pack, ignoring Nadine Boden. He prodded at the wall of vegetation with his metal stick.

"Are you all mad?" she demanded. "Peta?"

Magda looked uneasily from Nadine Boden to Gudenian. "We can't leave her to go back alone," she hissed.

"Why not? She wants to go back there so much —fine."

"At least give me a gun," Nadine exclaimed.

Gudenian snorted. "You're lucky I'm letting you keep your boots."

He stepped off the broken fragment of red pipe. Water slurped round his ankles.

He had pushed only a few steps into the soaking undergrowth when he heard the psychologist shouting. He smiled back at Magda and Chernitz.

They waited until she had taken her pack from Gento and then they pushed forward, Gudenian in front, using the metal prod to open narrow tunnels among the foliage, eyes flicking from side to side, leaving the others to keep pace. Scaly springtails erupted in jackknifing leaps from wet soil; small white moths fluttered out of dry hiding-places; red earthworms slithered like big, segmented snakes out of waterlogged burrows; dew drops hung like pearls on spiders' webs strung across little alcoves and grottoes.

Gudenian, like the three other guards, had been on enough field patrols to have lost his fear of the harmless insects that teemed in that strange, unknown world. He gave his senses full reign, eyes and ears responding to the heightened level of tension, enjoying a razor-edged awareness that made his whole body come alive.

He did not have to look back to know that she would be watching him in pure hatred, the white woman with the slanting eyes.

Nadine Boden, aged twenty-six, born Hong Kong of a German father and Chinese mother, educated at boarding schools in England, graduate in applied psychology, London; joining the WFC administration to specialize in pictograms, she was assigned to a special unit coordinating research into methods of population control; her passionate belief in the ideals of World Food Control, for which both her parents had worked as medical doctors, had been shaken by a growing realization that the psychological techniques used for remotivating imprisoned dissidents involved actual cruelty; she had joined various underground movements, all of them collapsing under the brutal reality of where power lay— in the hands of whoever controlled the sources of food. Volunteering for micro-cloning as her only escape from participation in what she began to regard as a dictatorship, she came face to face with an even harsher system. While carrying out her duties as the Colony's senior psychologist, she had helped organize the secret movement known as the Chalk Circle, a fact known only to four other people.

Ironically, it had been her own suggestion to Deputy-Commandant Lindsay that was responsible for her presence in the Rehabilitation Compound. How better to study the effectiveness of psychological shock treatment than by posing as a prisoner herself? Lindsay had seen it as a neat way of infiltrating her into the Chalk Circle. Spared the routine beatings suffered by other prisoners, she had otherwise been subjected to the punitive disorientation process. Her real aim had been to prove to Lindsay that she was worthy of promotion to executive status, possibly even to membership of the ICC.

Gudenian's reckless breakout had ruined everything. As she squelched through the swampy undergrowth she was trying to make up her mind which of the others would be most likely to help her escape from Gudenian. She had to get back to Glasshouse, that was all that mattered.

Most people made the mistake of taking Nadine Boden for a pleasantly self-effacing person, typically English in her outward lack of aggression. It suited her to go through life in this role. Of her own total ruthlessness she had no doubt whatsoever.

Using his boot to flatten hard, yellow stalks of grass, Gudenian's eye was caught by something brown and shiny. He thought it was a stone but then it moved. He stopped with an urgent gesture of his left hand. He gently parted tall grass with his prod, and found himself looking into four gold-flecked jewels. A broad yellow throat rose and fell in time to a heartbeat.

"What is it?" Delmer demanded, unshouldering his rifle.

Gudenian gripped the big man's arm.

Trapped in a narrow avenue under an arch of yellow stalks, the massive female toad had her puny husband riding in grotesquely intimate piggy-back, his squat hindlegs locked into the sides of her hugely swollen belly.

To turn she had to stand almost upright, towering above Gudenian, clawing with five-toed forefeet at the walls of grass.

She crawled away from them on four legs, her half-sized mate jogging on her wart-covered back. A bitter stench reached their nostrils, making them spit and rub their mouths in grimacing revulsion.

"Don't go near them—those warts are poison glands," said Peta Sandor. Chernitz gaped at her incredulously.

"Go near them? Jesus Christ!"

Gudenian looked for another way through the tall grass. Behind him he heard the blond Hungarian explaining that male toads rode piggy-back to the nearest water in the mating season, not because they were lazy parasites but to keep possession of the female.

"Toads have always aroused dark fears from the human subconscious," Peta Sandor told Lindop, enjoying the outright fear on the face of the aggressive young guard. "It may be something inherited from our primeval origins."

"Yeah, they did look evil," Chernitz said seriously, "you wouldn't like to hold my hand, would you?"

Peta Sandor, aged twenty-four, born in Vienna of Hungarian parents who both died in the second wave of famine; a qualified biochemist, she had joined WFC to serve humanity and almost immediately found herself in strident opposition to its rigid bureaucracy; given the option of dismissal from WFC —and therefore of inevitable unemployment and possible starvation—or of volunteering for micro-cloning, she had come to Colony One eight months before, again prepared to serve humanity, again reacting violently to authoritarian bureaucracy; caught with Chalk Circle pamphlets in her locker, she had been sentenced to six months hard labor in the Diggings. In her official psychoprofile—initialled by Nadine Boden—she was described as having a schizoid attitude to authority, resenting it partly from a sense of injustice, partly from her own latent power complex.

After the initial shock of Gudenian's breakout, she had begun to realize he was more than just a murderous renegade. She did not quite understand his relationship with Magda Hoessner but she had never yet met a man whom she could not use to her own purpose.

Already she had grimly satisfying visions of the little outlaw band bringing fire and destruction to the prison Colony where she had been humiliated and beaten.

When they came out of the wet grass they found themselves facing a steep slope of yellow builders' sand.

"If we stay in that wet stuff we'll get chilled," Gudenian announced. "We'll be out in the open, so keep your eyes skinned."

The dark-eyed Chernitz smiled at Peta. "If you start slipping just hang onto me, ma'am."

"I don't think I'll slip that far," she retorted.

Chernitz gave her a smile. At the moment his preference was for Nadine Boden, who reminded him of a schoolteacher who had once vainly tried to interest him in books, but with only two women and four men he was keeping all options open.

Abram Chernitz, aged twenty-four, born Chicago, youngest of a patrolman's five children; ran away from home at twelve, petty thief graduating to armed food-racketeering, sentenced to hard labor in Canal Zone construction camp; escaped, joined WFC cargo fleet as deckhand with papers stolen from a seaman in Barranquilla; jumped ship in Hamburg, enlisted WFC armed forces to escape mass roundup of unregistered civilians, served fourteen months in East African division, volunteered for Colony One as alternative to penal battalion after field court martial on charge of striking an officer.

Barely literate, he had not understood the implications of micro-cloning but had adapted quickly to the pseudo-military environment of the Security Guard. Sentenced to hard labor in the Diggings for rape, his natural optimism had never allowed him to doubt that he would escape in some way. As they started up the mound of weather-hardened sand he was thinking no farther ahead than how to make sure he got one of the two available women. He had no illusions about ever returning to Glasshouse, and very few about their chances of surviving for long in Beyond. On the other hand, since the age of twelve he had survived happily enough with a simple philosophy of screwing some satisfaction out of every day he managed to stay alive.

By now the air above them was alive with the flitting, darting silhouettes of winged insects; from all sides came a steady hum, as of a massed orchestra endlessly tuning up. After the chill wetness of the grass jungle they began to sweat, lagging behind the long-striding Gudenian, complaining of the heat and the dazzling glare of the yellow sand.

When they reached the shoulder of the hill Gudenian gave them a rest while he climbed higher. The others flopped down beside their packs, except Manuel Gento, who followed Gudenian, chewing methodically on a dry cake of concentrated amino-acid protein.

When he saw the stocky field worker coming up the slope Gudenian carefully hid the map in his jacket.

"There's a big dark patch ahead—you make out what it is, Manuel?"

Gento shielded his eyes with his hand. "It looks like an airport runway," he was saying when a dancing cloud of bloodsucker midges came at them from the blue sky.

At first the midges hovered above their heads, inspecting this new prey. Then the attack began, bloodsucking flies showing the cunning of a wolfpack, individuals darting in and being beaten off, only to be replaced by fresh maurauders zooming in from the opposite direction. They hit out with their prods but the midges were never where they'd been a moment before.

"Spray them!" Lindop yelled, swinging his prod like a broadsword.

Gudenian knelt down to fumble with his pack

straps. A hairy-legged midge dropped toward his face. He lashed out at its biting mouth but it flitted out of reach. Two midges came simultaneously at Delmer, who stumbled backward, arms flailing at empty air.

Gento swung his prod like a baseball bat. Poised to land on Delmer's face, the midge was slow in reacting. The metal stick smashed into its glinting wings.

The crippled body fell on Delmer's chest, broken wings buzzing ineffectually. Delmer twisted convulsively, shaking off the midge.

Gudenian crushed it under his boot. They started to run, hauling on their packs as they stumbled and floundered on a hard crust of sand. The cloud of midges rose and fell above their heads, effortlessly keeping pace.

They were running downhill when they felt the first stirring of a cool breeze. By the time they reached the bottom of the slope the sky had gone gray. The bloodsucking flies went as mysteriously as they had come. The breeze turned into a cold wind.

Gudenian kept them moving, heading across rough ground dotted here and there with broken bricks and bits of rusting metal and broken glass. At ground level on this harsh landscape the big dark patch was no longer visible—until they saw a wall of dark porous wood dotted with red fungus.

When Gudenian pulled himself to the top of the wall he saw that it was an old plank, stretching all the way to a distant horizon of blurred browns and gray sky, like a broad highway with neat lines of weed and grass forming a tall hedge on either side.

He was reaching down to grip Lindop's hand when Magda saw something and pointed, her eyes widening in apprehension.

Spinning through the air toward them was something white and ghostly, dreamlike, one moment rolling on dark wood like a gossamer snowball, the next launching into the air in a slow parabola.

They stared as if mesmerized as the wind carried the dandelion seed over their heads, low enough to see the white kernel and the silvery hairs, floating in a feathery roll that took it high into the buffeting air currents.

By the time they had all climbed onto the massive plank they had to brace themselves against the wind.

"It's blowing up a gale," Delmer shouted.

Gudenian pulled up his hood. "We'll keep going as long as it doesn't rain."

"It'll drive those goddamn bugs away," Chernitz shouted cheerfully.

As Gudenian began to pick his way along the uneven surface of slowly rotting wood, Nadine Boden hurried to catch up with him. "Have you *any* idea where you're making for?" she shouted.

He gestured ahead. Against the leaden gray of the sky she saw a darker blur of massive shapes as high as mountain peaks. "There's some buildings near the lake."

"And then you'll let us go back?"

"Save your breath."

"You can't live out here. How much food have you got?"

"You think the human race always ate in canteens?" Looking over his shoulder he saw Magda wincing painfully. "Something wrong?" he shouted, falling back.

"I feel sick."

His arm was reaching out to encircle her shoulders when the full blast of a gale knocked them off their feet.

John Lindop was bowled over and over by a thunderous avalanche of wind. His fingers clawed for a hold in crumbling wood. When he tried to look for the others his eyes blurred with tears. He fumbled for the hood of his warm-suit jacket but the moment he released his grip the battering gale rolled him across the huge expanse of wood.

John Lindop, aged twenty-three, born London, father unknown, mother a clerical worker in the WFC building; by the age of nine he took it for granted that his mother went with members of the WFC staff for food coupons; after minimal schooling he became a boy-messenger in the same building, rapidly making a name for himself as a pimp and all-round fixer; caught selling forged ID cards to unregistered civilians, his mother's influence saved him from hard labor in the northern coal fields and he was inducted into the WFC infantry; his ability to manipulate people and systems saved him from active service in combat zones, instead spending six years on garrison duty in Europe, reaching the rank of staff-sergeant; under interrogation for a variety of offenses—dealing in army stores, money-lending, forgery, organized prostitution—he had given the army Special Investigation Branch the names of six senior officers and fifteen civil servants in return for immunity for himself; part of the deal was his transfer to the micro-cloning project—he was assured that Colony One was an easy-going research establishment run by scientists without military intervention.

Finding himself in an oppressively strict regime where his acquired skills were of little use, Lindop's eye for commerce quickly spotted a commodity-opening, namely the total unavailability of alcohol; almost as a reflex action, for the Colony had no money, he had gone about the construction of a still, using an old drainage-sump he had discovered in the subtier pipe network; his attempt to blackmail an Allocations Office clerk for sugar out of stores led to his arrest and sentence of six months in the Diggings.

Any gratitude he felt toward Gudenian for freeing him from the brutality of the Compound had disappeared by the time the hurricane-force gale deposited his battered and bruised body in thick vegetation at the side of the plank; in a world of monster toads and flies the size of rats he had discovered genuine fear for the first time. A total and unabashed coward himself, he was already wondering if he could persuade one of the others to put a bullet in Gudenian's back and find some way of returning to Glasshouse.

One by one they found each other among the thick weeds until only Magda was unaccounted for. They huddled against a wall of rotting wood, watching leaves and dust and debris hurling overhead, communicating in signs against the deafening roar of the hurricane.

Pulling off his pack, Gudenian cautiously raised his head above their windbreak shelter. His eyes watered in a blast of cold air. There was no sign of Magda on the vast plane of the plank. Moving in a crouch he smashed his way along the wall.

Such was the violence of the wind whipping the tall stems he hardly noticed when his boots came down on something solid that immediately convulsed, throwing him sideways.

The huge olive-colored frog leaped high above his head its long, smoothly muscled legs and webbed toes like a grotesque parody of human limbs. The wind caught it on the upward curve of its leap and hurled it sideways. Landing on its back in the middle of the plank, its moistly shining body struggled to turn over.

Gudenian moved forward cautiously, poking into the weeds with his prod. On the plank the frog tried another hop—and again was thrown sideways in a jerking heap. It flattened itself against the wooden surface, then began to crawl on four legs, heading for the opposite bank of wind-whipped greenery.

Magda was cowering at the bottom of the wooden wall, clutching her knees.

She threw herself into his arms, clinging to him in desperation. For a moment he felt ashamed of himself; he had dragged her into this, the only truly innocent member of the group. How could they hope to survive out here? What right did he have to put seven lives at risk?

"Do you want to go back?"

He mouthed the words slowly, pointing in the

direction of Glasshouse. She shook her head, either failing to understand or saying no, which he could not tell. He helped her to her feet.

They were moving back along the wall in a crouch when the sky went dark.

Looking up, Gudenian had a glimpse of white fur and the black pads of a foot.

The huge furry body passed over them and then the thick red tail.

He held Magda down in a narrow trench, covering her with his body, hardly daring to blink.

Vulpes Vulpes came slinking through the wind, barely breaking stride as he took the frog with a gulping snatch of his jaws, champing almost absentmindedly on brittle bones and delicately muscled flesh.

11

Heads down against the gale, holding onto each other, they fought their way across open ground to reach a raised path border partly hidden under tough creeping grass. Gudenian pointed to a stony slope above which they could just distinguish the blurred silhouettes of huge bushes.

As he turned to lead them along the leeward side of the old stone border he caught Lindop's eye. His look was unmistakably hostile.

He guessed it had something to do with the fox. That was the trouble with guards—of all the colonists they were best trained for survival in the wilds but most of them would automatically settle a grievance with a bullet in the back.

The towering bush shapes came into focus, shrublike junipers with red-barked trunks growing at the summit of the craggy slope. He looked for a way up through the big cracks and fissures where rainwater had washed earth away from gnarled roots and buried stones.

They had barely started up the slope when something long and white came tumbling through the air above their heads. And then another . . .

Feathers!

A snowstorm of billowing feathers, white and gray and occasionally black, whirling up in eddies, spinning like surrealistic kites in the higher slip-streams, then drifting and rolling down the slope toward them like a soft tidal wave.

To Manuel Gento's surprise, Nadine Boden grabbed hold of his arm.

At the same time, through the gale, he heard a deep sound of organ music . . .

Manuel Gento, aged thirty-seven, born Barcelona, oldest of nine children whose peasant father had been murdered by army deserters; at fourteen a conscripted factory worker, by nineteen a section foreman in a fish-meal plant by reason of his physical strength; single-mindedly educating himself when others were drinking or sleeping, by twenty-one he was a workers' representative on the area industrial committee; by twenty-three he was a delegate to the Iberian Zonal Council where he kept silent on ideological and nationalist issues, creating an image of himself as a reliable functionary interested only in technical matters; by thirty-three he was deputy-controller of the Zonal Council, by thirty-five a member of the All-Europe Zonal Coordinating Council based in Geneva.

Throughout his rise through the bureaucratic infrastructure he maintained self-control to an almost inhuman level, making no enemies, achieving an aura of wisdom simply by keeping his mouth shut. He was promoted to the post of Industrial Adviser to the Supreme Council. People talked of him as a potential Commissioner.

His fall came suddenly in one of the struggles for power that had replaced the democratic process. The new Commissioner, Canetti, a lifelong bureaucrat posturing as a man of destiny, needed to create an illusion of dynamic change. In his ritual sacrifice of leading members of the hierarchy Manuel Gento found that the years of careful neutrality had won him no enemies—but no friends, either.

At thirty-six he was totally disgraced—allegedly for enforcing child labor in factories, although that had been official policy until quite recently. Being too squeamish for administrative murder, Canetti gave him the choice of expulsion into the Outlands, where nomads, indigenous barbarians, army deserters, criminals and political outlaws waged a grim war of survival, or inclusion in the micro-cloning project.

Quickly realizing that his previous prominence would only make him a potential threat to the tightly knit group that ran Colony One, he tried to submerge himself in anonymity as a field worker.

Until the day in the outfields when he beat unconscious a sadistic guard, Manuel Gento had never once committed a rash or impulsive act. Now, at thirty-seven, he found himself caught up with a bunch of renegades led by a triple-murderer through a savage nightmare world inhabited by monsters.

What astonished him was the fact that he had not felt so *alive* since his barefoot days in the streets of Barcelona. The feel of Nadine Boden's hand on his arm created a tingling warmth throughout his body, cruelly mocking the long, arid years of self-control . . .

They waded waist-deep through softly drifting feathers and then struggled up a narrow, stony fissure toward an overhang of exposed roots. Gudenian made them wait while he clambered over sharp rocks protruding from hard earth, shining his torch into the shadows of the cave.

Something moved. He stepped back into the wind and found a small stone, hurling it into the recess.

On thin, stiltlike legs, the daddy long-legs came to the mouth of the cave. Its twin antennae tested the air.

Chernitz threw a stone, hitting a finely veined wing. The crane-fly sagged, trying to turn. Gudenian jumped forward, grabbing one of the long, thin legs and hauling the big fly out onto the slope.

A current of air pushed it against a flint pebble. Splayed legs tried to get a foothold but the gale swept it off down the steep slope.

They climbed cautiously into the cave and slumped down, staring out in disbelief at a vast panorama of wind-lashed greenery.

"Where did all these feathers come from?"

Chernitz frowned moronically. "I don't know, Raoul—could they be from . . . *birds?*"

Delmer showed him a big fist.

"We'll stay here till the wind dies," Gudenian said briskly, crossing the cave to slump down beside Magda. She tried to smile.

"I don't feel so bad now."

"Could be your stomach rejecting the dry-pack rations—drink plenty of water and—"

"I don't bloody well believe it!" John Lindop snarled. "We just saw a bloody fox back there!"

Gudenian broke a bar of dry-cake and sprinkled it with water from his flask. He leaned back against the wall of the cave. "What's so terrible about a fox?" he said casually.

Lindop exploded. "You ever seen a chicken-run after a fox has gone berserk? They slaughter everything in sight—for fun! You told us the biggest animal we'd face out here was the bloody cat!"

"It wasn't interested in us, was it?"

Chernitz had his rifle between his knees, rubbing his forehead on the cool metal of the barrel. "What the hell would we do if it did get interested in us, Gudenian?"

He munched calmly on the protein-cake. "We've got three high-powered rifles."

"They wouldn't penetrate that thick fur."

"We've got other things going for us."

"Such as?" Lindop demanded.

"If it picks up our scent it's not going to know what size we are—"

"What if it just happens to step on us in the dark?" Chernitz drawled.

Gudenian took a sip of cold glucose. His pistol

was on his lap, the barrel resting between his drawn-up thighs. "We won't be stupid enough to be out in the open after dark. If it comes near us aim for its good eye—the cat clawed out its other eye."

It took a second for Lindop to pick up his mistake. The Londoner's face tightened. "You *knew* it was in the park? A bloody *fox?*"

Gudenian's hand closed on the pistol. "Yeah. That's how I got arrested—I tried to warn Lindsay." He was looking at Chernitz but keeping Lindop in his peripheral vision, tensed for the slightest movement.

Peta Sandor stared incredulously. "You brought us out here *knowing* about that monster?"

"If I'd told you—would you have come this far?"

"You bastard!"

Gento leaned forward. "I knew foxes when my father still had his farm. They are very clever and dangerous. You should have warned us, Gudenian."

It was the most aggressive thing he'd heard Gento say. "You want to make a quick dash back to Glasshouse?" he demanded.

Gento grimaced sympathetically. "I don't want to go back, of course—and you face hanging—"

"I'm never going back!" Magda flushed with anger. "I hated it in Glasshouse! What right do they have to treat us like criminals?"

"I hated every goddamn minute of it," said Chernitz, "but a fox . . ." he whistled soundlessly . . . "at our size we'd be no more than a quick snack!"

Gudenian looked at Nadine Boden. She was making a comb of her fingers, pushing back her thick chestnut hair.

"I think you know where I stand," she said calmly. "Perhaps the fox will bring the rest of you to your senses."

Gudenian's eyes narrowed to slits. "I can imagine why you want to go back, Doctor Boden!"

"I don't think you have any imagination," she retorted. "You were happy to brutalize other people when you were a guard—and murder them when you wanted to escape. Now you're just running for your life, smashing blindly in the dark."

He stood up slowly, letting them see the pistol. "Okay—I'm running because they'll hang me. First off, I only wanted people to carry enough equipment to give Magda and me a chance." He reached up his left hand, gripping a downward twist of cable-thick root. "I've realized since the more the better—I wish I'd sprung another dozen people out of the Compound."

"Yeah—but what the hell can we *do* out here?" Chernitz demanded.

Nadine Boden smiled ironically. "He sees himself as the fearless outlaw of the wilds, the great hunter—"

"I don't see myself getting whipped in the stinking Diggings, that's for sure," he snapped. "I've been out here on half a dozen field patrols, you don't have to tell me it's dangerous. But every time I left that prison I felt *alive*. It was like coming back to a place I'd lived in before but couldn't remember. Men lived in the wilds for thousands and thousands of years before they built cities and invented governments and got themselves trapped in all that crap. If they could do it, we can do it."

"What about the fox?" Delmer persisted.

"The hell with the fox! What about those primitive guys who took on sabre-tooth tigers with spears? We've got high-velocity rifles, armor-piercing bullets, electric prods, an acid spray—we're *equipped!*" He hung on the root, towering above them, deliberately creating an impression of size and strength. He touched Peta Sandor's leg with his toe. "What did they give you in the Colony? They let you fall in love? They ever ask your opinion on anything?" He shook his head. "They tricked us into micro-cloning because they needed specimens for a laboratory experiment! At least we can live like free human beings for whatever time we've got left."

Nadine Boden started to take off her boots. "Live like animals . . ."

The others looked uneasy, avoiding his eyes.

Through the wind he could still hear the strange new noise, a deep undercurrent of organ notes. He shoved the pistol in his belt—force wasn't going to settle this. Suddenly he grabbed the overhead root with both hands and pulled himself up to the roof of the cave in a cheerful display of gymnastic power.

"You want to know why Doctor Boden is so keen to go back?"

"There's no secret," she said, "I would have been back at work by now, I served my sentence. I know the rest of you were sentenced to the Diggings but if you go back voluntarily—"

"You know Area-Captain Steane, Doctor?" Gudenian jackknifed his body until his boots touched the cave roof.

"Vaguely."

"Vaguely? During the interrogation of subversives?"

"I didn't interrogate anybody—I simply prepared evaluations for psychoprofiles."

Gudenian used sheer arm-power to lift himself up and down, his body ramrod straight. "Steane and I were buddies. He told me you were planted in the Compound to infiltrate the Chalk Circle."

She snorted disdainfully. "You'll have to do better than that."

"Nadine was in the Compound like the rest of us," Peta protested.

"You ever see *her* getting a beating? You never wonder why they didn't give *her* a stretch in the Diggings?" He dropped neatly on his toes and stood over her. "You can *afford* to go back, Doctor, because you're one of *them*."

Lindop looked at her with a curious frown. She seemed unconcerned. "Yes, I was a spy—"

"You double-dyed bitch!" Chernitz snapped. Then he started to laugh. "We rescued a goddamn spy!"

"Yes, but not for the Security Guard," she said calmly. "I didn't have to infiltrate the Chalk Circle—I invented the symbol as it happens. I've been in it from the start, I'm one of the inner circle. I got myself into the Compound to prove my loyalty—Lindsay is going to nominate me for the ICC. We're getting ready to take over the Colony!"

"Anybody could make up a story like that," Gudenian growled.

She turned to Peta Sandor. "Your cell-leader is an SG section-leader called Empie." Peta Sandor blinked in astonishment. The underground cell-system was carefully designed to keep people anonymous in case of interrogation. Nadine looked up at Gudenian. "You threatened to plant illegal leaflets in Magda's locker if she didn't make love to you."

He whipped round, glaring down at Magda. "You told her that?"

"She told her cell-leader," Nadine snapped. "He's Bruce's personal assistant, Sasso the monkey." Magda nodded, wide-eyed. "She was instructed to compromise you, Gudenian."

For a moment he was going to hit Magda but Nadine jumped to her feet, pushing in front of him. "You blackmailed her first. None of us can claim any moral superiority in that respect. *But*—my reasons are legitimate. Maybe you could survive out here on some primitive hunting-band basis but how will that help five thousand people locked in a brutal system that's robbing them of every basic human right? You're simply running away. And if you want to keep me here you'll have to tie me up."

"Is that so?"

"Yes, it is so. And if I go back now, Lindsay will agree to an amnesty for everybody who comes with me."

He pushed her aside and went to the mouth of the cave, staring out at gray sky, vainly searching the horizon for the great mass of Glasshouse. Without looking round he barked at Chernitz to bring two rifles.

"Where are you going?" Lindop demanded.

"Up the hill. If any of you believe that crap you're welcome to go with her. Just make sure you're gone before I get back!"

Before Chernitz reached the top of a scree of loose stones he was almost deafened by the mighty honking noise. Gudenian was already flopped belly-down beside a red tree trunk. He ran at a crouch to drop at his side. The wind made his eyes water. He blinked, trying to make sense of the huge shapes moving between them and the leaden blur of the lake.

Then he gasped.

There were hundreds of them, a mighty army of black-necked geese, their brown bodies looming so close Chernitz recoiled in panic, already feeling himself being trampled under huge webbed feet.

Gudenian grabbed him by the scruff of the neck.

"You going yellow, you bastard?"

Crouched in a thicket of gorse twenty yards away, Vulpes Vulpes was watching the flock of Canada geese forced down by the gale, tensed to spring at the first goose which strayed from the flock.

He knew better than to rush into the heart of the honking army. One goose he could kill with a snap of his jaws but instinct told him they were nervous and wary at finding themselves pinned down in an unfamiliar resting-ground. Unable to take the air without a slow, ponderous take-off, they could easily find a collective bravery and turn on him in self-defense, scores of heavy beaks ripping into his flesh.

Then his one eye caught a movement.

He moved forward cautiously, head cocked sideways.

Avoiding the eternally aggressive geese, the brown mallard duck was taking her newly hatched brood to the lake, quacking softly to encourage her dozen babies.

The ducklings took each obstacle the hard way, little balls of yellow fluff waddling up smooth grass hillocks and sliding down the other side, budding wings spread in panic as they raced through the buffeting wind to keep their mother in sight.

Gudenian jabbed Chernitz. The brown duck was skirting the geese in a line that would bring her across the slope in front of them. "Aim for its head!"

"How the hell can we carry it?"

Gudenian gave him a mad grin.

The brown mallard's head was bobbing in their sights when the red fox came tearing across the slope.

Chernitz choked as he saw a flash of the killer's yellow fangs.

12

As his jaws snapped for the duck's neck, the fox's momentum slewed him round in a semicircle, his legs stiffening like brakes.

Squawking in hysterical indignation, wings threshing on grass, the mother duck fought until her feathers spewed up in the air. Yellow ducklings scattered in all directions, legs still running even when they rolled helplessly on their backs, tiny wing-buds flapping in pathetic parody of flight.

A warning honk alerted the flock of geese. Heads swivelled on craning necks. With lumbering steps they began to move. In zooming squadrons they began to take off, webbed feet running, huge wings beating the ground, each goose like a giant airliner boosting power for the big haul to get airborne.

The duck's wings stopped flapping. Confused by the hammering of wings above his head, Vulpes Vulpes was caught in a rare moment of indecision. The sky went dark with line after line of zooming geese. He looked this way and that, the lifeless duck hanging by her broken neck from his jaws.

At the first crack of Gudenian's rifle Chernitz blinked as if coming out of hypnosis. Gudenian's index finger pumped round after round of nylon bullets at the fox.

Vulpes Vulpes jumped as a searing pain ripped through his ear. Seeing nothing, he tightened his jaws on the duck's neck and bolted for the nearest shrubs.

"I hit him!" Gudenian shouted, pointing after the blurred red streak. "I hit him!"

All Chernitz wanted to do was turn and make a bolt for the cave.

The little yellow duckling kept flopping down on its belly, legs desperately paddling against grass and earth and stones . . . scaly legs still spotlessly clean from the egg.

Gudenian clambered to his feet, dropping his rifle.

The duckling saw him and turned away. He took it in a crash-dive, throwing his arms round its neck, dragging it sideways and trying to smother its struggles under his body.

"Get hold of it!"

Chernitz swallowed. The duckling was on top of Gudenian, webbed feet kicking empty air.

"Chernitz!"

He took a deep breath and sprinted down the slope.

"Use your knife!"

The duckling rolled over, starting to drag Gudenian across hard earth.

Lindop was standing guard at the cave entrance when he heard a shout. He came out to look up the slope. His mouth went slack. Chernitz and Gudenian were struggling under the weight of something big and soft and yellow.

Gudenian shouted against the wind. "Get wood for a fire—no more dry-pack rations!"

When Delmer's knife grated on stone Gudenian said the pit was deep enough. "Clear out all the loose stuff—we want these bottom stones red-hot."

Nadine Boden came to the edge of the pit, holding an armful of grass. "The way to cook a bird in an open fire is to seal it in a ball of clay."

Gudenian scooped out a double-handful of loose earth. "It'll taste just as good half-burned."

"You do realize a fire will attract every insect for miles?"

"Okay—so it's roasted bugs for dessert."

"You want to poison us all?"

"We'll draw straws for first mouthful—like those old kings who had a poison-taster." He got up off his stomach. "What's wrong, Doctor—you didn't really expect them to hightail it back to Glasshouse, did you?"

"I expected them to show some brains!" She threw down the grass. Magda came out of the cave, across which they'd draped the green nylon tent. Her sickness had gone but she felt a strange uneasiness, not painful, more like an intimation of pain to come. She saw David and the Boden woman standing together and frowned when she saw him smiling. As soon as he and Chernitz had gone up the hill Nadine Boden had promised them free pardons to help her back to Glasshouse, not caring if David lived or died. Why was he being so friendly to her?

"Does it remind you of the Boy Scouts?" Nadine sneered. "If so you've got a big shock coming, you can't—"

"I missed out on things like the Boy Scouts," Gudenian said ruefully, "I was too busy being a boy soldier. My mother hated me, Doctor—you think that's got something to do with it?" He threw back his head and laughed. Delmer stood up, slapping dirt off his hands.

"She said I should shoot you," he growled.

Gudenian patted the big man on the back. "What did you say, Raoul?"

Delmer shrugged him off, staring heavily at Nadine. Before he could say anything Lindop was calling at them from the flat ledge above the cave mouth. "They're coming back! They've got wood!"

Gento and Lindop were dragging a long branch with thin side-shoots. Peta Sandor had an armful of thin sticks and dead grass.

"Now you have another problem," Nadine said as they started breaking up the branch. "How do you light it?"

"Didn't they have something called a tinder-box in the old days?" Peta said. "I think they used flints . . . or metal . . ." Her voice trailed off.

"Of course, you could rub sticks together," Nadine sneered.

Against a rapidly darkening sky their faces were pale and apprehensive, all of them suddenly aware of the fragility of their lives in a world where nothing could be taken for granted. The breeze carried a faint whisper of nonhuman sounds from the encircling gloom.

Gudenian kicked some dry grass into the pit. He looked at each of them in turn and then pushed through the tent curtain.

"A simple thing like starting a fire?" Nadine shook her head. "What about all the other things we don't have?"

Gudenian's face was expressionless as he came back out of the cave carrying his black metal prod. Nobody spoke. He unscrewed the shiny tip from the insulated stock.

"It's called white man's magic," he murmured.

The metal prod broke into three sections, the handle grip with the battery casing, the insulated stock, and the live-wire tip. He handed the stock and the tip to Gento. His fingers seemed to grope aimlessly in the black battery casing.

"You're right about one thing, Doctor," he grunted, "these batteries won't last long so the sooner we switch over to natural technology the better."

His big fingers teased a coiled bedspring-wire out of the casing. He carefully stretched it out, then his right hand tightened on the grooved handle.

Somebody gasped. The coiled wire was giving off a faint yellow glow. Gudenian waved it to and fro above his head until it became a blur of brilliant red fire against the twilight clouds.

They crowded round the pit as he crouched over

the heaped grass and sticks. Wherever the red wire touched, stalks turned black and curled against the heat. There was a faint whiff of burning, an eddy of white smoke . . . and a flame.

He waited until there was an expanding circle of fire among the crackling grass, standing up when thick white smoke brought water to his eyes.

"Somebody start cutting up that bird," he growled, "I'm starving!"

In a few moments the pit was a sunken blaze. Chernitz and Gento hacked at the duckling, slicing off legs and wingbuds, ripping into downy skin to get at the soft innards.

Gudenian touched Delmer's shoulder. "Make sure they sling everything in, Raoul, bones and all. What we can't eat we burn or it'll attract carrion eaters. Okay?" He punched him on the bicep. "You buck-toothed old bastard!"

The big man gave him an exaggerated grin that showed off his protruding teeth . . .

Tiny feathers only recently dried from the egg sizzled into a bubbling black tar. Sparks cracked like fireworks in an upward funnel of flames and whirling smoke. The juicy smell of burning flesh mingled with the haunting smell of burning wood. A red glow shone on the faces that came and went through the dancing light.

Delmer carried out Gudenian's instructions with a fussiness that first irritated Chernitz and then amused him. When everything had been thrown into the blazing pit Delmer stood staring into the flames, feeling happier than he could ever remember.

Nadine Boden came to stand beside him.

"You're a very stupid man, Delmer," she said quietly.

"If it wasn't for Gudenian I'd be facing two years in the Diggings!"

"Not if you help me get back—"

His big hand closed round her arm, looking to see if they were being watched. He squeezed her arm until she winced. "Even if I believed you I wouldn't go back to that place! We'll survive out here if we stick together—"

"You think they'd stick with Johann Himst?"

Her slanting eyes stared up at him, mocking and vindictive. For a moment his hands itched to grip her throat . . .

Johann Himst, thirty-one, born Liège, father a steelworker; volunteered for WFC armed forces at sixteen, served twenty months occupation army of the Ukraine, transferred to penal battalion as drill-corporal; noted for his physical strength and unquestioning loyalty he was transferred to a secret unit attached to No. 3 Detention Center, Wahnerheide. When he discovered the nature of the special duties for which he was to be trained he applied for reallocation to the infantry but was informed that refusal to serve in the secret unit would be an act of extreme disloyalty, punishable with maximum severity.

In ten years as assistant and then as Senior Hangman he had participated in the executions of five hundred and thirty-nine men and women. He also became an alcoholic.

When Commissioner Canetti came to power in a wave of revulsion at increasing brutality by the previous regime, he disbanded the Death Unit; Senior Hangman Himst was allocated to the micro-cloning project and given a whole new identity to protect him from retribution; under the old regime he would have been quietly murdered but Canetti rationalized his own squeamishness by ridiculing the notion that a former hangman would boast about his exploits. The administration's dark secrets would be safe.

Ironically, it was Delmer's determination to bury Himst the Hangman that brought him to the Compound for possession of Chalk Circle leaflets; he had found them during a snap search of a Tier-Three dormitory and, taking pity on the field worker whose locker they were in, had hidden them in his own locker while he found a way to dispose of them. A fellow-guard had turned him in—there was something about Raoul Delmer, formerly Johann Himst, that did not inspire affection . . .

When the center of the pit looked like a white volcano, Chernitz shielded his face with his arm and poked into crumbling ash with his knife. His blade touched something solid. Slowly he brought up a speared lump of charred duck meat. He blew ash off the blackened skin, face shining triumphantly in the glow from red embers.

Tentatively at first, they licked their fingertips, then began to tear off slivers of white meat. Soon their lips and cheeks were oily and flaked with charred fragments. They got down on their knees, poking into hot ash.

"Don't overdo it—you'll be sick," he warned but they were too ravenous to pay attention. Seeing Delmer standing back, alone, he told him to grab some while it was still going. The big man nodded mournfully. Gudenian moved away from the dancing fire. In the very far distance he thought he detected a silvery glimmer—moonlight on Glasshouse or perhaps just imagination. Magda came toward him, licking her fingers.

"You feel better now?"

She nodded. "We'll have to find a better way to do our cooking—"

"Don't you like it?"

"We've wasted a lot. David—do you think they'll come after us?"

"It's a big park, plenty of places to hide. If they send out the wasps we'll hear the engines—"

"Get your hands off me, you ape!"

"Get your hands off me, you ape," Chernitz drawled, mimicking Nadine Boden's English accent. "Sorry, ma'am, must be all this meat bringing out the animal in me."

Gudenian shouted, "Time we were under cover. Build up the fire—"

"Just tell him I'm not available for general pawing," Nadine insisted, glaring venomously at Chernitz.

"General Pawing?" Chernitz lisped. "Whose army is he in, ma'am?"

"Don't be silly, Chernitz," Gudenian growled.

Lindop flicked a small stone into the fire. "What's all the fuss—nobody's been raped, have they?" Seeing how Peta Sandor took this joke, Chernitz pursed his lips and whistled softly. Lindop flicked a stone at Peta's boots. "You think we have any choice about being guards? You think I bloody well wanted to carry a big stick and stride about stinking fields—hitting people over the head for not working?"

"You did it all the same."

"Gudenian—tell her what happened to any guard caught being soft with field workers?"

Gudenian yawned. "That place was designed to bring out the worst in everybody."

"Well exactly," Nadine exclaimed. "That's why we've got to change it! What the hell can we do out here?"

"I have a plan," Gudenian said enigmatically.

"A *plan?*" She snorted. "Turn urban men and women into savage hunters? Reverse the whole tide of evolution?"

Delmer turned on her angrily. "We've survived a storm, we've eaten better than we ever tasted in Glasshouse, we have a warm fire. Why should we go back there?"

"Because this won't last!"

Delmer spat at the fire. "How many guns has the Chalk Circle?"

"We won't needs guns, we can change things by solidarity—"

"There are three hundred and fifty guards," Delmer said impatiently, "don't you think they know how the people hate them? They'd be fighting for their lives—is that what you want? Shootings and killings?"

She held his eyes across the flames. "I don't know as much about killing as you . . . anyway, I'm making it quite clear—at the very first opportunity I'm going back to the Colony but in the meantime—" she pointed at Chernitz—"tell him to leave me alone!"

"Abram," said Chernitz. "That's my name—Abram."

"It doesn't suit you," Peta said sarcastically.

"Just thought you'd like to have things on a friendly basis."

"With a guard—a *rapist?*"

Chernitz frowned indignantly. "I only ever raped two women in my life—I wouldn't have done it but I was feeling lonely."

"Okay—that's it," Gudenian announced. "Manuel—you and Chernitz—sorry, Abram—take the first watch. Keep the fire going—there's not many creatures like a naked flame. And if you're lonely try a little conversation."

When dawn came Gudenian was sitting cross-legged at the edge of the pit, head nodding forward on his chest. Shivering with cold, he shook himself and rose stiffly to throw the last of the wood on the smooth heap of white ash. He filled a pannikin with water from a flask and placed it on some red embers. Hearing a moan from inside the cave, he pushed aside the tent-curtain and saw Nadine kneeling beside Magda, coaxing her to sip some water.

He knelt beside her. Magda was trying to curl up, moaning softly. He put his hand on her forehead. "You don't seem to have a temperature. I'm boiling water for hot mash, you'll feel better with something warm—"

"Oh no," she groaned, "I'll be sick."

Nadine followed him out of the cave. There was a rosy light in the sky to the east but below them the night shadows were still black and impenetrable.

"What do you think's wrong with her?" His stomach was tight with anxiety. What if she required proper medical treatment? How could he get her back to Glasshouse without handing himself over? "I asked if you knew what's wrong with her," he said irritably.

Nadine made a little grimace. "You're not going to believe this—but I think it's morning sickness."

"I know she's sick!"

"Morning sickness is a specific term for what women suffer in the first stages of pregnancy."

He frowned. "*Pregnancy?*" He grabbed her arm. "I'm getting pretty sick of you and your—"

"You asked me what I thought and I'm telling you—"

"Pregnant? It's impossible at our size—"

"Why do you think they're running an AID program?"

The water in the pannikin had started to boil but he kept hold of her arm. "AID?"

"Artificial insemination—you did know she was one of the test subjects, didn't you?"

"She's a nurse!"

"Freedland originally ran a fertility program with selected couples but none of the women conceived. They thought it might be psychological—in theory there's no reason a micro-cloned woman can't be fertilized—so they devised an AID program where the subjects weren't supposed to know—"

"You're seriously telling me she could be pregnant?"

"Let me talk to her again."

Half an hour later, as the first slanting rays pierced the giant juniper bushes at the top of the slope, Nadine brought Magda out of the cave. The others were reluctantly tasting a hot mash of dry-pack concentrate and boiled water.

Magda smiled apologetically but the smell of the mash had an instant effect. She turned away in disgust, doubling up and moaning loudly. Nadine led her away from the cave to where she was sick. Gudenian snapped at the others to get ready to move out.

Nadine and Magda were sitting in warm sunshine. Magda blinked up at him through moist eyes.

"Tell him," Nadine said firmly.

"They did a lot of tests under anesthetic. They said it was something to do with bacteria—"

"She is pregnant and they'll have checked her blood sample by now so it's almost certain they know."

He felt confused. "How *could* they know? She hardly knows herself yet—"

"I'll try to explain about hormones . . ."

A few minutes later he strode back to the cave. As he kicked loose earth into the pit he barked at them to hurry up.

"This is a good place," Lindop said, "the cave's dry and nothing can get near us on this exposed slope—"

"We're too conspicuous from the air. Come on—get that tent rolled up!"

"You said they wouldn't come after us," Chernitz said suspiciously. "What's wrong with your girl?"

"She's pregnant!"

"What difference does that make?" Lindop demanded.

"*Difference?* I'll tell you the goddamn difference! No micro-cloned woman has ever conceived. They're going to want her back, Christ knows they are. You want to be stuck out here on a bare slope with a fire leading the SG wasps right to us?"

The thought of SG helicopters was enough.

When they had covered all traces, he led them up the slope toward the massive trunks of the junipers. He made them flatten themselves below the skyline while he crept forward to survey the slope that ran down toward the huge lake. From its banks came the discordant squabbling of ducks but the army of geese had gone.

He felt in his pack for the black transceiver unit. He was extending the aerial and tuning the receiver band to the field patrol channel when Nadine Boden slithered up beside him.

"You didn't tell us you had a radio," she said.

He listened to the faint roar of unbroken static. "I've also got a map. Knock me on the head and you can steer yourself back to Glasshouse."

Her brown, slanting eyes looked at him in surprise. "I don't want to go back now—not on my own." He frowned. "Don't you see—Magda has changed everything."

"You're too devious for me—"

"Our first pregnant woman? They'll be so desperate to get her back they'll agree to anything!"

"Yeah? And lock us all up as soon as they've got their hands on her?"

She frowned. "You're right. We'll have to think of something."

He looked back, waving at the others to come up the slope. "I have a plan," he said quietly. When the others were crouched beside the red trunk he pointed out across the slope. "There's a house marked on the map, west of the lake. Keep close to the bushes—and if the fox shows up, aim for his one good eye!"

13

Rotor-blades picked up speed and the black and yellow SG helicopter rose from the Colony's heliport platform jutting from the glass wall above Tier-Six of the Control building.

The pilot swung it away from Glasshouse. Through the perspex canopy, Bruce saw the whirling windmill vanes that gave the Colony most of its electricity. Below he saw the Net stretching over the Colony's outfields. He rubbed his eyes, feeling a slight sensation of nausea caused by distorted vision.

The pilot looked normal, the young section-leader sitting beside him looked normal, so did the guards squatting in the belly of the helicopter. Yet, when he looked out, it was to see a huge escarpment of glass in which the reflected helicopter looked no bigger than a toy.

The next time he looked he could see Glasshouse as it really was, a shabby relic of the park's pre-famine days. The young section-leader touched his arm. He was trying to tell him something, pointing at his helmet. Bruce shook his head. With an apologetic smile the young section-leader stretched out and touched something on his helmet chinpiece. The roar of the engines was immediately replaced by voices.

"You're plugged into the intercom now, sir. Just speak normally, your strap-mike will pick it up."

"Thank you."

The pilot looked back, raising his hand. "We're passing over the Net heading due south," came his cheerful voice. "We'll hit the old walled garden in about five minutes."

"We'll follow the line of the high wall going east until we find—"

"Company on the port side!"

He followed the section-leader's example, craning to see through the nose canopy. A dark scimitar-shape swooped past the helicopter, and then another. He recognized the forked tail and white breast of a swallow. The next darting bird was so close he could see its beak snatching at flying insects.

His brain told him it was a perfectly normal swallow.

His eyes changed focus slightly and it became something else—like a supersonic jet fighter buzzing their SG helicopter as if in preparation for aerial combat.

He sat back, telling himself he had been cooped up in Glasshouse so long he'd forgotten the enormity of their situation.

"Something wrong, sir?"

He shook his head. "I haven't been up for some time," he said.

"It's sensory distortion, sir, we always get it at the beginning of a field patrol. Look, sir—"

He followed the pointing finger and saw ahead a sheer wall of dark red brick partly hidden by ivy. His stomach turned and his hands trembled as they soared up the huge cliff-face. For a moment they were staring up at limitless blue sky and then they were into the old ornamental garden. Here and there stone-flagged paths were still discernible among the greenery. The pilot tilted the nose. Greenery and red brick and blue sky whirled in a nauseating kaleidoscope.

It took him several moments to realize the helicopter's engines had been shut off.

"The Controller's air sick," he heard a voice saying.

He blinked. Through the perspex canopy he saw giant leaves and yellow flowers. The young section-leader motioned for him to take off his helmet and they climbed through the front hatch, dropping down onto hard stone dotted here and there with copper-colored lichen. Some of the guards jumped out of the rear hatch and ran straight toward a patch of spongy green moss, laughing and shouting as they tried to trampoline on the waist-high layer of velvet.

"Why have we landed?"

"The pilot thought he saw some wild cavies, sir."

"We met recently, didn't we?"

"In the machine shops, sir, you were doing an inspection. My name's Empie."

"I remember." The section leader's hazel eyes looked at him steadily. Without his helmet he had jug ears and the face of a boy. "We're supposed to be checking the high wall, Empie—what is the significance of cavies?"

Empie shifted uncomfortably. "We always land when we sight them, sir, the men look on it as a kind of—"

"Fringe benefit?" Empie nodded. "What about radio contact?"

The pilot leaned down from the cockpit. "The old garden's a dead area, sir, they expect us to be out of touch."

By now the guards had spread out in a long line, advancing shoulder to shoulder through deep green moss toward a huge plantation of broad-leafed dockens, holding their rifles across their chests. Bruce rubbed his scalp, feeling the warmth of the sun. He heard shouts—reckless and violent and unmistakably happy. The authentic sound of young males temporarily free from restriction.

The pilot yawned and stretched out.

"I'm sorry, sir," Empie said.

A blunt-nosed cavy with smooth sandy hair burst from the dockens. It took five shots to knock it squealing on its side. The guards went leaping through the moss. There was an agonized squealing as they descended on the fallen animal. He saw the flash of metal in sunshine and the squealing stopped. He heard raucous laughter.

"If I'd tried to stop them we would have had a mutiny on our hands, sir," Empie explained.

"What do they expect to do now?"

"They're cutting off meat to take back to Glasshouse, sir."

"And if I told them they were all on a Section Six . . . ?"

"I don't know, sir—but I wouldn't tell them. Not till we're back in the Colony."

Bruce looked across the velvety patch of moss. Black and red figures were swarming urgently round the brown carcass. "I hadn't realized the guards were so near to open disobedience," he said quietly. "Of course—I could have you charged."

"Yes, sir."

"Let's do a little horse-trading. I have some unofficial business of my own on this trip. I need a transceiver . . ."

"That's easy, sir—" he took a few steps toward the moss. "Okay—we're getting airborne, you men."

Bruce frowned. It wasn't only the boyish face that was familiar . . .

They did a steep climb out of the old walled garden and exploded into blinding sunshine.

At first the other side of the high wall—the outside world to which they could never return—looked much the same as the park, trees and shrubs and open spaces, with distant blurs that might be clouds or deserted buildings, a vast hinterland of greens and browns. They flew along the top of the wall with the nose tilted, scanning the barbed-wire strands. A shimmer of light on the port side resolved into the great river, an expanse of rippling silver so wide the far bank was beyond their range of vision.

"There's something ahead," came the pilot's voice. "A goddamn tree!"

They flew back and forth over the branches of the dead poplar which had toppled against the high wall, forming a perfect gangway up into the park.

"We can't move that," Empie said. "We might as well go back and report."

"I want to do a complete tour," Bruce said. He held out his hand, pointing at Empie's transceiver. Empie unclipped the black casing from his OD jacket. Bruce took off his helmet.

"Bruce to Gudenian . . . Bruce to Gudenian . . . do you read me, over?"

Saving the pregnant girl was all that mattered, he told himself, the others were thugs and criminals. Gudenian was everything he feared and despised in his fellow men, a uniformed bully and triple murderer, the eternal psychopath who had corrupted all human societies. And yet . . . was it possible that a brutal murderer could carry the torch of freedom?

"Bruce to Gudenian . . . this is Controller Bruce calling Section-Leader David Gudenian . . . come in, Gudenian."

The midday sun was directly on them now. Stones were already too hot to touch with bare hands. Their boots scraped on hard, gritty soil. They began to sweat but Gudenian refused to let them take off their camouflage suits.

And then, as the slope evened out toward a forest of green stems and blue flowers, there was a sudden transition from harsh sunlight into somber shadow. The sky above was still bright blue but something had cut off the sun. The ground started sloping up again as they skirted the forest of bluebells. Ahead loomed darkness. The air grew cold.

Magda clutched Gudenian's arm.

"It's a thunderstorm," Lindop snapped, "we've got to find cover!"

Gudenian pointed upward.

"Trees!" Chernitz snorted. "It's a goddamn forest!"

The Dark Area.

At first it was agreeably cool, then it began to frighten them. For a long time as they moved toward the giant trees nobody spoke. They walked on rotting leaves, boots sinking down into a soft, damp carpet. Gudenian felt a hand on his elbow. He looked around at Chernitz's puzzled face.

"We're safer in here than out in the open," he growled.

Chernitz pulled him back. "I'm not scared, Gudenian, but I think you ought to know there's an SG wasp buzzing around up there."

They stopped instantly, tense and alert, peering up through a vast gloom at little patches of blue.

"They're looking for us," Peta whispered.

Gudenian gestured irritably. "They're probably checking the high wall. Keep moving."

"Try the radio," Chernitz said eagerly. "We should pick 'em up if they're on field-patrol channel."

"What good will that do?" Gudenian was angry at not having been first to hear the helicopter engine through the general buzzing of insect life.

"Try it—what's the danger?" Chernitz insisted.

"Once we're higher up—these trees will block out transmissions."

The Dark Area grew even gloomier. They began to look for a place to rest. Gento pointed to a dark, solid shape that seemed too wide for a tree until the blurred outlines sharpened focus into the multitrunk bole of a giant yew. Clustered columns towered in eerie resemblance to the stone work of some vast gothic cathedral, blocking out sun and sky, an awesome monolith that silenced them in chilling awareness of their own puny insignificance. The distant noise-horizon of insects buzzings and clickings receded. In the oppressive gloom of the Dark Area the only immediate sound was the scraping of their boots on layers of rotting leaves and dead twigs.

Gudenian led them to a natural alcove formed by the gnarled bole of the red-barked giant, dropping his pack, apparently oblivious to the all-pervading sense of foreboding stillness. Hesitantly, the others pulled off their packs. The ever-restless Chernitz could not be subdued for long, however.

"Tune in, Gudenian, let's hear the bastards!"

"Why do we want to hear them?" Gento asked wearily.

"You need a reason for every goddamn thing?"

Gudenian produced the black radio-unit from his pack and extended the aerial. "These trees will make it a dead area—"

"Yeah yeah, so switch on!"

There was a fuzzy roar of static. He turned the casing this way and that. "Nothing—"

"Listen!"

Through the static they heard a man's voice.

"*... calling Gudenian. Do you read me? Over.*"

Magda clutched his arm. "They're looking for us!"

"Listen, for Christ's sake," Chernitz growled.

Again they heard the voice.

"*Bruce to Gudenian ... Bruce to Gudenian ... this is Controller Bruce calling Section-Leader David Gudenian ... do you read me? Come in, Gudenian ...*

He switched off, ramming in the aerial.

"That was Bruce himself," Nadine said excitedly. "He wants to talk to you!"

"He didn't want to talk when I told them about the fox. The hell with him."

"We should listen to what he says," Delmer said.

Lindop put his hand on the big man's shoulder. "They could get a fix on us, they got equipment that can locate an active receiver—you don't even have to transmit."

"But why Bruce himself?" Peta asked.

Nadine looked at Magda. "I think we know the answer to that. They *know*—and Bruce realizes how important it is. He isn't like Khomich or Lindsay, he—"

"Forget it," Gudenian said calmly. "I have a plan."

"What is this bloody plan?"

"I'll tell you, John, when I'm—"

"Look! I saw it!" Peta was pointing back down the slope. Her face had lost all color. "The fox! I saw it! I tell you, I—"

"Keep quiet," Gudenian hissed, shoving her to the rear of the alcove among the gnarled columns of the yew, grabbing for his rifle.

"Aim for its eye," he told Chernitz and Lindop as they fumbled to replace clips of nylon bullets on their rifles. To penetrate the fox's brain would need armor-piercing bullets.

Up the slope came a snake-smooth head covered with gray fur. Before they got a proper sight it darted sideways out of vision. Gudenian gestured angrily at Delmer to keep the others back in the recess.

Suddenly they were looking up into a dark and beady eye. A paw with long, sharp claws rested on the red bark just above their heads.

Lindop began to laugh.

14

The gray squirrel stopped a yard from the tree, bushy tail fully erect, each silver-tipped hair quivering with a fine tension that suggested some form of antennae.

Without any warning, Lindop dropped his rifle and ran out from the yew tree, waving his arms. Gudenian roared at him to come back—the others watched open-mouthed as he did a crazy war dance in front of the squirrel, which sat up on its hindlegs, drooping forepaws giving it the air of a dog begging for biscuits.

Londop let out a whoop.

The squirrel charged him, teeth bared, ears flattened. It hit him chest on, knocking him flat on his back.

Chernitz fired first, hitting it in the soft fur where long whiskers fanned out in front of a bunchy cheek. The squirrel leaped in the air.

Gudenian hit it somewhere about the shoulder. It squealed and started running in a demented zigzag. They fired at random. Dark stains appeared on gray fur, then it sank to the ground.

Lindop was sitting in a daze, head lolling between his knees. Blood was pouring down his neck. Chernitz gently lowered him to the ground.

"Jesus . . ."

The squirrel's claw had opened Lindop's cheek to the jawbone. Through sliced flesh and blood Gudenian saw a white tooth. "Get him back to the tree," he snapped, "don't let the blood fall on the ground."

While they carried Lindop back to the giant trunk, he watched the squirrel until it gave a last twitch and lay still.

Magda was tenderly wiping blood from around the jagged gash. Lindop was moaning. "It needs stitches," she said.

Gudenian spat. "It needs sterilizing first—with the dirt those brutes collect under their claws he'll get blood-poisoning." He touched Lindop's leg with the toe of his boot, eyes narrowing vindictively. "There's good old-fashioned iodine in the survival kits—pour it on the bastard."

"We don't have anesthetic," Magda said.

"Too bad." Gudenian straddled Lindop's legs, then sat down, pinning him to the ground. "Get his arms—he's going to regret his little moment of fun."

When Lindop saw Magda opening the bottle of iodine he tried to struggle. "Yeah, it'll hurt," Gudenian snarled. "Get a stick for him to bite on. Sure, it'll hurt, Lindop, risky being an animal lover out here." Lindop twisted violently, head jerking from side to side. Nadine Boden forced a length of dead twig between his teeth. Magda poured dark iodine over the brighter red of blood seeping from the ragged edges of the gash. Lindop's struggles became cataclysmic.

Gudenian smiled. "Is it hurting, John?"

"Show a little sympathy," Peta said reprovingly.

"He cost us twelve rounds of ammunition. The whole park knows where we are. *Sympathy?* Pour it on, Magda, make the bastard *suffer*. He thinks this is bad wait till he feels the needle!"

Standing on guard at the front of the alcove, Chernitz moved cautiously, shielding the transceiver with his chest. He flicked the switch.

". . . to Gudenian, Bruce to Gudenian—do you read me? Over."

He looked over his shoulder. They were all busy holding Lindop down. He switched to *Transmit.*

"We read you, Bruce . . . drop dead, I say again, drop dead!"

When they had only fifteen minutes fuel left, the SG wasp turned over the southern end of the lake, flying low enough to scatter white-crested coots and red-billed moorhens for the shelter of reeds. Looking down into the dark green water the pilot saw a lazy flotilla of big red and silver carp. Bruce went on transmitting.

The return vector took them up the juniper slope and then due south toward the distant shimmer of Glasshouse. He sat close behind the pilot, scanning the ground below, seeing the ruins of an old hut under green creeper and a stack of red drainpipes.

His thumb was on the switch again when he heard a faint American voice.

"We read you, Bruce . . . drop dead, I say again, drop dead!"

He held the black casing to his ear. There was an unbroken crackle of static. He flicked to *Transmit.*

"Receiving you weak but clear. Come in."

The faint voice did not break through again but he had heard enough. He crouched forward to shout in the pilot's ear. "Make for the north wall of Glasshouse."

They changed course and flew into the shadow under the endlessly towering glass wall, descending in a spiral to the level of yellow dandelions growing beside the white-brick base wall. Empie came forward. "What's wrong?"

Bruce pointed at the narrow strip of weeds. "I want to see the escape tunnel."

The pilot tilted the nose until they saw a black metal pipe jutting out among the dandelions. Bruce motioned at him to touch down. They landed on the edge of the great expanse of concrete. Easing past the pilot's seat, Bruce asked Empie for a torch and climbed out.

Empie looked down from the hatch. "You don't intend to go up that pipe, sir?"

"The torch, please."

Empie reached back into the shadows. Bruce frowned. Something had jogged his memory. He reached up his hand to take the rubber-cased field torch. Empie was reluctant to relinquish hold of it.

"I don't think—well, sir, I am responsible for your safety . . ."

The voice on the phone!

He stared up at the boyish face with the big ears. But there was no doubt—that was the voice which had enticed him down to the machine shops!

"If you're responsible for my safety you'd better come with me, Empie." He smiled up at the pilot. "Tell them we'll be coming by the pipe—no shooting!"

They watched the black and yellow SG helicopter zoom up the side of the huge glass wall, until its engine roar was lost in the endless swell of insect noise. Bruce opened out a map of the park, finding the north wall of Glasshouse.

"Gudenian said they were on that stack of drain-pipes we flew over when they saw the fox." He peered out across the gray expanse of concrete.

"A fox could have jumped up on that fallen tree I suppose," Empie said. He grimaced. "I wouldn't like to be in their shoes—if they're still alive."

"Let's try the tunnel."

They pushed through the dandelion stalks. The female Segestria had rebuilt her web. Empie picked up a stone but Bruce held his arm.

"Live and let live, son . . ."

They crawled under the silken strands and stood up in the hollow gloom of the iron tunnel. Bruce shone the torch beam on rusting walls and then on scattered Compound fatigues. "I don't suppose prison uniforms have much sentimental value."

"Were you hoping to find some sort of—*clue,* sir? We've had the pipe examined—"

"There's no mystery about how they escaped," Bruce said, shining the beam directly in Empie's face. "But I have found one clue, now that you mention it. Amazing—you look about nineteen but on the phone you sounded as old as me. You are the anonymous Chalk Circle delegate who invited me to the machine shops, aren't you?"

"You're blinding me, sir."

He lowered the beam. "Well?"

Empie coughed. "I don't know what you're talking about, sir, actually."

"Every human voice is unique, son."

"An anonymous phone call? That isn't much to go on, sir."

Bruce sat down stiffly, resting his back against the curved iron wall. "How long do you think you'd stand up to interrogation by Commandant Khomich, son?"

"Is that what you've got in mind for me?"

"That's up to you. Nobody seems to want to help me, so . . ."

Empie squatted down. Bruce placed the torch on the dusty floor, the angled beam lighting their faces from below. "Maybe nobody trusts you," Empie said calmly. "After all, you helped trick everybody in the Colony—"

"So now I want to make amends—is that wrong of me?"

"It's wrong if all you're offering is mild reformism from the top, a palliative that will merely reinforce the existing power structure—"

"For Christ's sake! We're alone in a three-inch waterpipe under an old hothouse—can't we forget the crap jargon and speak like human beings?"

Empie grimaced sheepishly. "It's how we tend to talk in the . . ."

"In the Chalk Circle? I bet it is. Frustrated intellectuals and pseudo-revolutionaries—"

"We did organize a strike!"

"A few arrests and the workers were trampling over each other in the rush to pick up their spades! Did none of you ever stop to think that without the guards you didn't stand a chance?"

"I can tell you, sir, the guards are near to mutiny and—"

"I've never known any soldiers who weren't near to mutiny—if you believed their habitual moans . . . you offer the guards a chance to join in a libertarian democracy and they'll blow your head off! They don't want to be *workers* for God's sake!"

"We're winning converts all the time," Empie said stubbornly.

"There are five thousand people up there, Empie. They're living on the most dangerous frontier Man ever opened up. You can pump 'em full of propaganda, inspire them with dreams of justice—and first sight of a red centipede they're running to kiss the boots of the nearest guard! No, son, in my considered opinion this Colony is beyond redemption—from the inside anyway." He picked up the torch and slanted the beam up into the pitch blackness of the tunnel. "But Gudenian's shown us the way . . . *escape . . .*"

"Escape to certain death?"

"Oh no—he's still alive—he called me on the radio. Told me to drop dead."

"Why didn't you tell me?" Empie demanded.

"I didn't know I could trust you then. We're going to break out of here, Empie, you and me and as many of your Chalk Circle friends who have enough guts."

"Break out? What good will that do?"

Bruce slowly pulled himself to his feet. "It'll put us in a position to lay down terms. Come on, they'll be suspicious if we don't get back, we can talk on the way up. It's going to need careful planning."

Empie grabbed the torch from his hand and shone it into his face. All boyish deference had gone from his voice. "Listen to me, old man—"

"Old?" Bruce shrugged. "If you say so. But just remember, son—old men can be pretty ruthless. You're going to help me because one word from me and you're strapped to that big chair in the Interrogation Chamber." He smiled and patted Empie on the shoulder. "You can do the same to me, of course. We've got a realistic basis for mutual trust . . ."

Vulpes Vulpes moved cautiously from tree to tree through the Dark Area. Even when his nose led him to the stiffening carcass of the squirrel he controlled his aching hunger, sniffing the wind, cocking his head this way and that for the slightest movement. The scent of Man was still warm and instinct alerted him for a trap.

Hunger finally overcame fear. He touched the squirrel with a forepaw, then jumped back. He touched it again. Satisfied there was no iron trap to be sprung, he dragged the dead squirrel into deep shadow and wolfed down flesh and bones and fur alike. Man meant danger but Man also meant food and soon he picked up the scent-trail again . . .

15

The Dark Area.

In their fear they crowded together, touching each other for reassurance.

They came onto a soft bed of rotting pine needles, staggering as their boots sank into an uneven, yielding surface. Each jarring step sent a stab of white pain through the crudely stitched gash in Lindop's cheek. His incessant groans became a rhythmic litany to unimaginable dangers lurking behind every gigantic tree trunk.

When their eyes moved, each empty shadow instantly became the blurred shape of a giant predator.

A dark green shadow ahead became a moss-covered log from whose towering side jutted fawn discs of rock-hard fungi. It stretched out of sight in both directions. They hesitated, terrified at the prospect of a detour which would take them into the deepest regions of that dark-brown world under the trees. Gudenian stared up the steep incline of moss and lichens.

The others flopped down on decaying wood pulp, only too glad to leave all decisions to him.

"We'll be able to see where we're going from

up there," he said with an attempt at enthusiasm. Nobody wanted to catch his eye. Even Magda seemed to be blaming him for what had happened to Lindop. For a moment he felt lonelier than at any time in his life. "I can't do everything for you," he snapped. Still their eyes avoided him. He prodded Chernitz with the toe of his boot. "What would you do if I wasn't here?"

Chernitz was wiping water from his chin and neck. "If you weren't here I wouldn't be here, Gudenian," he drawled. "But if you're asking my opinion on what the hell we do now—"

"We keep going, that's what we do," Gudenian growled, dragging off his pack and jumping onto a ledge of hard fungus.

He stamped his boot. The jutting plate of what looked like fossilized mushroom took the impact without a tremor. He flattened himself against damp moss and started pulling himself up. The moss pulled away from the rotting tree with a tearing sound and he crashed back to the ground.

On the exposed section of moldering wood, caramel-colored and riddled with small, neat holes, they saw a scattering family of gray woodlice as big as armadilloes.

Gudenian dusted himself and climbed onto the lowest fungus again. This time he had his knife, cutting footsteps in the soft fibers of rotting wood. His toecaps spewed out a fine brown dust.

"It's easy," he called down, looking over his shoulder. They looked at each other. Lindop was on his side, with his knees drawn up, moaning spasmodically. Nadine pulled at Delmer's sleeve.

"You could take him on your back."

The big man frowned. "I thought you wanted to go back to Glasshouse," he muttered.

She looked up at Gudenian's disappearing feet. "I still do," she said quietly, "but not yet. Don't worry —I won't tell him who you are . . . not unless I have to."

Gudenian shouted from the top of the log. They

stepped back until they could see him above a shoulder of soft green moss. He was pointing in the other direction. "I can see sunshine! Get the packs up here!"

"John isn't fit to go any farther," Peta protested.

Gudenian stared down at them, hands on hips. Surrounded by dark browns and deep shadows Nadine had a strange sensation of being in an amphitheater. For a moment Gudenian was remote, god-like. His voice was without emotion.

"That's bad luck for John."

Peta turned angrily on Chernitz. "Are you going to leave him to die—your friend?"

Chernitz spat, shaking his head. "My friend?" he said. Then he shrugged. "Maybe you're right." He touched Lindop with his boot. "The best favor we can do him is put a bullet through his head."

To the astonishment of the three women, Lindop immediately struggled to his feet, mumbling indignantly through swollen bruising. Chernitz gave Nadine an innocent look. "I guess you'd call that the psychological approach, Doctor . . ."

The packs were passed from hand to hand up the mossy log. Their boots gouged crumbling footholds in rotting wood. From the top of the log they could see a low horizon of brilliant yellow. One by one they slid feet first over the edge, clutching at moss to brake their hurtling descent onto soft pulp.

Chernitz was last. Slinging his rifle across his back, he sat down. Just before he slid over the shoulder of the log he looked in the direction they had come. His eye caught a movement but he was already tobogganing down through the moss.

Not sure what he had seen—or whether he had seen anything at all—he caught up with Gudenian, speaking in an urgent murmur.

"There was something back there in the trees—it could have been the fox."

"Don't say anything," Gudenian hissed. He raised his voice. "Make for that big tree with the round lump. Keep moving, we'll be out of this wood soon."

Vulpes Vulpes slowly let his head protrude from a tumble of green moss at one end of the moldering log. His body stiffened.

Against a distant brilliance of white petals, his eye registered the movement of small creatures. Only the ever-stronger scent of Man stopped him from bursting out for the kill . . .

A sickly sweet stench of rotting flowers filled their noses and mouths as they crushed through a carpet of pink-tinged petals toward the rugged old crab apple tree. Ahead was blinding sunshine.

This time it was Peta who looked back. Her breath choked in her throat. Her voice was a shrill rasp.

"The fox!"

Gudenian took one look. "Get to the tree!"

They broke into a jog, boots smashing down on silky white petals. Chernitz and Gento were half-carrying, half-dragging Lindop by the elbows.

New grass was waist-high around the misshapen trunk. Flies buzzed above their heads. Gudenian pointed to a hole, about two feet off the ground, accessible up a natural gangway formed by the crab apple's gnarled bole.

"Manuel—make sure there's nothing hiding up there!"

Gento clambered onto the fissured bark, crawling upright on all fours. He pulled himself up onto the rim of the hole, head and shoulders disappearing inside. Then he pulled himself into the hole and reappeared, waving down at them.

"Leave the packs here," Gudenian snapped. "Raoul—Abram—you go first, get up there and cover us with the rifles!"

"What about John?" Peta hissed anxiously.

Gudenian grabbed Lindop, who collapsed against him and slid to the ground. The others hesitated. Gudenian swore at them to get up the tree. He tried to drag Lindop to his feet but realized he could never get his dead weight up to the hole.

"It's coming!" Gento shouted, dragging Magda and then Peta into the hole.

Gudenian drew his pistol.

Chernitz threw himself off the gnarled trunk, crashing heavily to the ground and snatching at Gudenian's arm. "You're not going to shoot him!"

Gudenian pushed him away and swung the butt of the pistol against Lindop's temple.

"Drag him into the crack—cover him with the packs!"

"But the fox—"

"It'll get *us* if you don't fucking *move!*"

They were clambering into the hole as the fox's head appeared among the daffodils. Gudenian shoved the others back into the gloomy little chamber. Its floor was soft and damp, like old sawdust. Above them hung ragged stalactites of hard wood.

"Give us room to fire," he snarled.

"You left John down there?" Peta gasped incredulously.

"He's out cold—we won't let it get near him. Just shut up!"

He knelt beside Gento and Chernitz, sighting the fox in their rifles. "Our bullets won't penetrate that fur," Gento muttered.

"Aim for his good eye."

"Wounded animals are said to be more dangerous—"

"They're all dangerous," Chernitz growled. "What about that goddamn squirrel?"

The red fox padded cautiously in a zig-zag line that inexorably brought him nearer the tree. He lifted his head, wet nose scooping at the air. Over the shoulders of the three kneeling men, Magda saw once again the huge bulk of red fur and the dark pointed ears. Her throat was dry but she had no saliva to swallow. She saw a sharkfin tooth on the lower jaw, yellow and pointed, a steel-trap canine which drew her eyes like a magnet. She let out a low moan, turning blindly to clutch at Nadine Boden.

The fox took a few hesitant steps, so close below

them now they could see each lustrous hair of the rippling red coat. A musky smell reached their nostrils.

Gudenian cursed under his breath. The fox had its blinded eye toward them, a weeping, encrusted socket over which buzzed three or four green-tinted flies.

"Look this way, damn you . . ."

The fox sat back on his haunches. He flicked at the poisonous eye-socket with a dark forepaw, shaking his head. The dark-furred triangles of his ears were almost level with their little chamber in the trunk of the crab-apple tree.

Still the good eye refused to present itself.

Gudenian spoke in a low whisper. "Try for the socket, maybe we'll get a shot right into his—"

The fox suddenly stiffened, pointed ears flicking forward, forepaw frozen in midair.

They heard a drumming noise. The fox raised himself carefully off the ground, tail going rigid.

For a moment they thought it had located Lindop. Three rifles came into line.

The fox bolted. Its head-down dash took it to the edge of the daffodils. It started jumping forward in a series of high springs.

Suddenly it changed direction. Out of the yellow flowers shot a big brown rabbit.

The fox sprang out of the daffodils and overtook the zig-zagging rabbit before it could reach the shelter of a huge bramble bush.

The rabbit turned, losing its balance, hind legs kicking up spumes of dirt as it scrabbled desperately on its side. The fox slewed round in a right semicircle. The rabbit bounded toward the tree, big spring-kicks projecting it forward like a missile.

They saw the fox's full array of teeth as he charged toward them. Even in the electric madness of the chase to kill his long jaws seemed to be grinning.

At the tree the rabbit changed direction. They had a flash of its white scut and felt the pounding vibrations of its hind feet.

For a moment they ran in tandem.

The long, pointed jaws snapped down in mid-stride.

The squeal they heard then was like that of a tortured child.

There was no single moment of death. A violent tremor shook the big brown rabbit from head to tail. Yellow urine sprayed from under the white tail.

They stared in silence, each of them paralyzed by one thought . . .

"Try and shoot its eye out," Gudenian snapped.

"It isn't near enough—"

"It's as near as I ever want it!"

They fired simultaneously. At that range they had no way of telling if their bullets had found a mark but the fox seemed to start up abruptly, snatching the dead rabbit and loping off into the heart of the Dark Area . . .

Lindop was sitting against the base of the gnarled trunk, gently touching at the purple bruising on his cheek and lips. His dazed eyes stared up at them.

"What happened? Where have you been?" he mumbled.

Chernitz helped him to his feet. "You missed a great show, John . . ."

They emerged finally from the Dark Area into a massive plantation of daffodils.

They waded through tender new shoots of grass, telling each other they had survived the worst, holding up their faces to the warm sunshine. As they penetrated deeper into the daffodils they found themselves walking in narrow tunnels between crossed arches of smooth green leaves, bathed in a soft yellow light.

Sheltered from any movement of air, they made all the gestures and noises of people ruefully recovering from a tense ordeal which, in retrospect, makes them quite glad of the chance to boast. They felt safe in the green tunnels and archways under a sky of yellow petals. They breathed deeply, savoring the fleshly sweet aroma of the daffodils, a scent that was both fresh and cloying at the same time, a mystic scent that seemed to awaken long-dead memories and sensations . . .

Gudenian shook his head. He blinked stupidly. He was still walking yet it felt as if he had been asleep. He looked back.

Delmer was grinning happily as he made little slaps at the big leaves.

Gento started to speak, then his knees buckled. Like a drunk man, he kept upright on momentum alone, feet moving just fast enough to stop his body from crashing face-first to the ground.

Peta Sandor was walking with her eyes closed!

Gudenian took a step back, gesturing at Magda. His head seemed a long way off from his hands. Greens and yellows spun round him in whirling walls of shiny color. He felt himself falling into a pastel-colored vortex . . .

16

He was drowning!

Cold water filled his nostrils. His arms flailed desperately, lungs fighting for air.

He surfaced to look up at a white face that had no nose or mouth—only eyes.

Nadine slapped him again, slopping more water from her flask onto his face. Through the wet cloth covering the lower half of her face she was shouting his name. He tried to push her away.

"It's the scent," she shouted, "it's putting us to sleep! We must get out of the daffodils!"

He understood the spinning dream then and took the wet towel she was offering him and clamped it over his nose and mouth . . .

At the first touch of cool air on their faces they threw themselves to the ground, breathing in urgent, rasping spasms to clear the last traces of daffodil scent from their lungs.

Gudenian sat up, blinking against brilliant sunshine from an open blue sky. His body felt as if it had been pulverized by some massive exertion yet he was strangely relaxed. Slowly the others shook themselves and got to their feet. Chernitz shook his head, blinking his eyes clear. "What the hell happened?"

"We walked into a pocket of concentrated perfume," Nadine explained, "at our size all that scent was just too much for—"

"I broke my own rule, that's what happened," Gudenian snapped. "It only takes one careless moment out here and you're *dead.* Ask John Lindop."

"You weren't to know *flowers* would put us to sleep," Magda said.

"Well, I know now. I hope the rest of you take the lesson. This isn't our world. You have to consider *every* angle before you make your next move. One mistake—that's enough. Take nothing for granted." He opened out the map. "We must be near the lake now . . ."

Soon they found themselves coming down a gentle slope onto soft, marshy soil, facing a solid bank of gently swaying reeds. Checking the map again, Gudenian calculated they were at the southern end of the park lake and led them diagonally across the slope. By now the full orchestral hubbub of insect buzzings and hummings and clickings was reassuringly familiar. The glint of a patrolling dragonfly's huge wings and the sheen of its brilliant blue body seemed like a welcome sign that they were out of darkness.

When they came to a narrow finger of shallow water between the grassy slope and the reeds, Gudenian told them to fill their flasks.

Intending to splash her face, Nadine took a step into the clear shallows. Immediately the surface surged and frothed with urgent movement. She caught a glimpse of fat brown bodies churning up fine mud on the bottom and came splashing out of the water in a panic.

"I have always heard that clever people are the most stupid in practical matters," Gudenian drawled. "Only frogs and toads—but you weren't to know that, were you?"

"People weren't intended to live like this," she said defensively.

"People lived like this for thousands, maybe millions of years!"

"You can't turn the clock back. We've adapted to civilization—"

"We'll adapt to anything. For years I thought *war* was the normal way to live. Give me your flask." He took the water bottle and stood in the water.

"I wish you'd tell us what this plan is you're always mentioning."

He stooped over the water, finding a patch that hadn't been muddied by the diving frogs, submerging her flask. "I'll spell it out once we've found a safe place to live."

"You make it sound as if we'll be out here forever—"

"That's a possibility."

She came to the edge, lowering her voice. The others were flopped back on the grass. Chernitz had his boots off, tentatively dipping his bare feet in the water. "You do realize they'll agree to anything once they know Magda's pregnant—"

"Hand over Magda for those bastards to study in a laboratory?" He waded back to the edge and handed her the flask. "In return for which we might be lucky enough to be welcomed back into the prison?"

"It doesn't have to be like that."

"No?" He pulled off his black and red jacket and started throwing handfuls of water over his chest and shoulders. "How do you see it, Doctor?"

"Obviously they'll make it top priority to find out why she conceived and nobody else did. It opens up a whole new range of possibilities."

"Sure it does." He lowered his head, cupping water over his blond hair and face. "You take us back with the big prize and you'll be top girl, maybe a seat on the ICC, maybe—"

"I'd be in a position to protect you—"

"Out here I'm in a position to do my own protecting."

"Yes, but for how long? For God's sake—"

"Tadpoles would taste all right, wouldn't they?" he said briskly. "I mean, what do they eat—green stuff, isn't it, nothing poisonous. The French eat frogs, maybe we should try and spear one . . ." He smiled at her, wiping water from his eyebrows. "Nobody else wants to go back but you're welcome to leave any time, Doctor." He pointed at the distant blur of trees. "I think you know the way now . . ."

"You know very well I can't go back on my own. I don't *want* to go back on my own! I want you to be sensible and admit that eight of us don't have any future out here."

He stepped up out of the water, reaching for his thermal undervest to dry himself. For a moment she saw him against the blue sky, his wet hair flat on his skull, his arm muscles rippling as he rubbed at his chest and shoulders, a blond giant of a man, freed from all constrictions, Man the animal, the most fearsome predator of all.

"I guess I'm just too dumb to worry about the future," he smiled. "I just want to stay alive for a little while longer."

For the rest of the afternoon they moved slowly across the open slope. Repellent ointment and the HASG spray kept biting insects away and soon they lost their fear of the huge shapes that turned out to be harmless and easily frightened ducks and waterhens. A movement of cool air off the lake beyond the reeds made the blinding sun tolerable.

Distance was the enemy.

What looked like short stretches on the map proved to be endless vistas of grass and stones, with no visible landmarks on the horizon. The sky became a deep purple. Gudenian watched his own shadow lengthen. He led them higher up the slope, looking for natural shelter, eventually having to settle for the overhang of a big flat stone sticking out at angle from the sloping bank.

They hurried to pitch the tent, racing against a quickening darkness, too exhausted to think of finding wood for a fire, driven only by the need to get under cover from the mysterious dangers of the night.

Wearily Gudenian said he would take the first watch.

The others crawled gratefully into their sleeping bags. Magda came outside with him, mixing dry-pack concentrate and cold water in a field tin.

His first mouthful made him feel sick.

"You must eat," Magda said sharply.

"What's bothering you?"

"I want you to eat something."

He pushed her hand away, squeezing her wrist until she hissed with pain. "What is it?"

"You're hurting me."

"Tell me why you got that look on your face."

"You were discussing me with Nadine, weren't you?" she said accusingly.

He released her wrist, letting his head loll forward, groaning wearily. "That's all I need—"

"I saw you, don't deny it, you were talking about me."

"*She* was talking about you. She thinks we could do a deal because you're . . ."

"Because I'm pregnant? She's probably right."

"The hell with that! I told her she can go back any time but we're free of that stinking Colony forever." He looked at her doubtfully. "That's what you want, isn't it?"

She put down the field tin and came into his arms, snuggling against his chest for warmth. "She's much more intelligent than I am," she murmured. "When I was watching you, back there at the water, you looked . . . well, you looked as if you enjoyed talking to her . . ."

He made a little growling sound. "Go to bed!"

"I'm too frightened to sleep."

They stared out at a silvery shimmer of moonlight on the huge lake.

"Maybe it would be better for you to go back," he said slowly. "They'd take good care of you—"

"But it wouldn't be safe for you."

"It's a pity you ever got yourself mixed up with me, Magda . . ."

Her hand reached up, feeling for his face. "Don't say that. Tell me about your plan."

"I'm still working on it."

"If they know I'm going to have a baby they'll send guards to capture us, won't they?"

"You can bet on it."

They sat in silence, holding each other, looking out at a limitless night-world they could guess at from an incessant rustling and the singing of ghostly voices, some calling softly, some harsh and threatening. The silver light of a Moon that was beyond the range of their vision cast a hard-edge shadow from the big stone overhead. He kept scanning the ghostly panorama for any movement that might mean danger but his eyes saw shapes where there were none. He thought of the big dormitories of Glasshouse, crowded and sweaty and loud with bickering—but safe. It was madness—how could a little band of eight people break away from the anthill and challenge a world that had been waiting down through the eons to wreak vengeance on Man the Destroyer? He snorted.

"I'm a fool—we can't survive out here!"

She was fast asleep.

He got his arms under her and carried her into the tent . . .

When his eyes opened he was looking into a green sky. He felt warm and relaxed and pleasantly stiff. He blinked. The green sky was almost touching his nose. He tried to stretch out his hand and found it was imprisoned.

For a moment he thought he had been captured and tied up. He raised his head.

He was in his sleeping bag. The green sky was the wall of the tent. He struggled to free his arms and sat up. The other sleeping bags were empty.

When he crawled out of the tent they were eating cold mash from their field tins. Chernitz was stripped to the waist, pouring water over his head.

Beyond the overhang of the flat stone the sky was blue and the huge lake sparkled in the sun.

"How long have I been sleeping?"

"About an hour," Nadine said.

"Christ—why didn't you waken me?"

Chernitz tapped him lightly on the bicep with a clenched fist. "You needed the rest, Gudenian, we decided—"

"Who the hell said you could make decisions?" Before he could hit Chernitz, which seemed momentarily inevitable, Gento stepped between them, putting the flat of his hand on Gudenian's chest.

"We all made the decision," he said with quiet authority. "We are not fools, you know."

"You've wasted an hour of daylight at least, that's what kind of fools you are!" He went to sweep Gento's hand away but to his surprise found that the stocky Spaniard could not be budged. He was ready to lash out then, annoyed at himself for having shown weakness, but Gento gripped him by the hands. For the first time in his adult life he was up against a stronger man! Blood tightened the veins on his neck and turned his face a dark red.

"We are not escaping from one dictatorship to start another. You must listen to advice." Gudenian tried to jerk his hands free but Gento merely tightened the grip of his short, thick fingers. "You are no good as a leader if you are too exhausted to make proper decisions. Do you understand?"

Gudenian glared down at him, puzzled and humiliated by the smaller man's unshakable grip. It made no difference that Gento was talking sense—it made it worse!

He nodded. "Okay," he said, relaxing.

Gento released his grip and stood back, ready to smile. "Sometimes we all need—"

Gudenian's fist smashed into his belly.

It was as if he was taking a last deep breath before diving into water. He rocked forward on his toes, mouth opening and closing.

Gudenian hammered another punch into his face.

Recovering from shock, Chernitz and Delmer made to grab Gudenian. He held up his left hand, palm outward.

"Don't make me draw my pistol on you," he warned. They stopped in their tracks. Gento made gruesome choking noises, trying to force air into his lungs. His nose dripped blood.

"What did you do that for?" Chernitz demanded.

"The next time anybody puts a hand on me I'll blow his head off! Get the tent rolled up, we're moving out."

"For Christ's sake, man, he was only trying to give you some advice!"

"I'll give you some advice—all of you. The moment you want another leader for this party just say the word—but while I'm responsible for your lives you'll do it my way. That understood?"

Gento straightened up. His face was impassive. "You cannot go round hitting people," Delmer said threateningly.

Gudenian shrugged but his eyes never left the big man's face. "Maybe that's the kind of person I am, Raoul. You want to do something about it?"

"I feel sick," Magda said apologetically.

Shielding their eyes from an endless dazzle of sunlight coming back at them in reflected rays from countless millions of dewdrops, they left the shelter of the flat stone and headed on up the slope. They found that the flat stone had been part of some kind of old wall or ledge. Ahead they began to make out a sheer face of mossy stone. The ground underfoot became softer and they began to hear the rustle of moving water. They walked in silence, each trying to make sense of Gudenian's behavior, each a little frightened of him.

He turned them up the slope, skirting a patch of emerald-green grass shoots growing on wet ground under the wall. Peta looked curiously at Magda, as if she could explain Gudenian's ferocious outburst. Magda looked away, embarrassed. Not knowing if he would be angry, she said nothing about the churning queasiness in her stomach.

When huge drops of water came hurtling down on them from the top of the stone wall there was nowhere to find shelter. Gudenian grabbed Magda's hand and waved at the others to run up the muddy slope. From above came a deafening uproar of screaming and chattering.

17

From the shadows under massive dock leaves, they watched the sparrows splashing in shallow water under what looked like a curtain of green slime. Feathers fluffed out, the sparrows used their beaks to flick water over their wings, or rolled on their backs, threshing so violently that big drops sprayed down on the green leaves.

Peta smiled. "It's only sparrows having a bath."

Gudenian pointed at the crude stitching on Lindop's bruised, swollen cheek. "Last time it was *only* a squirrel," he snapped. "When are you dumb bastards going to learn?"

Peta blushed. "I didn't think it—"

Chernitz aimed his rifle at a chocolate-headed dock sparrow preening his wing feathers on the stone ledge round the flat stretch of water. Then he grinned at Gudenian. "S'okay—I wasn't going to fire."

Gudenian folded the map. "It's an old ornamental waterfall—there's a fountain up there somewhere. We'll kill when it's necessary, Chernitz."

"What's all that green stuff?" Nadine asked.

"Algae by the looks of it. Keep close under that

wall and hang onto each other—it'll be goddamn slippy."

Delmer frowned. "We don't know how deep it is."

"Not too deep for those sparrows."

"We don't have wings," Peta snapped. She saw the aggression on Gudenian's face. "I'm simply suggesting it would be safer to make a detour."

Delmer nodded, pointing at the wall of green algae. "There's water coming over the edge—"

"It's the overflow from a natural spring, it isn't moving fast enough to carry us away."

They weren't convinced. Faced with another challenge to his authority, Gudenian's face tightened implacably. Then Gento spoke—for the first time since the fight.

"The fox was following us through the Dark Area—we may still smell of duck meat, I don't know—but we won't leave any scent if we cross moving water."

Gudenian gave him a rueful smile.

The moment their black and red figures emerged from the dock leaves the sparrow family froze, heads cocked for a fraction of a second before they went screaming and chattering off into the blue sky. Water showered down on them.

"That's what it is to be *wild*," Gudenian said. "You don't wait around to satisfy your curiosity, you just get the hell out of it at the first *sign*. Everything that moves is dangerous until proved otherwise—and you don't make yourself available for capture while you're finding out!"

They hurried across a broad flagstone path, blinking against a dazzle of reflected sunshine from the smooth stretch of water.

Looking down into the shallows where the sparrows had been splashing they saw the soft movement of long green tendrils. Gudenian sat down on the edge of the stone and lowered his boots into the water. "Keep the weapons dry," he said, sliding forward up to his waist.

Green slime.

It slithered against their legs as they started out across the flat stone ledge. It undulated in the gently moving water like the long tresses of storybook mermaids, sinuous tendrils that rubbed against them in clammy, intimate caresses. When they got nearer the high wall down which water ran from the next level of the old ornamental waterfall, it seemed to writhe under their boots, softer than silk, more treacherous than ice. It hung over the edge of the sheer drop in long skeins that moved to the delicate rhythm of the flowing water.

As soon as they tried to wade faster through the flat sheet of water they found themselves slipping. When they slowed down the long tendrils seemed to be coiling round their legs and waists. Gudenian led them close to the smooth wall of water, reaching out to grip the green curtain of hair-algae. The smooth cascade of water was strong enough to push his hand down.

They waded forward like skiers, each leg swinging forward from the hip to find a firm balance before bringing the other leg into place. Their faces began to look cold. Heat loss!

He forced his thighs through the chilling water, trying to hurry. Magda slipped and clutched desperately at his pack. The whole line came dangerously near to toppling, heels skidding as if they were novice ice skaters.

Gudenian held firm. "Take it easy, we've no—"

There was a huge swooshing noise and a beating of wings that sent small ripples slapping against their waists.

Webbed feet hit the flat surface with a series of choppy, chin-high waves.

They clutched at each other in panic.

The mallard duck and drake paddled their flat bills in the water. Magda's feet slid forward. She grabbed at Gudenian's arms, almost taking him down with her. For a second he was looking at her face through water.

Another big wave smacked against the algae-covered wall and came back at them in a swirling undertow.

Delmer got a handful of Magda's jacket and pulled her to her feet. Gudenian seized hanging tendrils of green slime with both hands, water churning over his face and arms as he held on grimly, feeling their clutching hands clamping round his arms and waist.

The huge mallard drake stretched his bottle-green neck to snap at the duck's nape. She flopped down in the water.

Another series of waves raced toward them, smashing against their backs as they clung to Gudenian, exploding back into their faces from the wall. Gudenian threw back his head to gulp for air. So cold was the water flowing down the slimy wall he could no longer feel his hands.

With a terrifying threshing of wings that drove wind and water in a storm that threatened to sweep them away, the drake lifted himself onto the duck's back, his stiff tail-feathers quivering with the electric drive of copulation . . .

For half an hour Khomich said nothing at all.

But Bruce knew a fuse had been lit.

"It isn't so simple as you suggest." Engineer Grouchy's hand made rapid passes over the chalked diagram of the fallen tree that was forming a natural gangway into the park. "If we burn these supporting branches . . . here . . . the trunk may only slide half-way down . . . so . . . the full weight would be pushing sideways against the wall, which is more than a hundred years old at that end of the park . . . the wall might topple sideways, thereby creating a gap which would be much more dangerous than the situation we're facing now."

"May I make a suggestion?" asked Chief-Technician Masopust, a rangy Austrian whose hairline was severely disfigured by white scar-stitching.

Bruce nodded. "That's why you're here."

Still Khomich said nothing.

Masopust went to the big blackboard and faced the emergency committee that had come to the Technical Office on Tier Two for a final decision on how to deal with the fallen tree. "Why don't we douse the *bottom* of the tree with oil . . . here . . . then if we start the fire at ground level the whole tree will burn up."

"Once we start a fire of that magnitude we would have no control over it," said Chief Administrator Bogaert.

"There's been too much rain for it to spread—"

"I have to make a comment from the Security angle," said Deputy-Commandant Steane. "Those woods on the other side of the river will probably be crawling with hooligan elements now that the London garrison has been withdrawn and there are no outer-limit checkpoints."

"The sight of a burning tree and they'll immediately dive into the river and swim across?" Lena's sarcasm had apparently no effect on Steane.

"People foraging for anything they can loot? A burning tree will only draw their attention to the existence of a walled-in park where they might expect to find something."

"They'll be scared off by those fake notices about biological research—"

"Provided they can read."

Still Khomich said nothing.

Masopust suddenly snapped his fingers. "Got it!" He regretted his outburst and grinned sheepishly. "Tell me if this is stupid . . . but would an industrial laser have the capacity to cut through a tree that size?"

The hubbub was instantaneous.

"Brilliant!"

"How do we get a laser over there?"

"Dismantle it—fly it across in sections—"

"Power's the problem—"

"We can rig up a generator—"

"Or connect it up to the helicopter's electrical system—"

"It means a visible presence on top of the wall."

"How long would it take?"

"A day to set up—"

"Those lasers can punch holes in granite!"

Still Khomich was silent.

Lena tried to question Bruce with her eyes but the wintry smile that passed quickly over his face gave no clue to his reaction.

Grouchy went excitedly to the blackboard. Chalk squeaked as he made a quick sketch of the wall from an overhead angle. "We can position the laser here . . ."

Then Khomich spoke.

"Thank you, Masopust."

He waited until the tall Austrian had closed the door.

Grouchy was still chalking angled perspectives of the tree and the wall. Khomich told him to sit down. Lena gave Bruce a puzzled frown.

Khomich stood before the blackboard, hands clasped behind his back. "You can consider this an extraordinary session of the Internal Coordinating Committee."

"I hate to be pedantic but isn't it the Controller's responsibility to convene meetings?" Bruce drawled.

"That is correct." Khomich pointed to the door. "Bring him in, Steane."

"Yes, sir."

When Steane opened the door Bruce saw Empie's boyish face. He marched into the room and came to attention in front of Khomich, who acknowledged his salute with a curiously effeminate little hand-gesture. "Make your report, Area-Captain Empie."

"Yes, sir. All of it, sir?"

"I will tell you when to stop!"

"Yes, sir." Empie cleared his throat. "Acting under the orders of Deputy-Commandant Lindsay—"

"*Former* Deputy-Commandant," Khomich snapped.

"Yes, sir. Acting under the orders of former

Deputy-Commandant Lindsay I joined a cell of the illegal movement known as the Chalk Circle. My cell-leader and contact was Education Officer Annette Rosa—"

"Now under arrest," Khomich snapped.

"Yes, sir. She informed me that Controller-in-Chief Bruce had asked her to put him in touch with the organizers of the Chalk Circle. I had a conversation with the Controller by telephone—I did not reveal my identity. He said he wanted to overthrow the whole system. During an inspection flight of the high wall he recognized my voice and threatened to expose me as a Chalk Circle activist unless I helped him to organize rebellious elements in the Security Guard with a view of overthrowing the system—"

"Overthrow *me!*" Khomich growled.

"Yes, sir."

Startled faces stared at Bruce—but only for a moment. Men like Bello and Wisnovsky had lightning instincts for danger and their immediate reaction was to obliterate him from sensory record; already he was untouchable—in a few moments he would become invisible . . . dead and buried and expunged from official memory.

Khomich nodded for Empie to leave the room.

Steane closed the door and stood guard.

"I deny everything," Bruce said coolly.

"*Deny?*"

Khomich's rage was turned on with terrifying abruptness. "Who cares what you *deny?*" he screamed, smashing his boot into the front panel of the nearest desk. "I saved your life ten times and you betray me!" He picked up a drawing-board stool and hurled it at the wall. "I saved you when these fools would have helped Lindsay bury you!" He heaved the drawing-board over on its side, scattering pens and pencils and blueprints. "The Colony is in danger from all sides and you start a lunatic conspiracy against me!"

Bruce folded his arms. "I will leave it to this Committee to—"

"This Committee no longer exists!"

As quickly as Khomich had exploded he stiffened again. "I have declared a state of emergency. All functions of the Controller-in-Chief and the ICC are now under my jurisdiction."

Lena jumped to her feet, glaring at the others. "Are you gutless creeps going to—"

"Sit down, *woman,*" Khomich snapped.

"I will not sit down. I refuse to be—"

"Sit down, Lena," Bruce said, "he'll only smash up more furniture." Reluctantly, Lena took her seat. "Okay, Khomich, what happens now?"

"I am placing you in custody."

Bruce snorted. "You got enough cells for all the people who're as sick as I am of the way you're running this Colony?"

Khomich's pale blue eyes tightened imperceptibly. He became expansive, as if addressing children. "It may be a little crowded in the Compound—we have arrested every member of the so-called Chalk Circle conspiracy." He shook his head. "Did any of you imagine I would allow this gangrene to fester unhindered? From the start I have had infiltrators among these social gangsters. Bruce will be among friends in the compound . . . his pet monkey, Sasso . . . the black woman Annette Rosa . . . and perhaps a friend he did not know about . . . yes, we have the name of the chief traitor . . ." He looked at the ceiling . . . "It is very difficult to have a *cautious* revolution, Chief Administrator."

Bogaert's jaw dropped.

He was alternately weeping and shouting his innocence as the guards marched him and Bruce to the elevator.

Bruce said nothing, although he knew Bogaert was telling the truth. He was still pleading for *someone* to listen to him as they were escorted across the huge concrete floor of Glasshouse to the shabby Compound building.

As they waited for the main door to be opened, Bruce looked up. Brilliant sunlight was flooding through the towering walls of glass.

They were marched into a dark corridor. The door behind them was closed and locked by someone he did not see. Ahead of them, behind a barred gate-door, a disgruntled-looking white-strap section-leader checked their names against a list before unlocking the grill-door. They filed through into the hall of cells.

"This one can go anywhere you like," Empie said, touching Bogaert's shoulder with his stick. "This one—" he pointed the stick at Bruce— "must be kept in solitary confinement."

"A whole cell for one man?" the jailer protested. "Have you any idea how many—"

"Those are the Commandant's orders," Empie said.

"For God's sake—I never had anything to do with the Chalk Circle," Bogaert whined. "Tell them, Bruce, I implore you!"

Bruce shrugged. "I wouldn't know, Bogaert, I wasn't in it either."

The jailor pushed the escort guards aside and jabbed Bogaert on the chest with a forefinger whose nail had been bitten almost to the cuticle. "Nobody talks in here without permission." He pointed the dirty forefinger at Bruce. "I don't care what you were upstairs, here you are only a numbered unit. I tell you this once only—you will move when ordered and speak when spoken to. At all other times you will sit to attention on your bedplanks with your hands on your knees. You will not close your eyes, talk, sing, or tap the walls. First offense—six lashes. Subsequent offenses—twelve lashes."

Bruce was steered roughly into a dark wooden box. The door slammed. The only light and ventilation came from a transom of mesh-netting above the door. The only furniture was a bunk of greasy planks without bedding. There was a nauseating smell of disinfectant.

The door was thrown open and Empie stood in the harsh light from the corridor. "I have given orders that you are allowed no communication whatsoever either with prisoners or guards," he snapped.

"I'm innocent, damn you!" Bruce shouted, trying to force his way past Empie.

For a moment they struggled together, then Empie shoved him back onto the hard planks.

"I hope nothing happens to you," Bruce hissed, "I'm scared to death already!"

"No talking!"

The door slammed.

18

Zzzz . . .

Peta Sandor stared up into a haze of blue. The buzzing noise faded into the distance. She found that she was lying on rough stone. All around her patches of water were evaporating in steamy wisps.

She had been dreaming of floods and dark skies and dead bodies floating in a rising torrent. Until she felt the sun burning her face she actually thought she had been drowned.

The dark-eyed, city-sharp face of Abram Chernitz grinned down at her, blocking out the blue sky. He was humming a little tune. He clicked his fingers. "Just my luck, I love a duck," he chanted.

She sat up abruptly, pushing him away. The others were stretched on the stone where they had thrown themselves after floundering out of the waterfall. They began to stir as the sun brought life back to their chilled bodies.

Far across the open expanse of the massive flagstone she saw Gudenian and Gento climbing down a mossy bank.

"You want me to dry your hair?" Chernitz asked.

She gave him a tight little smile. "That won't be necessary, thank you."

He put on a little boy's hurt face. "Just my luck, I love a duck . . ."

She struggled to her feet, careful not to touch him . . .

"You might as well say it—we're in trouble and it's my fault," Gudenian said bitterly.

Gento stopped, wiping his forehead with a handful of green moss. They had found that the massive flagstone was part of a stepped path that climbed away from the ornamental waterfall, following the line of a series of linked pools. The house that had been Gudenian's obsessional goal—so seductively near on the map—now seemed unreachable.

"Are you asking my advice?"

Gudenian sighed ruefully. "I'm sorry I hit you back there—"

"No, you were right. I should not have put my hands on you. The leader of a group like ours must preserve his authority at all costs."

"Leader? All I ever wanted to do was bust out of the Colony—"

"Listen to me," Gento said seriously. "You *are* the leader now, it is too late to change your mind. You must show no signs of doubt! All our lives—"

"I was the one who talked about carelessness and then I almost had you all drowned!" He smacked the map with his knuckles. "This is scaled for full-size people. I was reading in inches—I should've been reading in *miles!*"

"We can't go back—so we go on. Simple—unless you're suggesting we sit down and wait to die."

Gudenian squinted across the flat expanse of stone. The others were sprawled out in the sun. "How long can they keep going?"

Gento shook his head. "You will feel even more guilty if you let anyone die. That is the basic truth about leadership—how do you think Khomich justifies to himself the Colony's brutality? He is keeping alive people who would otherwise be dead. He does not expect to be popular and neither must you. They will thank you . . . in time."

Gudenian stared at the stocky Spaniard. "How come you were stuck out there in the fields? You sound more like a—"

"I have not always been a field worker," Gento said dismissively.

"Maybe you should be leading us—"

"There is a chemistry about leadership—you have it, Gudenian. I spent most of my life *talking*. If I was leader we would still be discussing the moral implications of killing Markstein."

"I've got to be just as big a bastard as the ones we're escaping from?"

"To keep us alive, yes. Follow your instincts, Gudenian, take risks, if necessary drive us with a stick!" He smiled. "Hating the man in authority usually gives people new strength."

Gudenian took a deep breath. "Thanks."

He was already snapping at them to get their packs on as they came back across the flagstone. Peta said they should rest, at least to give John Lindop a chance to recover.

"John's only got himself to blame. We're going to make that house before night—with or without him!"

They were looking tired and bedraggled as they set off across the massive flagstone. They climbed the mossy bank and found themselves facing another, identical expanse of stone. Half of it was in shadow from a looming bank of greenery—to keep in the warmth of the sun they veered toward the edge overlooking a deep, dark pool. Its limpid surface was immediately criss-crossed by pond-skater beetles fleeing on splayed legs from their dark silhouettes on the high ledge. Looking down Gudenian saw a perfect mirror-image of sky and clouds. Yet when he looked up he could see only a purplish-blue haze.

Chernitz hissed, pointing toward the center of the pool. In the deep, still water they could see the slow, majestic movements of red and silver fish.

Chernitz lobbed a dry-pack cake out onto the

pool. They saw a flash of red and silver scales. The surface swirled and white lips groped up into the sunlight, noisily smacking at the cake. There was a twist of a huge tail and a splash and the koi carp dived in a frothy vortex of broken water.

"We could catch small ones with a net," Delmer said.

"The hell with small ones!" Chernitz drew his knife, holding it between his clenched teeth. He mimed a dive into the pool. "Swim up behind a big one then—" he showed them how he would thrust the knife up into a fish's belly.

"You got energy to spare, you can take a turn of Lindop's pack," Gudenian growled. Delmer gave the extra pack to Chernitz.

"Teach me to keep my big mouth shut," Chernitz grumbled cheerfully.

Gudenian again saw white clouds in the water—yet those same clouds were beyond the reach of his vision when he looked up. Magda saw him frowning. She waited until they had climbed the next mossy bank onto yet another massive flagstone. "What's wrong?" she whispered.

"Nothing."

For the first time she became afraid of him, no longer certain of his moods.

He led them diagonally across the flagstone toward a mountainous swell of green leaves and white flowers. First they had to climb a short bank of delicate green plants. Chernitz had started chanting again . . . "Just my luck, I love a duck . . ."

"Don't you know any other songs?" Peta snapped as they waded waist-deep in heart-shaped leaves, poking ahead with their prods.

Chernitz frowned. "Now if I had my old guitar—"

Zzzzzzz . . .

Peta looked up quickly, catching a glimpse of something dark passing overhead.

"It's only a busy little bee," Chernitz told her, "but if you're scared feel free to hold my hand . . . you're free to trust me, my busy little bee . . ."

"I need a doctor," Lindop mumbled. Nobody paid any attention. "I need a doctor! My face is killing me!"

Chernitz nodded casually. "Tough."

Gudenian's prod met something hard. He carefully pushed soft leaves aside to reveal a cable-thick shoot with sharp pointed thorns the shape of shark fins.

"Careful here— these spikes will rip right through to the bone!"

At ground level the huge outcrop of brambles was a dead forest where no flowers grew, a dark brown place, silent, malevolent. Here and there a thin ray of sunshine penetrated the overhead canopy of leaves, giving them just enough light to move among the thick stems, on which the wicked points of shark-fin thorns seemed to be waiting patiently for impaled victims.

Magda shivered, clutching his elbow.

"I'm scared!"

"I need a doctor," Lindop moaned.

"Why the hell don't you—"

The ground vibrated to an urgent drumming.

They had time to hide before there was a crashing of leaves and a pounding of feet.

Ahead of them, through a tangle of massive stems and dead stalks, a big black and white rabbit darted into the shadows.

Suddenly the dead forest exploded in a frenzy of hurtling shapes.

Then came the squeal.

"Get down!" Gudenian hissed.

In his rush to push Nadine and Peta into the protection of a cluster of bramble stems, Delmer caught his jacket on the spike of a dead thorn. The fox came looming out of the shadows. From his jaws dangled the broken body of a rabbit.

He cocked his head, sniffing at the close scent of Man.

Chernitz, face pressed against a bramble stem

as thick and rough as a tree trunk, felt a tap on his arm. Gudenian was gesturing urgently, sliding his own rifle off his back.

The huge flank of red fur passed almost overhead. Where the long brush of the fox's tail touched the branches, fragments of brittle leaf floated down in a slow shower of dust.

Chernitz fumbled for his rifle. Nadine made a small gasping sound.

Delmer quickly pulled her face against his chest, smothering her sneeze.

Even as he fired, Gudenian realized the real reason for the bitterness that had been growing in him all day.

Two rifles fired simultaneously. Both bullets buried themselves in the fur under the fox's eye. He felt a hot stinging sensation and ran off, the rabbit bouncing under his long jaws . . .

Zzzzzzzzz . . .

Gudenian cautiously pushed back a finely veined leaf.

"Holy shit!"

ZZZZZZZZZZZZZZZZ . . .

Across a flat expanse of grass cropped to carpet-smoothness round scotch thistles towering as high as giant redwoods they saw a line of square wooden boxes standing on stilts.

Above them the blue sky was criss-crossed by zooming brown bodies looking as deadly as a random hail of tracer bullets.

Gudenian pointed. Beyond the line of beehives was the dark blur of the house.

"That's it," he said wearily, "we've made it."

When he looked round the others were flopped down in the young grass under the great wall of bramble leaves. Magda was flat on her back, eyes closed, panting and moaning with exhaustion. He stooped to shake her by the shoulder.

"We'll have to make a detour," he said. "Come on, we want to reach that house before night." Nobody moved. "Let's go!"

"I'm finished," Lindop groaned, "just let me lie here and die!"

Nadine tried to get to her feet. She smiled ruefully and held up both hands. He hesitated, then pulled her up. For a moment she clung to him, wincing at the stiffness in her legs. He turned away quickly and helped Magda to her feet. Why the hell hadn't he left the other women in the Compound—it was for Magda he'd brought them all this way—it was Magda he loved!

"My father kept bees in Cyprus," Nadine said, "They're fairly harmless unless you try to get into the hive."

Chernitz snorted. "We'll take your word for it!"

"What I mean is—we'd be perfectly safe going straight across—"

"They'll sting us to death!" Peta protested shrilly.

"You sure about that?" Gudenian spoke directly to Nadine. She nodded. "All right—"

"You're out of your mind, Gudenian!"

"I would rather face the bees than the fox," Gento said.

They left the shelter of the brambles, blinking in brilliant sunshine as they advanced slowly in a tight group across tightly mown grass littered with the flecked cannonballs of rabbit droppings.

Gudenian spoke quietly. "Keep in step, don't talk, don't wave your arms about . . . if they come near push them away with your prods . . . start running and they'll be on you in swarms . . ."

ZZZZZZZZZZZZZZZZZZZZZZZ

They held onto each other, mouths dry, walking almost on tip-toe. They passed a spew of soil from a round hole cut into the grass. Delmer pointed at it, saying something that was lost in the deafening drone from the beehives. Gudenian shook his head.

They came under two flight paths converging on the hive directly in front of them, one of fast-moving bees climbing away from the hive, the other of honey collectors lumbering home under the weight of leg-baskets tightly packed with yellow pollen.

Nadine touched Gudenian's elbow. She pointed at the hive to their right. Even to look at her made Gudenian feel ashamed of himself. His hand tightened on Magda's. Nadine jabbed him again, gesticulating at the other hive.

He saw then that there were no bees coming or going from the narrow entrance slit. He pointed and they changed direction.

Close to the hives they began to see that, far from being perfect flying-machines, the heavily laden bees had great difficulty in landing on the narrow ledge. Some of them crashed head on against the slat above the entrance slit, bouncing off and crashing upside down on the ledge. Some collided and fell in a confusion of glinting wings and hard, furry bodies. There was a deeper drone now, like the steady whirr of an electric fan.

Approaching the empty hive they began to see the shells of dead bees. Passing into the shadow between the big wooden legs they disturbed a swarm of green-tinted flies buzzing over a mass of strewn bee carcasses. They swiped at the flies with their prods, grimacing as they caught a reek of ammonia. Above them, the underside of the hive was mottled with red fungus spores. They hurried out into the sunshine on the other side, crossing more flat grass toward the dark gray cliff of a stone wall.

Gradually the droning receded to a low whine. Gudenian let go of Magda's hand. "At least we know where we can lay our hands on some honey," he said gruffly.

The old wooden gate was hanging at a lurch from a rotten post. Through its bars they saw a dark red wall towering so high their eyes could not distinguish where it merged into blinding sunshine. They helped each other over the bottom bar of the gate, avoiding the high-tension cables of a spider's web.

The ground beneath it was littered with the dry husks of dead flies.

They were in a stone-paved courtyard. Out of the sunlight the air was chilly and damp. They heard the chattering racket of sparrows high above their heads but nothing moved in the gloomy shadow of the house. They stuck close to a red-brick wall, cautiously advancing round a huge water-butt. Where water leaked from the slimy staves the side of the butt was encrusted with a hard, red scum.

Delmer pointed ahead. "That's the doorstep," he hissed.

Suddenly Chernitz was pulling back against the wall.

They froze, watching a red ant dragging a dead moth twice its own size across a hillock of green moss growing from a crack between the paving-stones. It stopped, its twin antennae flicking this way and that, then its big vertical jaws seized the white moth again, hauling its huge burden across an endless landscape of flat stone.

"If we were as strong as that we could lift mountains," Nadine said in awe.

It was exactly what Gudenian had been thinking. It was as if everything she said or did was deliberately planned to disturb him. He took Magda's hand again as they came toward a sheer wall of rough sandstone.

To climb onto the doorstep, he clasped his hands for Chernitz to stand on. Delmer crouched down to let Manuel stand on his shoulders. Two of them lifted Lindop, brutally ignoring the Londoner's incessant complaints that nobody knew the pain he was suffering from the inflamed stitches on his obscenely gashed face.

They passed up the packs.

An almost overwhelming urge to reach out and touch Nadine Boden made Gudenian so angry with himself he hurled one of the packs up at Chernitz, making the dark-haired American stumble backward.

"What the hell . . ."

Gudenian crouched in front of Magda. Seeing his bitter expression she asked what was wrong. He gestured impatiently putting his arm round her knees and standing up. For a moment she was looking at him, her fingertips on his shoulders.

"Hurry it up," he said irritably, straining to hoist her into Gento's reaching hands.

Delmer had lifted Nadine onto the step. Gudenian told himself the attraction was purely mental—she was much the most intelligent of all of them. It was Magda he loved.

Why could he hardly bear to look at her?

He was last, jumping up to get his elbows on the ledge, then lifting himself with sheer strength of arms, hoping that Nadine was watching and immediately cursing himself for being childish.

From there, looking out across the gloomy well of the courtyard, they saw more ants, moving in lines that converged toward the garden wall.

"They give me the creeps," Chernitz shuddered. "If we're going to set up in this place I'll burn them out!"

Gudenian turned on him viciously. "I'll say what we do, Chernitz!"

"All I said was—"

"Shouldn't we get inside before we start bickering?" Peta snapped.

They crossed the step in silence, craning to peer up a sheer escarpment of weathered wood, a few curling flakes of green paint still adhering to panels that were warping and cracking.

Far above them, mockingly familiar and totally out of reach, was a jutting door-handle. Delmer scratched his neck.

"I once saw an old newsreel of a man climbing the Empire State building in New York."

"Can we send for him?" Chernitz drawled.

Gento got down on his knees beside the heavy cross-timber at the foot of the door and lay flat on his stomach, reaching into the space between the door and the stone step.

"We can squeeze through here," he grunted.

Gudenian dropped his pack and lay down beside Gento. He snapped his fingers. "Give me a torch."

When he looked up it was Nadine who was handing him the rubber-cased torch. He almost snatched it from her hand.

The torch beam rested on what looked like a pile of shredded rope. He gestured at them to keep quiet, listening for sounds from inside the house.

"There may be rats inside," Gento murmured.

"The rest of you wait here," he said, "don't wander—keep your eyes open!"

Magda shook her head. "I want to come with you—"

"Stay here I said!"

Compared to Nadine she was a dumb peasant —the very softness and shyness that had first attracted him now seemed cloying—her big warm eyes made him feel smothered, trapped.

Pistol in one hand, torch in the other, he went in sideways, on his back, sliding and wriggling on rough stone, nose almost touching solid wood, trying not to imagine hinges that might suddenly sag and bring the immense weight of the door down on the wet stain that would be his body.

When his hand touched rope fibers he found he could raise his head. He squeezed up through a narrow space. The torch beam showed him that he was standing on a doormat. Gento rose beside him, dusting himself off.

They stood together in a soft gray light coming from far above their heads, a light that drained color from all surfaces, making the old kitchen look like a faded, two-dimensional photograph. The silence was timeless, tomblike.

On the vast plane of a stone floor they saw immense fragments of what they realized was a broken china mug. Beyond there was a fallen chair and a heap of disintegrating rags. The gray light gave an eerie impression of falling, like soft, dry rain. Familiar objects filled them with a deep, disturbing fear—

the broken mug, a filigree of delicate cracks on the porcelain of a looming kitchen sink, a table that towered so high it might have been in the sky . . . all of it bleached in the gray light of a world that had simply been switched off . . .

19

Gento shuddered audibly.

The echo of their voices rose into the vast heights of the gloomy kitchen.

"It's only an empty house," Gudenian said loudly, trying to convince himself.

"There has been violence done here."

"Somebody kicked over a chair is all—"

Gento shook his head. "It is not a home for us. There are other buildings in the park—"

"We've come a helluva long way and we can't go any farther."

He crouched down to shout under the door. One by one, dragging their packs, the others emerged onto the doormat.

Cheerful voices died away as they felt the cold stillness of a house that had been waiting silently . . . but not for them.

Nadine Boden could have explained their fear but she knew that bringing it out in the open and giving it a name would probably make it worse. The planners of the micro-cloning project had learned to lessen the trauma of micro-replication. From the moment of replication, crossovers were allowed no further visual contact with full-size objects or people. The proportionally scaled rooms and corridors and workshops of the Colony had been designed to induce an illusion of normality—which was why, apart from field workers, few colonists were ever allowed a sight of the huge world outside Glasshouse.

This first confrontation with human artifacts—a broken mug, an ordinary kitchen knife—brought a chilling terror that transcended physical fear. Face to face with what they had once been and could never be again, they were made to feel like ghosts trespassing on their own past lives; the living dead.

Gudenian was afraid.

When they looked to him for strength he wanted to let the words pour out, to admit that their fears were his fears, their weakness his weakness, *I am no hero, don't look to me . . .*

Something died in him at that moment . . . there was a new emptiness inside . . . a loss . . . or a casting-off.

"We have nowhere else to go," he said grimly. He shook himself. He could still feel his body, his physical existence. He blinked. The fear had gone! "It's only a *house*—people used to live here. I want to see the rest of it . . ."

When Magda's hand slipped into his, Gudenian forced himself to give her a reassuring smile, although her touch now irritated him. He told himself things would be okay now that they'd reached the house . . . his goal.

As they set off across the stone floor, Chernitz's image of a huge descending foot dominated their imaginations. The fallen chair and the pieces of broken china and the kitchen knife and the crumbling rags all seemed like hastily abandoned relics of an extinct species of giants. Nobody spoke.

They stopped before another monolithic door, open a few inches. Beyond was pitch-darkness. Gudenian switched on the torch.

Feathery white fungus formed fuzzy haloes round lumps of dried food still adhering to the two halves of a broken plate. The floor was covered in a soft layer of dust that was like dry snow, gray and powdery.

Nadine Boden had experienced many moments of fear during their long trek across the park but outside, in the sun, danger had been specific, recognizable. She told herself that the sensation of deep, dark terror was purely superstitious, visual images releasing sense-memories of childhood nightmares.

The rational mind, however, was no match for the phantoms of the subconscious. The house was frozen in a moment of long-ago time, an evil moment preserved by the gentle, smothering dust. When Gudenian led them between the two halves of the broken plate she closed her eyes and clutched at Manuel's arm, fighting to hold back a scream.

Moving along a brown wooden wall that the torch beam showed to be a skirting board, they turned a corner. Ahead of them was an angled shaft of pale sunshine. They hurried along the side of the wall toward the open doorway.

Under a blaze of sunlight they looked out across an endless prairie of red and yellow tufts.

Outside they heard the muffled chatter of birds. The air on their faces was oven-warm.

Gudenian climbed onto a thick woolen pile that came up to his knees. His boots kicked up little sprays of dust. Small particles rose in slowly spiralling eddies into the blinding sunshine.

"It's a rug," he said cheerfully, "this is the livingroom."

One by one they climbed onto the thick woolen pile. To escape the dazzling light, he led them along the wall until they came into shadow under a vast curtain of yellow cloth trailing on thick tufts of wool. They stared up in awe, recognizing it as a sofa.

Delmer touched the heavy material with his prod. The brittle fabric cracked, releasing a smell of dry mold.

"Dust and decay," Manuel said quietly, shaking his head, "this is not a home for us."

Chernitz opened his jacket, blowing cool air down at his chest and armpits. "We'll be dry-heated to a frazzle, Gudenian."

"It's too big," Peta muttered.

Gudenian waded out into brilliant sunlight from an unseen window high above. "We'll soon get used to these big spaces—you'd rather be out there with the fox, would you?"

Nobody followed.

He stared out toward the middle of the room. Through the haze of dusty sunlight he could vaguely distinguish the dark surfaces of towering furniture. He pulled off his jacket and his undervest, feeling sun on bare skin. He looked back.

"Houses were made for people," he said.

His voice echoed up through the vastness of the room. Still nobody moved.

He shrugged and turned away, walking quickly with high steps that didn't kick up dust in clouds. He left red tufts for yellow tufts. Peering ahead through sunlight so intense it ceased to illuminate he caught glimpses of something white.

Behind he heard a voice.

Nadine Boden was coming first with the others hurrying to catch up. Like sheep, he thought with a sense of grim satisfaction, scared of facing the unknown but even more scared of being left alone. They came straggling toward him in a rising cloud of dust.

"I haven't made up my mind whether you're brave or stupid," Nadine muttered.

He allowed himself to touch her then, just a quick pat on the shoulder. "Maybe both," he growled.

As he led them out in the center of the room, Magda tried to apologize. "I was scared, David."

"That's okay."

They passed the mahogany leg of a looming chair. Through dazzling sunshine he made out a line of white spars, sticking up from the rug like the curved ribs of a derelict wooden ship. He changed direction. There had obviously been some kind of panic when the house was abandoned. The white spars were in a jumbled line of oddly-shaped lengths, ivory he thought, probably the wreckage of a broken ornament.

Then he saw a round dome, dull white and broken in places. A raft of dust particles glinted like sequins in the downward flow of sunshine. There were gaping holes in the white dome. He screwed up his eyes against the dust and the dazzle. The holes made a sort of pattern that was vaguely familiar—

His throat tightened.

Stretching towards them across thick yellow tufts of wool were the knuckle bones of a human hand.

The white dome loomed out of the brilliant haze in a towering grin of big yellow teeth and gaping eye-sockets . . .

Not daring to look back at the vast house of death, they hurried across the shadowy floor of the courtyard and under the sagging gate.

Out in sunshine, under the darkening purple of the sky, they flopped down on grass.

He stood apart, face set in a tight scowl.

"You weren't to know," Nadine said briskly.

Gento looked along the gray cliff of the garden wall. "We must find a cave of some kind . . ."

Chernitz wiped water from his face with the back of his hand. Peta Sandor dabbed some healing ointment on Lindop's tortured cheek.

Magda's big, reproachful eyes exasperated Gudenian into speaking.

"We'll put up the tent against the wall. Tomorrow we'll try to kill something . . ." Delmer got to his feet, peering out across the lawn at the line of wooden boxes among the giant thistles. Gudenian scratched his neck. ". . . I might as well admit it—getting to the house was the only plan I had. Maybe you should—what is it, Raoul?"

The big Belgian hesitated. "I was just wondering . . . why do you think the bees abandoned that hive?"

"Rain could be coming through the roof," Nadine said irritably, her eyes never leaving Gudenian.

"It would be safe from the fox," Delmer said.

Chernitz glared incredulously. "A goddamn *bee-hive?*"

Zzzzzzzzzzzzzzzz . . .

The drone was deeper and more contented now as the bees settled down for the night.

Gudenian's boot struck Manuel Gento's ear as he launched himself up from the Spaniard's clasped hands, scrambling in midair to get his knee up onto the ledge, clawing at rough wood then dragging himself up onto the landing slat.

Facing him was a low, dark opening.

Looking out across the mown lawn and the slanting shadows of the huge thistles he could see the dark blur of the brambles. Night was coming in fast. The big shapes of birds returning to their roosts whirred past in the purple sky.

Kneeling at the low entrance, he switched on the torch. The beam rested on thin perpendicular boards. He swallowed, then went under on hands on knees. The beam picked out a dead bee, its legs sticking up in the air.

He stood up, shining the torch this way and that. Big rectangular honeycombs hung from the roof in rows. He took a deep breath and stamped his boot down on the wooden floor.

20

In his dark wooden cell, Bruce had no means of telling whether it was night or day when he heard voices from the corridor. There was a rattle of metal gates and the ominous squeak of rubber soles on concrete.

Deprived of continuous sleep by a half-hourly inspection system, he had used the old trick of concentrating his mind on the compilation of lists ... of his longterm aims for the Colony, of the food sources an unsupported group would find in the park.

When his door was thrown open he was sitting on the edge of his greasy bed-plank.

"On your feet," barked Pedder, the Compound section-leader.

Bruce rose stiffly. The white-strap tapped him on the elbow with his stick. In the overhead light of the corridor he saw Empie flanked by two SG men. Pedder put the stick in the small of his back and pushed him out of the cell.

Empie, his boyish face grim and severe under his green beret, made a tick against a list of names on a clipboard sheet. "There's one more—Maurice Sasso."

"Cell ten," Pedder grunted, striding along the corridor. He threw up the heavy wooden latch which secured the cell doors from the outside. "Sasso—outside, on the double!"

It was still a source of astonishment to Bruce that Sasso—his own personal assistant—had been a member of the Chalk Circle. He had grossly underestimated these people.

Sasso came blinking into the light of the corridor, pulling on the shapeless blue fatigue jacket worn by all Compound prisoners, male and female.

Pedder pushed him roughly at the two guards and made to close the cell door.

Empie drew his pistol and pressed it against the back of Pedder's neck. "Take his stick and tie him up," he told the two guards. Pedder turned, frowning incredulously.

"What the hell's going on?" he demanded.

The two guards pushed his arms behind his back while Empie unhooked the small bunch of keys from his white belt. "Call the others out here, Pedder."

"You breaking out?"

"Just do what I tell you and I won't have to shoot you!"

Empie motioned at Bruce and Sasso to get out of sight in Bruce's cell.

"I never guessed it about you, Sasso," Bruce muttered to the small, swarthy man he had always dismissed—with a proprietorial affection—as monkey-bright in the petty routines of bureaucracy but of limited imagination.

They heard Pedder calling through to the jailers' quarters. "Everybody outside for a cell search!"

"I'm glad you joined us in the end, Bruce," Sasso said warmly. It was the first time Sasso had ever called him by anything other than his rank.

They heard more voices and doors being opened and a man's indignant voice demanding to know what the hell was going on.

When Empie told them to come out into the corridor, Pedder and three other jailers were leaning on the wall on outstretched arms, legs spread behind them, covered by the pistols of Empie's two guards.

Empie and Sasso went down the corridor, throwing up the wooden latches and shouting into each cell.

Confused, sleepy prisoners came shuffling out into the light. Bruce saw Annette Rosa and a field worker he remembered from some recent conversation, a powerful man with a broken nose. And Bogaert—trying to cower back among the other prisoners. There were others he recognized vaguely, men and women he remembered seeing in corridors and offices, all of them with cropped heads and frightened faces. Some of the faces were cut and bruised.

He found he could not meet their apprehensive eyes. He felt almost sick with embarrassment, knowing that he had personally signed a detention order for every single one of these cowed, beaten people.

In the crowded corridor it was soon apparent which prisoners belonged to the Chalk Circle—those who had been arrested the day before on the strength of the list Empie had given to Khomich; *they* were not cowed. He saw Sasso talking urgently to Empie and the broken-nosed field worker. Sasso said something to Annette Rosa, who began moving among the other prisoners. Sasso came toward him.

"Empie has four men packing survival kits in the Field-Patrol stores. I think you should talk to thse people now, Bruce—let them know what's happening. We don't want any holdups once we start."

"There's bound to be some who won't come with us."

Sasso grimaced, scratching at the tight, wiry curls on his broad head. "That's going to be a problem—"

"We'll lock them up again—nobody can blame them for—"

"The problem is we're going to set fire to this building."

"Why?"

"It will keep the guards occupied while we're in the tunnel. There's no danger of it spreading across the concrete floor to Control—"

"It's hardly the way to make a silent escape!"

Sasso raised his hand, catching Empie's eye and pointing to Pedder and the three jailers still braced against the wall at gunpoint. "Talk to them now, please."

Bruce clenched his fists and forced himself to look along the rows of frightened faces.

"I was arrested yesterday," he began. "Commandant Khomich has taken complete control of the Colony. Whatever you may have thought of me in the past I hope you will believe me now. The Chalk Circle opposition is, in my judgment, the true voice of the vast majority of the Colony, but while Khomich controls the Security Guard a direct challenge would lead only to severe loss of life . . ." He looked over his shoulder, seeing Empie and the two guards pushing the four jailers into a cell. ". . . I know you've all been fed a lot of scare-propaganda about the dangers of Beyond but as you probably know a few of us survived for more than a year in the wilds and it is not the living hell you've been brainwashed into believing. We will have enough food and weapons and equipment from the stores to carry us over until we locate sources of food. What we do then is for us all to decide—once we set up a viable alternative to the Colony other people will join us. We're all victims of a system which I, to my shame, allowed to turn sour. I hope now to make amends. Ask any questions you like."

Prisoners exchanged nervous glances.

"Are you sure we won't starve to death out there?" came the voice of Annette Rosa.

Bruce smiled reassuringly at the nearest faces. "That was the whole point of mivro-cloning in the first place—the food resources at this level are unlimited. That park out there must be teeming with rabbits and cavies and birds—there's a lake that's probably crammed with fish—not to mention fruit and plants. It has its dangers, of course, but—"

"Are you saying all this was premeditated?" demanded Chief-Administrator Bogaert, pushing his way to the front. Bruce nodded. "Then who included *me* on any list of Chalk Circle traitors? I want everyone here to know that I had no part in it! Lindsay was right, Bruce—you're deranged! I demand that—"

"Your objections have been noted," Sasso said firmly.

Bogaert glared wildly at Sasso. "You stupid little man, you're a *clerk*, you don't speak to me like that! Is this the riff-raff you're siding with, Bruce?" He turned on the lines of prisoners, waving his arms. "We must all get back in our cells! These people are lunatics and renegades, they will get us all killed. Where is the alarm? We must—"

"You put me in here, Bogaert you bastard!" screamed a female prisoner, raking her nails at the tall man's eyes.

With instant savagery the prisoners, male and female, became a snarling pack, kicking and gouging and tearing at Bogaert. "Get Pedder as well!" somebody yelled.

Bruce fought against a wall of bodies. Bogaert sank beneath the clubbing fists. An elbow hit Bruce in the mouth and he was spun round and forced back out of the melée. He saw Sasso and Empie just standing there, doing nothing.

"They'll kill him!" he shouted.

Sasso nodded. "Better stop it, Empie, we need him with us."

Empie and the two guards rushed into the heaving mass of bodies, shoving people against the wall until they were standing over Bogaert's twisted, cowering body. They dragged him to his feet. A prisoner tried to tear at his eyes. Empie jabbed his stick into the man's stomach. "He's a hostage," he shouted, "he's no good to us dead! Stand back!"

"Yes and keep quiet," Sasso barked. "We must not alert Control Security! Is there any of you who wants to stay here?"

"No," growled a man's voice, "we're all with you!"

Other voices joined in a pulsing chant, hatred

for the Compound mixed with a rising exultation. Until Sasso—no longer the quirky jumping-bean but a charismatic powerhouse of a man—raised his hand.

"From now on—total silence. This is the dangerous part. First, the Field-Patrol stores. Then, the escape tunnel. On our way we will set fire to this abominable building. Our days of slavery are finished!"

Bruce felt the first nagging doubt then. What did Sasso know of slavery? He tried to catch him, to demand answers and explanations, but his former secretary was quickly lost in the crowd that pressed along the narrow corridor toward the outside door.

He turned, seeing Empie. Bogaert was slumped against a wall, holding his battered head and groaning.

"What do you intend for the jailers?" he demanded.

The boy-faced Empie gave him a reassuring smirk. "Don't worry about them, sir. You'd better come, sir, there may be extra equipment you'll want us to bring from the stores." He began steering Bruce along the corridor. "It's all worked out well so far—"

"Why was Bogaert's name added to that list?"

"Khomich wouldn't have been satisfied unless he thought he had our leader. I don't think we'll have any trouble at Field-Patrol stores—actually I'm the duty security officer tonight . . ."

And then they were sprinting across the vast floor toward the dim light from the upper tiers of Control and he was faced with the exhilaration of physical challenge. He ignored the voice that nagged him with the questions he should have asked, letting himself be carried along in the silent rush of tense, excited faces, getting caught up in the feverish looting of the storeroom and the silent march back across the concrete floor of the huge glass building, refusing to heed the questions that would have isolated him once again, glowing with the tingling sensation of comradeship, of *belonging* . . .

There was a red glow from a raised ventilation grill on the Compound's flat roof but long before the low, shabby building erupted in flame he was just one anonymous figure in the line of escaping men and women whose footsteps echoed down the slope of the old iron tunnel . . .

A field mouse had invaded the hive and been promptly stung to death.

Unable to move its heavy body, the bees had carefully sealed it in a transparent sarcophagus of propolis, a resin they collected from trees to seal off draughts and damp.

The bees in that hive had long since gone, joining the other colonies when their own new queen was found to suffer from a peculiar form of infertility which produced only useless male drones. The perfectly preserved mouse, however, still lay where it had finally died on the floor of the hive, hygienically encased from tailtip to whiskers in propolis.

When the pencil-beam of Gudenian's torch touched the amberish cocoon, it was as if a switch had been pulled. Refracted light made the propolis glow from within, bathing the mouse in a liquid light, like that of a yellow diamond. Caught in its moment of death, the mouse seemed only to be resting peacefully. When he moved the torch, the shiny cocoon gave off a jewel-like radiance.

For several moments he simply stared, not trusting his weary senses, thinking it might be a hallucination. Finally he reached out and touched it. His hand caressed the hard, smooth surface.

Only then did he call out to the others.

They all touched it—and jokingly told each other it was a lucky charm.

For some reason he did not understand, Gudenian found himself wishing he had kept it a secret.

Dawn brought luck to Vulpes Vulpes. Moving through reeds, his one eye scanning shallow water for frogs, he did not see the flattened moorhen until she was almost under his nose. His jaws snapped but she was off the nest and sliding among the tall reeds. He ate her eggs in a few slurping gulps, shells and all.

Shortly after that his jaws smashed down into muddy water to seize a big female toad with her mate riding piggy-back.

The toads' poison glands filled his mouth with a foul bitterness but handicapped by the loss of his left eye he was no longer able to pick and choose his prey. The cavies had scattered from their old nests —the lake's ducks had taken their newly hatched broods across to the safety of the island. He ate anything that moved now . . .

Book Three

"In that moment Vulpes Vulpes had become a man-eater."

21

"Hey. Gudenian—wake up—quick, I got something to show you!"

Gudenian sat up in his sleeping bag. His eyes were red and crusted and his hands felt cold and grimy. His teeth were furred and his thermal underwear was clammy against his skin.

"Don't shine that torch in my face," he growled. "What is it, Chernitz?"

"Something to kill! Come on, man . . ."

Scratching his heavily stubbled cheeks, he crouched beside Chernitz in a cold draft at the low entrance slit. Outside it was a dark gray morning, with heavy dew silvering the grass. Chernitz pointed.

In the middle of the lawn he saw a movement of brown shapes. He rubbed his eyes.

"Rabbits."

"It's a mother and babies. If we could get near enough for a shot . . ."

Gudenian bared his teeth, rubbing them clean on his sleeve. Gento emerged from the dark interior of the hive, pulling on his red and black jacket. He squatted down beside them. Chernitz pointed at the doe rabbit and her four youngsters cropping grass among the towering thistles.

Gudenian stood up. "They'd spot us long before we got in range." He felt his way back among the hanging combs to where the others were still in their sleeping-bags against the rear wall of the hive. Seeing a small chink of light between the overlapping slats, he inserted his knife into the crack and twisted it until he made a small hole. Cold air made his eye water. He gouged into the wood, pulling off splinters. He felt numb. His stomach was queasy. They were down to two days' rations of dry-pack protein and their water flasks were empty. All the ingenious ideas he'd had for hunting and trapping now seemed futile. He stabbed at the splintering wood. Getting to the damned house was all he'd thought about . . . a new life for Magda and him . . . now he could hardly bear to look at her.

"Is that you, Gudenian?" muttered Lindop from the huddle of sleeping bags.

"Yeah."

"I'm hungry, Gudenian," Lindop said, dragging himself out of his sleeping-bag. He stepped over Delmer and crowded beside him at the jagged aperture. His fingers touched at the swollen stitching on his cheek. "Would you look at my face, Gudenian?"

"What about it?"

Chernitz turned his head, pointing at Lindop's mangled cheek. Stubble was growing between the bright red weals. "It's not healing right—it feels inflamed. Tell me the truth, Gudenian—I need a doctor!"

"Magda's a nurse, she—"

"What does she know? They only *called* her a nurse for the AID program! She hasn't even been trained in—"

"Shut up!"

Delmer woke with a start, struggling to sit up. "What is it?"

"Oh nothing," Gudenian sneered. "John Lindop is

worried about his good looks!" He pulled off another big splinter with a loud cracking noise. There was enough light now to see the three women stirring in their sleeping bags. He glanced at Lindop's cheek. "If you had blood-poisoning you'd be dead by now. It'll heal—you'll probably look like Frankenstein's monster but—"

Gento was calling urgently from the front of the hive. "Come here, Gudenian!"

He tapped Lindop's shoulder. "Get your knife and cut a window here . . . Frankenstein."

When he crouched down beside Gento and Chernitz the light had improved. The mother rabbit was sitting upright, ears cocked forward.

"Tell him, Manuel," Chernitz hissed.

Gento pointed out toward the middle of the lawn. "You remember we passed a hole in the grass? The doe rabbit dug that hole to keep her litter safe from the bucks in the warren. We used to dig out these nest-holes when my father had his farm—the mother comes to feed them at night—"

"Manuel says it's got to be a dead-end hole," Chernitz said enthusiastically. "If we frighten them, she'll run for the brambles and the babies will bolt down the hole!"

"You sure about that, Manuel?"

Gento nodded. "I think so."

Gudenian looked back into the darkness. "Hey—Raoul. Lindop!"

When they dropped down onto the wet grass he looked back up at the ledge. Lindop was standing above them with a rifle. "You cover us, John—if you see the fox fire one shot. Get the women building a fire—under the hive here. Use all that wood, rip up the combs—just pile it on. Okay?"

Lindop nodded.

He watched them hurrying toward the nearest towering thistle. His fingers touched at his stubbled cheek, tenderly tracing the inflamed scar that was going to disfigure him for life. He needed proper medical treatment from a doctor but they didn't care. None of them liked him . . .

They sprinted from thistle to thistle until only open grass lay between them and the big baby rabbits. One of them did a little scamper, kicking up its hind legs. The doe scratched her ear with her hind leg and pulled the ear down with her fore-paws to lick it clean. In the shadow of the brambles they saw the moving shapes of more rabbits.

"Shouldn't we get between them and the brambles?" Delmer whispered. "They might stampede into the hole before—"

"We don't want to meet the mother rabbit down there," Gento hissed, "she will fight viciously in defense of her young."

Gudenian scraped fur off his tongue with his teeth. Above them on the giant thistle stretched the dew-pearled hawsers of a meta spider's web. He cupped his hands and ran them under one of the web strands, catching the broken dew-drops. He swilled water round his mouth and spat it out.

"I could drop one from here," Chernitz muttered, gesturing at Delmer for the rifle.

Gudenian shook his head. "We got to start saving on ammunition. How many shots did it take to drop that squirrel? We have to find out sometime—"

"Find out what?" Chernitz hissed.

Gudenian stooped to pick up a small stone. "Find out if we've got any goddamn future out here!"

He hurled the stone.

It fell far short of the grazing rabbits but his movement alerted the grazing family. The mother sat up, ears flicking forward. For a moment it looked like a big brown kangaroo.

Gento clapped his hands.

The four baby rabbits ducked and scampered for the hole, disappearing into the ground. The mother's white tail flashed across the dewy lawn and disappeared into the brambles.

They sprinted across wet grass, their boots kicking up little sprays of water. Something big and black passed overhead but they kept running until they were jumping down an earthen slope into the black tunnel.

"Gudenian caught hold of Delmer. "Stay here, Raoul—if you see the fox, *whistle!*"

Gento switched on the torch when a downward slope took them out of gray daylight. They advanced into the pitch-black tunnel.

Gudenian drew his knife. "Kill them all if we can —we won't get a second chance!"

The round hole was straight and narrow. It rose again. The torch-beam flicked across dry earth and stones.

It came to rest on a scatter of dead grass and fine gray hairs.

The four brown rabbits were huddled together in the warm ruins of a nest their mother had made with mouthfuls of hay and fur plucked from her own belly. The plump bodies jammed together, cowering, ears flattened.

Gento put the torch on a jutting stone, shining the beam on the nest.

Gudenian shifted his knife to his right hand and carefully reached into the soft, warm flanks.

Furry bodies erupted in a desperate bolt to escape.

Gudenian got both arms round a strong hind leg that kicked him up and down until his neck seemed ready to crack.

Knives rose and fell in the shadowy torchlight . . .

From his vantage point on the landing ledge of the hive, John Lindop saw two brown rabbits come darting up onto the flat lawn and bolt into the brambles. Hungry as he was, he smiled vindictively.

Then he saw a black and red jacket.

From the hole in the lawn they emerged, dragging two dead rabbits by the hind legs.

He looked down at Nadine, who was breaking lengths of wood with her feet. "They caught two!" He crossed the ledge and stooped to look into the dark interior. "Hurry up with the wood!"

Nadine came out in front of the hive. "We're not in the Colony now, you know, we don't need a guard giving us orders. Why don't you lend a hand?"

"I'm on look-out."

Peta ducked through the entrance slit with an armful of wood. "That scratch won't last much longer as an excuse," she said, throwing the wood down to Nadine.

"What do you mean—an excuse?" he demanded.

"An excuse for not working."

"I got this scratch as you call it trying to kill a squirrel single-handed," he said indignantly. He pointed out across the lawn. They were dragging the dead rabbits between the giant thistles. "It took four of them to knock off a couple of baby rabbits!"

"He was trying to *kill* the squirrel, Peta," Nadine said, smiling up at Lindop. "We all thought you'd found a friend."

Through the damp, still air came the sound of a man's laughter. Magda came out of the hive with more wood. She looked pale and tired. "Feeling sick again?" Lindop asked sympathetically.

"I'll be all right."

"Women are much braver," Peta smirked.

"Take this," he snapped, shoving the rifle at her and ducking through the low entrance.

When Gudenian and the others reached the hive with the two dead rabbits they heard a violent crashing noise from inside. A spew of dust billowed through the entrance slit.

"John's tearing those combs to pieces," Peta explained. "I'm afraid we upset him."

Lindop appeared above them on the ledge, blinking through a mask of dust. He lowered a long, thin spar to Delmer and Gento. "Hey, Gudenian—that big barrel beside the house, remember where it was leaking? Want me to take the flasks and fill 'em up?"

Gudenian nodded approvingly. "You're doing a good job in there, stick to it. Raoul—how about you and Abram going for the water? We'll get a fire going and cut up these animals—the sooner we get all this meat stored safely inside the better. Manuel—you know how to dry a pelt?"

Gento nodded. "Scrape off all the fat and flesh, then peg them out, fur down. It's a pity we don't have salt, we could keep the meat in brine."

"There might be salt in the house," Delmer said quietly. They shivered, shaking their heads.

Nadine suggested smoking the meat over the fire but nobody was too sure if this would work and Gudenian said they might as well fix up some kind of roasting-spit and cook the lot. Lindop went back into the dark, dusty interior of the hive, whistling cheerfully.

Peta grimaced at Gudenian. "I think he's trying to rehabilitate himself."

Gudenian prodded a dead rabbit with his boot. He grunted and drew his knife. "That's just as well—the rule is if you don't pull your weight you don't eat."

His blade ripped into fur and skin. From the floor of the big wooden structure overhead came a banging of wood.

Lindop knelt quickly beside the packs, hearing the vibration of voices from below. Rummaging in Gudenian's pack he found the black transceiver and shoved it under his belt. On his way back across the floor he made as much noise as possible, kicking broken slats, stamping heavily. It had always been his way to let people underestimate him and then to plan the clever move that would leave all the superior bastards gasping.

He listened. From below came Nadine's voice, ". . . twist dry stalks into ropes and make a ladder . . ."

He braced himself against the wall, holding the black casing to his ear. Diffused sunlight glowed softly on the amber cocoon. He needed medical treatment but none of them gave a damn—betraying them would be a pleasure. He held his breath, then switched on to *Receive*.

Through static he heard something.

He closed his eyes. Gudenian was saying something to Magda. He turned the volume up.

"*... read me? Bruce to Gudenian, this is Bruce calling Gudenian. Do you read me? Over.*"

In his surprise he switched off, shoving the transceiver into his jacket. His heart was pounding. He rested his head back against the wall, breathing in short, shallow gasps . . .

Bruce jammed his boot down on the deep red segments of the big earthworm's twisting fore-end. The shiny segments bunched together, trying to find enough force to throw him off.

Bruce glanced round the startled, apprehensive faces. "Lumbricus—the common garden worm," he said reassuringly. "We ate a lot of them in our year in the wilds. Sliced up and grilled over an open fire they taste not unlike octopus." He saw the revulsion on Sasso's face. "What's wrong, Maurice?"

"We don't have time for nature lessons," said the small, swarthy man.

"On the contrary—it's nature lessons that'll keep us alive." He looked round the party of escaped prisoners and deserters. "It's something you'll have to get used to so we might as well start now. May I have a knife? Thank you. The way to kill them is to start at the front end here, the prostomium as it's properly called . . ." He grunted, dragging the knife through blood-red cuticle and muscle. The severed mouth-tip went on convulsing. He jammed his boot down on the threshing worm again . . . "We work from head to tip forcing the earth in the gullet back to the anus . . . I know it isn't pretty to watch, first time, but that's the world we're in now. When we stop tonight we can start a fire and then you'll—"

"It's them!" Empie shouted. He was standing up in the huge expanse of wooden plank, his transceiver aerial extended. "He's calling Bruce!"

"Never mind the worm," Sasso snapped, "speak to him, Bruce!"

He shook his head, methodically working his way down the long, shiny body. Its violent twistings and threshings began to subside. Thin black earth oozed out of the tail. He straightened up. People were looking ready to vomit.

"Wrap the pieces up in leaves," he said, only then climbing onto the huge platform of rotting wood. Sasso crowded close to Empie, cocking his head to hear the voice on the transceiver.

"*. . . this is John Lindop calling Bruce. Do you read me? Over.*"

"Speak to him," Sasso hissed, "find out where they are!"

"Who's John Lindop?"

"He was one of the guards who escaped with Gudernian from the Compound," Empie said.

"I remember—a thief, wasn't he?"

Sasso held his arm. "Don't give him any information—as far as he knows you're still Controller."

Bruce took the transceiver. Before he switched to *Transmit* he looked down at the rest of the party. "Better tell them to get the worm bundled up—good red meat soon attracts predators out here."

"You heard him," Sasso growled. People reluctantly approached the jagged tube-lengths of dead worm.

"This is Bruce calling John Lindop," he said into the transceiver. "Come in, Lindop."

He switched to *Receive*. Sasso opened out a map, urgently stabbing at it with a gloved finger. "Get the location."

"*Lindop to Bruce, receiving you loud and clear.*"

"Bruce to Lindop—what is your position?"

"*Lindop to Bruce—I have been wounded and need a doctor. Gudenian does not know I am calling you. I say again, Gudenian does not know I am calling you. Over.*"

Sasso blinked rapidly. He jabbed the air with his forefinger. "He wants to betray them," he muttered urgently. "Promise him anything—just get the location!"

Bruce shrugged. "Bruce to Lindop—make your transmissions brief. Are you being held prisoner by Gudenian?"

"*Affirmative.*"

"What is your location?"

There was a roar of transmission but no voice. "He's thinking how to do a deal," Empie hissed. Then Lindop's voice came through the static.

"*Do I get an amnesty? I say again—do you guarantee me an amnesty?*"

Bruce raised his eyebrows. Sasso nodded urgently. "It's our only chance—promise him what he wants!"

Bruce took a deep breath.

"Controller Bruce to Lindop. Affirmative. Full amnesty for your cooperation."

A din of chattering sparrows passed overhead, drowning Lindop's reply. Sasso clenched his fists in frustration

"Bruce to Lindop—say again please."

"*We are close to a house in the northeast section of the park,*" came Lindop's voice. "*How far away are you?*"

Sasso and Empie pulled the map taut. "Got it," Sasso snapped.

Empie's finger traced a route from the big planks past the tip of the lake to the house. "We won't make that today."

Sasso grabbed the map. "It's not far, we can make it by late afternoon."

"It's taken us six hours to come this far," Bruce drawled, "you have to multiply these map distances thirty-five times. I'd say it's the equivalent of another twenty miles. These people look exhausted already, Sasso."

The small dark man grimaced angrily. "All right, all right. Tell him we'll be there by midday tomorrow!"

Bruce flicked to *Transmit* again . . .

When the sky darkened Sasso still wanted to push on up the slope toward the giant shapes of the juniper bushes but Bruce had regained full authority—at least in matters affecting their safety on the long trek across the park.

"We'll put up the tents in this grass," he said firmly, "we'd be too exposed up there." While Empie supervised the preparations for encampment he drew his former assistant aside. "Lindop's only helping us because he thinks I'm still Controller. What's he going to do when he finds out?"

"It will be too late them."

"He was careful not to give us the exact location."

"He'll tell us tomorrow. He's scared!" Sasso peered up through the tall forest of grass at the darkening gray sky. Mingling with the steady noise horizon of insect life was a deeper, sighing sound, as if the earth itself was breathing. He shivered. "This Gudenian must be a savage! First he breaks out of Glasshouse—to make love to some girl! Now he thinks he can exist out here? How could they choose such people for the first colony?"

"The same way as they chose you and me, Sasso—people they wanted to get rid of. Expendable people. What was your crime?"

Sasso rubbed his tightly cropped curls. "It's easy to make enemies in Geneva. Will we be safe in these tents?"

"As safe as we're likely to be. Strangely enough, most creatures find the scent of man repellent. Don't go for any midnight strolls—owls got one or two people back in Arcadia."

Sasso started, glancing up apprehensively. "Owls! Earthworms as big as snakes!" He shook his head. "Hurry up with those tents!"

"I'm puzzled, Sasso," Bruce said quietly.

"You expect me to throw up my arms in glee?"

"Not that. I had you in my front office for—how long? Six, seven months? All the time you were the brains of the Chalk Circle . . ."

Sasso smiled. "You only saw me as some kind of licensed court jester."

"So I know now how clever you are. So tell me why you never stopped to think I wanted to make reforms only I didn't have any help."

Sasso patted him on the arm, a gesture at once friendly and dismissively patronizing. "You were more use to us acting as a focal point for Lindsay's suspicions."

"And now you're using me as a patrol-guide—the environment expert. What happens afterward, Sasso? What happens when we meet up with Gudenian?"

The little dynamo of a man gave him the frank, open look that he had seen on the face of every conniving, lying, double-dealing swindler he had ever met. "Have I made any secret of it? Once we have the girl—Magda Hoessner—we can bargain with Khomich. We will return to the Colony on our own terms. There are too many of us now to be treated like a bunch of criminal renegades. You've read our pamphlets—you know the sort of Colony we want. Let's get inside the tent—"

Bruce caught him by the arm. "Yeah, I read the inspiring message, Sasso. Justice, democracy ... the usual crap. I'll tell you one thing—Khomich at his worst would never have let four guards burn to death!"

Sasso shrugged. "Is that what is worrying you? Well, if it makes you feel any better—they were strangled first."

He strode toward the tents. "And what happens when Khomich comes after us?" Bruce demanded.

"Like all thugs, his guards are cowards. They will only leave Glasshouse by helicopter. We will hear them a long way off."

Bruce stood back, alone, shutting his ears to the voices of twenty-seven men and women preparing for their first long night out in Beyond.

The same old story, he thought, promise them happiness tomorrow . . . only *this* time I won't be there . . .

"I could've made it really cozy if I'd had a hammer and nails," Lindop said modestly, showing them the sheltered sleeping compartments he'd made out of piled wood in a corner of the hive, away from the draft from the gaping hole in the rear wall.

After their orgy of meat-eating they were still groaning with tight bellies, too tired to show appreciation of his efforts.

Gento pulled himself into his sleeping bag. "There must be a garbage dump near that house—we might find some glass for a window . . ."

Chernitz burped.

"I beg your pardon," Peta said briskly.

He grinned. "Why—what did you do?"

Gudenian shone the torch into the corner compartment. "Magda, Peta and Nadine can sleep there. Come on, I don't want to waste the battery." He shone the torch up into the open vault Lindop had cleared in the middle of the hanging combs. "We can check the roof for leaks tomorrow . . ." The beam moved down until it hit the glowing incandescence of the dead mouse's amber cocoon.

"That thing gives me the spooks," Peta said, "can't we get rid of it?"

"Get rid of it?"

Gudenian put on a display of astonishment which puzzled the three women but which Chernitz and Lindop appreciated . . . a soldier's joke. He strode across the wooden floor, shining the torch at various angles to show off the dead mouse. He caressed the hard resin. "This is our lucky mascot, we can't—"

Without warning the big wooden structure shuddered, hurling him back into the corner.

There was a terrifying sound of splintering wood and the floor-slats erupted like the opening of a jagged trapdoor . . .

In the gray light of dusk, Vulpes Vulpes had come on a familiar combination of scents—Man and animal blood. After only a few days, the birds and mammals of the park had been fully alerted to his presence, making hunting more and more difficult. Cavies had taken to nesting in impenetrable rat-holes; in daylight, when sight became crucial, the missing eye was proving a severe handicap in the chasing of rabbits and birds.

He had waited till dark, crouched in the shadow of the garden wall, watching the wooden box. Man had killed rabbit and brought it across the grass. Man's scent was everywhere but he had lived close enough to Man all his life to know that after dark Man would be safely inside his big house. The wooden box was where the rabbit scent ended.

In his hunger, his yellow canines snapped through the thin floor-slats as if they were wafers.

22

His broken ribs encased in a steel corset that allowed no movement from chest to hips, heavy bruises turning yellow round his eyes and nose, former Deputy-Commandant Lindsay marched stiffly under escort into an office on Tier Six of Control.

The shaken Doctor Freedland, senior medical officer, was just leaving. Andrew Steane, Lindsay's successor, nodded for the two white-straps who had brought Lindsay from the Clinic to follow Freedland out of the room.

Khomich turned from the big wall-map of the park.

By way of apology to the man he had kicked and beaten senseless in full view of the Internal Coordinating Committee, Khomich gestured at Lindsay to sit.

"It's less painful if I stand, sir," said the red-haired man, eyes blinking nervously at the cold appraisal he was getting from Khomich and the burly young Steane.

Khomich shrugged. "You have heard of this latest outrage?"

"There was a rumor—"

"Bruce and a number of prisoners and Chalk Circle conspirators deserted the Colony last night. And Bogaert—did you know he was the ringleader of this gangster element?"

"Bogaert?" Lindsay said doubtfully. Steane nodded in confirmation.

"They let four guards burn to death in the Compound," Khomich went on, his voice almost frighteningly unemotional. "This all started with you, Lindsay, the man Gudenian came to you with a warning—" he shrugged—"that is past. We must deal with the situation as it is. Do you wish to return to duty?"

"Yes, sir," Lindsay said eagerly.

"How fit are you?" Steane snapped.

"I have this steel corset but otherwise—"

"I could have had you shot for conspiracy, Lindsay," Khomich said, "you may consider yourself lucky." He glanced at the map. "Luckier than those renegades—a patrol-flight has confirmed the existence of Gudenian's fox. In the ordinary way these criminals would have done us a favor—we now know exactly who they are and where they are—I would simply leave them to the fox. However . . ." He nodded to Steane.

Lindsay gave his full attention to the young SG officer whom he had picked out of the ranks and who had then betrayed him. Hope was already stirring in him that he was getting a second chance and not far behind was the thought of sweet revenge.

Steane addressed him like a subordinate whose views were of no interest. "Doctor Freedland has just confirmed that the girl Gudenian took outside—Magda Hoessner—is pregnant. Bruce knew this but did not inform us. Freedland assures us it is *not* the result of the AID program—we have to presume—" He hesitated, hearing footsteps and loud voices in the corridor—"We have to presume she conceived in the normal way and that Gudenian is the father. This represents a major advance in the whole microproject and we must—"

There was an urgent knock at the door.

"Enter," Khomich growled.

The duty white-strap looked into the room. "Sir, there's—"

Engineer Grouchy pushed past him, angrily confronting Khomich. "I warned you, Khomich—now it's happened. There's a mutiny in the Diggings—they've killed at least one guard and they're holding two of my assistants hostage! The whole Colony is ready to—"

"Get a grip of yourself, man. Handle it, Steane—no negotiations, they surrender or we flood them out!"

Steane saluted and hurried out of the big room with Grouchy. Khomich closed the door and faced Lindsay.

"If you had listened to Gudenian, you fool!" He regained control. "Look at this map. Come nearer, man!" Two threads stretched from the big pin that marked Glasshouse. One stretched to the northeast boundary of the park, the other to a pin stuck in the northern boundary. "These are bearings taken by Surveillance monitors on field-patrol channel transmissions made this afternoon. At that range the transmissions were too weak to be deciphered but it's obvious—Bruce's party is somewhere here between us and the lake ... and Gudenian is somewhere up here in the northeast corner. I assume they have arranged to meet. I cannot spare guards for a full-scale search-and-destroy patrol—"

With a lightning eruption of temper he smashed his fist against the map. His broad, pink face went dark with a rush of blood. Lindsay swallowed, wincing in anticipation of the big, hairless fists smashing against his corsetted ribs.

"How can I help you, sir?"

"*Help me?*" Khomich ranted. He started to stride up and down the room, oblivious to Lindsay's presence, waving his fists and apparently addressing an audience that existed only in his own head. "I do my job. Did I ask for this? I carried out orders. I have to keep them alive. They conspire against me when my hands are tied. Am I protecting my own interests? Answer me that. I could go after them with an army but who would guard the outer wall? Who would guard the fields? My father was a peasant farmer and his father before him. We must guard the crops. Should we play games when the high wall has been breached? Am I a murderer who burns men alive? Bruce is a treacherous hypocrite. He calls me 'The Butcher.' He smiles and fawns and they like him and he sneers at me. He knew this damned girl was pregnant. But I had the floods to handle. I have to safeguard the whole Colony. Do I get thanked for keeping them alive? Thanked?"

In a final paroxysm of frustration his fists clenched and his eyes closed and his neck tightened in an ape-like grimace of such violence Lindsay moved stiffly toward the door.

Khomich grabbed him by the collar and hauled him round. "You want to help me?" he screamed.

"Of course, sir—"

"Well help me then!"

"Just tell me how, sir."

Khomich blinked. He stepped back, putting his hands behind his back. He straightened his shoulders with little, birdlike motions of his big, broad head. When he spoke all anger had gone from his voice. It was as if they had been in a sane, business-like discussion.

"In the long-term interests of the whole micro-cloning project it is vital that this girl Hoessner and Gudenian are available for medical study. They will have to be brought back by force. You made a gross error of judgment, Lindsay, but you are still the most experienced officer at my disposal—and you know the guards as individuals. We need ten reliable men."

"You want me to lead a search-patrol, sir?"

"No, I will be in command. Have them equipped and mustered by nine hundred hours. We can spare one helicopter for a limited operation—dealing with that fallen tree is paramount." He moved closer to the map. "If you were Gudenian—show me a safe place."

Eager to rehabilitate himself, Lindsay forgot

about his broken ribs. Reaching up he felt a stab of agony—but it would have been impolitic then to remind Khomich of his beating. His index finger followed the thread that ran to the northeast corner—until it reached the outline of the house.

Khomich nodded approvingly. "We will take an RDF monitor for more bearings when they start chattering to each other."

"If we follow the eastern wall and get beyond the house for our approach we may surprise them, sir."

"A good suggestion. You should never have meddled in politics, Lindsay, soldiering is your trade. I will reinstate you at the rank of Area-Captain."

"Thank you, sir, I assure you—"

Khomich waved impatiently. "Just find ten reliable men."

"By reliable, sir, do you mean . . . ?"

"I mean men who are not tainted with the disease of squeamishness."

"And Bruce, sir?"

"Bruce wants the girl so that he can bargain with me. If possible we will get to her first . . . if not, what happens to Bruce is entirely of his own making." Khomich's voice dropped to a murmur. His clumsy fingers touched the red thread that ran from Glasshouse to the top right hand corner of the map. "It goes without saying that he and his friends have declared war on this Colony . . ."

They left the office on Tier Six together, meeting a hurrying guard who told Khomich that the Diggings mutineers were threatening to kill their hostages one by one unless they were allowed to put their grievances to a full ICC meeting.

Lindsay left Khomich to find men for the search-patrol. His initial astonishment at being brought from the Clinic, where he had been under armed guard, to be pardoned instead of sentenced had soon worn off. Khomich *needed* him.

Cautious as the words had been, the order was perfectly clear: Find ten guards who will commit murder without hesitation!

23

Another wooden slat cracked and broke upward in jagged splinters.

Their screams mingled with the explosive cracking of dry wood. The torch disappeared under their struggling bodies. Gudenian punched and clawed, snatching down at a momentary flash of the torch.

Frustrated by a strong cross-beam running under the floor, the fox withdrew his jaws, probing with his fangs for thin board.

The torch flashed across hysterical faces.

"Hold it!" Gudenian snarled, shoving the torch into the nearest hand. For a moment there was enough light for Lindop to see the gaping hole they had cut in the rear wall. He clawed his way along and clambered head-first out into the darkness.

Gudenian grabbed for the HASG pack.

Nadine shone the torch directly in his face.

"You're blinding me," he snarled, "shine it in the middle!"

Magda grabbed at his legs. "Don't David—"

He kicked free of her arms. "Shine it in the middle." He was shouting when wood splintered with a deafening crack and the hive seemed to stagger on its stilt legs. Lindop was thrown to the floor.

Thrown against the wall in a jumble of threshing bodies, Nadine fought to stay upright, holding the torch up in the air.

Gudenian saw yellow canines and incisors snapping down on a thin slat. Red fur pushed up through the opening.

He ran down one side of the hive, hand feeling for the mesh-nozzle of the spray-gun. The floor heaved beneath him.

A slat rose on end and then the top half of the fox's head came up into the torchlight.

Gudenian ripped off the mesh-cap and started jumping from one sagging slat to the next until he was being shaken off balance by the fox's desperate heaving. He stumbled to his knees.

A big yellow fang crunched down into wood.

The fox was growling. Splinters pushed into thick red fur. A dark-pointed ear emerged through the widening gap and flicked upright.

Gudenian rammed the open nozzle of the spray-gun's short rubber coil into a damp, black nostril and rammed down the release plunger.

Designed to release short bursts of hydrocyanic acid in a fine spray to drive away insects, the pressurized tank voided its burning contents in one long jet—deep into the fox's most sensitive nose membranes.

Under the hive the fox's body convulsed with such force the big wooden structure tilted sideways on two legs, hurling Gudenian backward through the brittle parchment-cells of a hanging comb.

A yowling scream choked in the fox's throat as splinters speared into his wet gums. Like a hooked fish he jerked this way and that to free his jaws from the jagged opening.

His thin yelps faded into the distance.

A shattered wooden slat sagged down into the dark void of the night below.

Chernitz and Nadine were the first to reach him. He was on his knees, trembling uncontrollably. The skin had been ripped off the bridge of his nose. Blood ran down into his thick blond stubble.

When Magda reached them Nadine was cradling him in her arms.

She knew the truth then and in her bitterness she almost wished the fox had killed him.

They spent the rest of that long, dark night sitting close together in the dark corner. When his hands stopped shaking, Gudenian asked for the torch and shone it into the center of the broken floor. The beam touched the resin-cocoon of the dead mouse, radiating a warm, glowing halo.

"Didn't I tell you?" he said in a hoarse whisper. "Our lucky mascot . . ."

"We won't be so bloody lucky next time," Lindop growled.

Gento grunted angrily. "It was not luck! One man risked his life while you were trying to run away, Lindop!"

"The only reason you didn't run away was you were petrified with bloody fear!"

"I keep telling myself it's all a nightmare," Magda whispered, hugging her knees. "I wish—"

"It is a bloody nightmare!" Lindop snapped. "And in the morning it'll be just as bad and it'll go on tomorrow night and the night after and—"

"Shut up, Lindop," Delmer barked. "Gudenian—you think the fox will come back?"

"He smelled the dead rabbit," Gento said. "We will have to store our meat in a different place."

"I wouldn't think that acid will leave him much sense of smell," Gudenian said, switching off the torch. "He'll have to hunt by his ears and his one good eye now. We're going to have to kill him."

Lindop banged his head against the wall. "Kill him? How the hell can we kill a monster that size? What's wrong with you people? I say we should go back to Glasshouse and give ourselves up and take what's coming to us—anything would be better than this! Kill a bloody fox? You must be insane!"

Gudenian yawned. "All right, John, if that's how you feel—you know the way now, you can set out at first sunlight."

"You don't think I would, do you? Well, you're bloody wrong!"

"That's settled then," Gudenian said cheerfully. "Anybody else?"

Nobody spoke.

In the darkness Nadine felt for his hand and raised it to her cheek.

By dawn Bruce was halfway up the juniper slope. After the enclosed life of the Colony his body and legs soon began to ache but he resisted the temptation to rest in a dark little cave under some exposed roots, scrambling on up the rough slope toward the huge bushes.

Sitting with his back against a red-barked trunk, he saw the first rays of sunshine touching millions of dew drops. Looking back over the vast expanse of greens and browns he saw the blurred shimmer of Glasshouse. He chewed on cold meat that had been grilled on the fire the night before. For water he pulled down a tall blade of grass and carefully sucked at dew-drops, avoiding the hard edges that would have sliced through his tongue. When he stood up, keeping in the shadow of the juniper, he could see sunlight glinting on the vast lake. Through a soft buzz of awakening insect life he heard the quacking of ducks and the gossipy chatter of sparrows. He checked his position on the map, orienting himself for the next leg of the journey that would take him across the vast spaces of the park. Below him on the open slope that ran down to the reedy bank of the lake strutted a pair of powder-blue wood-pigeons; from far off came the bell-clear notes of a blackbird; above him in dancing flight a holly-blue butterfly swooped low enough for him to see the black spots on the pale-blue scales of its underwings.

He loosened his black and red OD jacket to let his chest feel the sun.

"You've burned your bridges now, old boy," he drawled, pulling on his pack and shouldering the high-powered rifle he had stolen from a sleeping guard in Sasso's camp, knowing that Gudenian would welcome him for the extra weapon if nothing else, vowing to himself that he would fire at only one creature in the park . . . the fox. Rifles, radios, acid sprays—those were the very things he was escaping from . . . Man's gifts to the butterflies!

Keeping just below the skyline, he set off on his long, lonely race to reach Gudenian, his legs falling into a striding rhythm that he could keep up all day.

To the best of his knowledge he had never met or spoken to this man Gudenian. What did he know about him? A former soldier, a guard and therefore a thug—a triple-murderer? But also a man who had taken a girl out into the wilds to make love to her. A man who risked certain punishment to warn them about the fox. Above all, a man who had consciously chosen the hunted life of an outlaw in preference to the prison-society for which most humans seemed genetically programmed.

"Aren't you a bit old to be looking for a hero-figure?" he muttered ruefully.

He smiled, answering himself in a loud, cheerful voice. "You used to be a bit of a hero yourself, old boy."

He stooped to pick up a heavy yew twig, using his knife to trim off its side-shoots.

The moment he broke away from the towering line of junipers, the big, overfed wood-pigeons burst up into the sky.

Just for a moment, on the vast, open slope, he saw himself for what he was . . . a moving dot, dwarfed by every poisonous outcrop of buttercups, forced to change direction at every big pebble.

Two hours later, moving cautiously through long coarse grass toward the tinkling sound of running water that he knew must be the ornamental waterfall marked on the map, he heard a splash and froze in midstride, only putting his boot down on rotting vegetation when he distinguished the slurping sound of a tongue lapping up water. Easing carefully between the yellow-sheathed stalks, he saw gray stone and green moss and a sparkle of sun on disturbed water.

He crouched, prodding forward at young grass shoots with his yew stick.

There was a short slope of emerald-green moss and black earth and then a flat paving-stone beside a wide pool of shallow water fed from spring water trickling over a slimy green ledge.

Standing with his forefeet in the water, splashing his nose and mouth from side to side with urgent jerks of his head, was the red fox.

24

The moment Gudenian had been evading finally came as the fierce afternoon sun began to cast longer shadows across the rabbit-mown lawn.

He was staggering under the awkward bulk of a huge sheaf of grass stalks he and Manuel had been cutting beside the garden wall. Peta was escorting them with a rifle, enjoying the role of a field guard.

"Move it, you scum—miss your quota target and I'll cut your rations!"

"But if we don't eat how can we work?" Gudenian pleaded. "We'll grow weak—"

"So I'll cut your rations again!"

"I used to be a guard myself," he whimpered.

"Don't expect any favors!"

It was a new side to Peta. The shrillness seemed to have gone. They all sounded eager to get the hive repaired and explore the place they were going to inhabit . . . all except Lindop. He had stuck to his word, setting off at first sunlight for Glasshouse, showing a bravery Gudenian had not expected. Maybe he would make it, maybe not.

"Maybe I should've stopped John from going," he said. He was bent forward from the waist, the bound sheaf of silica-bright stalks balanced on his head and back, dancing plumes of seed-heads obscuring his forward vision, steering himself by following her boots.

"What could you have done?" he heard her saying, "tied him up? We're better off without him."

Then he saw another pair of boots.

"David . . . ?"

He grunted something, glad to be out of sight under the sagging sheaf. When they reached the hive he threw it down—and found himself looking into Magda's accusing eyes.

"That's our last load today," he said to Nadine who was spreading the long stalks out to dry on open grass. "Hey, Raoul—"

He moved under the wooden floor but her hand was on his arm. "You've been avoiding me all afternoon," she said quietly.

He frowned, pretending innocence. Delmer called down. He was edging sideways onto the upraised angle of the most severely damaged slat, moving one sliding step at a time as it flattened under his weight. He looked down over the jagged edge.

"That's the best I can do, Gudenian—we need to cover this hole."

"Maybe we can find something inside the house," he said cheerfully. Delmer grimaced. Magda's hand tightened on his arm.

They walked out onto the grass. Angled sunlight shone on their reddened faces. His blond stubble had a bleached quality. "What is wrong?" she demanded. "Did I do something?"

"I don't know what you're—"

"I know you think I'm stupid but I'm not blind. You don't want me any more, do you?"

"For Christ's sake—"

"You were hoping I'd go back with John Lindop, tell me the truth, I know you were. Just so that you could have Nadine—"

"Shut up," he growled. "We don't need—"

"Hey—Gudenian!" Chernitz was shouting from

the landing ledge on the other side of the hive. He raised his voice without taking his eyes off hers. "What is it, Abram?"

"A cavy—out there!"

He took Magda by the elbow and steered her back to the hive. "There's a lot of things we have to get settled—"

She pulled herself free. "It's your child I'm carrying. I just want to know!"

His face tightened but he said nothing.

Chernitz was pointing to the northern end of the lawn. He jumped onto a pile of broken comb-slats and pulled himself up. Beyond the line of wooden hives he had a quick glimpse of a bullet-smooth, brown body before the cavy ran quickly toward the other end of the garden wall.

Chernitz's eyes glinted. "Let's go hunting!"

Gudenian nodded patiently. "Tomorrow."

"There's still plenty of light—"

"Tomorrow."

"One shot—"

"We got enough meat for a couple of days. More important, we learn how to kill them without using up ammunition." Delmer ducked out from the last section of the entrance that Chernitz had not blocked up with broken wood. "Raoul—Abram saw a cavy. Isn't there some way of making spears by hardening the pointed tip of a branch in a fire?"

The big man nodded, squinting against the slanting rays of the sun. "Guinea pigs we used to call them, I kept them as pets when I was a boy, then we had to eat them!" He smiled ruefully. "I was ill."

"Better get everybody inside," Gudenian said. "When that grass is dry we can make a ladder—you know—twist the stalks into ropes and . . ."

He peered out at the towering thistles that dotted the wide lawn between them and the big dark blur of brambles.

Delmer pulled off his red and black jacket. "We could make the roof watertight with grass-thatching . . ." He followed the direction of Gudenian's gaze out over the lawn. The angled rays of the setting sun threw long shadows behind the towering thistles, making them look like trees standing against a racing flood. Gudenian was still staring. "What is it?"

"I thought . . . nah, just sun in my eyes." He sat down, dangling his legs over the edge. He called down. "Manuel? Time to get everybody inside." He yawned, stretching his arms. "You know, Raoul, that house must be full of stuff we can use—yeah, I know it's pretty spooky but—"

Chernitz squinted into the sunlight. "Hey—"

Gudenian's big hand clamped round his ankle. He crouched down on his haunches. "I just saw somebody out there in an OD suit," he hissed.

"I know—behind the middle thistle in that row of three. Pretend we haven't seen him." He leaned down. "Hurry it up, Manuel, going to be dark soon." He gestured at Delmer, motioning for him to get inside. "Just keep it casual—get a rifle but stay back in the shadow," he murmured.

The others were coming under the hive, comparing aches and blisters, telling each other how red their faces were. "It's only John Lindop trying to sneak back," he murmured. Chernitz breathed sharply.

"It could be a patrol."

"No, they think we're long dead." He smiled down at Magda and Peta. "This is a good time for midges," he said. They began to climb up onto the ledge. Chernitz took a deep breath.

"Gudenian," he whispered, covering his mouth with his hand, "they do know we're alive . . . I spoke to Bruce on the radio." Gudenian's head turned slowly. "When you were all stitching John up—I heard Bruce calling us. I didn't say much more than piss off but . . . they know we're alive."

Gudenian gave him a long steady look. He mouthed something unintelligible, then he let himself drop to the ground. Peta was laughing as Gento hoisted her up on his shoulders.

"Go through to the back and drop me out a rifle," he murmured up at Chernitz. "Don't say anything—keep everything looking normal."

"What are you going to do?"

Already his blue eyes had a preoccupied look. "I'm going to take an evening stroll—what do you think?"

From the cover of a spiky thistle-trunk, Bruce saw black and red figures climbing onto the wooden ledge. He counted four of them.

A beehive?

He had pushed himself well beyond the limit to get this far by nightfall and he did not trust his senses. There was a band of pain across his lower ribcage and his legs were numb. One minute blood pounded through his head, sending dark waves across his eyes, the next it seemed to drain away, leaving him weak and giddy.

A *beehive?*

Chest heaving, he put both hands against the spiky thistle-trunk and leaned wearily, head down.

The sky was almost black now to the east and the angled sunlight was turning a brilliant red. He estimated another twenty minutes of daylight at most.

"If you walk straight toward them they'll shoot on sight," he muttered.

He thought about trying to raise them on his transceiver but Sasso would pick up the transmissions. And several times during the day he'd heard a helicopter engine.

By now the aerial traffic to the other hives was one-way, the last stragglers returning with heavy loads of pollen and honey-nectar. When he squinted against the red sunset he thought he could make out three of them on the ledge.

Gudenian was a triple-killer. He would be expecting a search-patrol. To stay alive this long he must have learned the basic truth about survival in the wilds—at the first hint of danger you either ran away or you cocked your gun. To hesitate was to die.

He peered across the wide expanse of grass. There were still two figures moving on the ledge of the big dark structure. He snorted at the irony of being forced to wait for darkness before he could approach the hive; night was the most dangerous time of all, when guns were no match for the predator's far superior senses of smell and hearing—yet it was only in darkness that he would be safe from his own species . . .

Gudenian sprinted from thistle in a red furnace glow, following a wide semicircle from the rear of the hive. He remembered a boyhood story, of a peasant whose king had rewarded him with as much virgin land as he could run round in a day.

All his life he'd puzzled over what he would have done. Try to cover too much ground and burst a lung? Be cautious—and then find he could have covered twice the distance?

He made the next thistle and merged into its shadow, checking his position against the landmark of the hive. The steady daylight buzz of insects had changed to a more sinister rhythm of clickings and scrapings. From the other hives came a quiet hum, as of a throbbing generator.

He ran to the next thistle with the rifle across his chest, running face on to the blazing sunset. The whole world was on fire.

He was more than halfway across the lawn now, beyond the group of thistles where they'd spotted the skulking figure. Blood pulsed through the open scar on the bridge of his nose. He stopped in shadow, taking deep breaths, holding them down until his lungs had extracted all possible oxygen.

He moved slowly round the spiky trunk, one step at a time, gently feeling down onto each patch of grass in case his weight cracked a dry stick.

The man was a black silhouette against the blazing sky. He was leaning against a thistle-trunk.

Gudenian quietly pulled the rifle-belt over his head. Then he drew his knife.

That was why he had come on his own. Lindop had caused enough trouble. No matter how angry the others might be, he could not trust them to make the kind of decision that would keep them alive.

He moved out from the huge thistle-trunk. Overhead the sky was black. To the west the red sunset was dying in a last explosion of fire. He moved forward on his toes, the knife poised in his right hand . . .

At last the two figures disappeared into the hive. The dark wooden structure merged into the blackness of the advancing night, only one wall bathed in a wintry red glow.

Bruce winced as his legs took their first step toward sanctuary. Once under the hive, safe from their weapons in darkness, he could shout up to them, let them—

From nowhere there was a rushing presence behind.

Before he could look round, a big hand clamped over his mouth, pulling back his head to expose his throat to a steel blade that glinted red as it came up in an arc.

Gudenian rammed his knee against Lindop's spine, right hand tightening on the knife handle. One quick slash into the throat and . . .

He hesitated. It didn't *feel* like Lindop.

The big hand twisted Bruce round and he was looking into the stubbled, scarred face of a bearded Viking.

The torchlight showed him a ring of hostile faces. He chewed on cold rabbit meat, gulping at a flask of cold water. He recognized Nadine Boden and Peta Sandor—which meant that the dark-haired girl with the big worried eyes was Magda Hoessner.

"How did you know where we'd be?" Peta Sandor demanded.

He looked at the hostile faces, counting four men and three women. "Which one of you is John Lindop?"

"Lindop set off back to Glasshouse this morning," said a big man with protruding teeth.

"He came through on the radio yesterday, wanting to do a deal. We didn't tell him we were on the run ourselves. You can take it he's gone to meet up with Sasso."

"Bastard!" Chernitz smacked his fist into his palm. "I should've known that creep was too yellow to—"

"What's this guy Sasso want with us anyway?" Gudenian demanded.

Bruce sucked at his teeth. "You took something valuable from the Colony—very valuable . . . that's why I broke away from Sasso—I thought we wanted the same things but it's the same old story, another hungry ego looking for power—"

"Something like yourself?" Nadine said.

He smiled ruefully. "It's Doctor Boden, isn't it? People can change, you know—one thing you behaviorists won't admit is the human will . . . I said you'd taken something valuable—nobody going to ask me *what?*"

Magda spoke for the first time.

"They know I'm pregnant."

Gudenian enjoyed the surprise on Bruce's face. "Yeah, Bruce, we know about Magda. We've killed a couple of rabbits—we even survived a visit from the goddamn fox. Did you think we'd be trembling in a dark hole, waiting to follow you home like sheep?"

Bruce smiled. "I did tell you we burned down the Compound, didn't I? Things are blowing up back there, it's all going to be different—"

"You do want to go back then?" Peta demanded.

He raised his hands. "Who knows? Maybe we can make a life out here—"

"What good would you be to us?" Nadine asked.

He thought it was a joke until he saw the unchanging hostility on the torchlit faces. "What's wrong with you people? Didn't I come all this way on my own—just to warn you?"

Chernitz yawned. "Or just to get here before that monkey Sasso? It's all politics with you bastards—"

"Are you saying you don't *want* me?"

They exchanged quick looks. The circle began to break up. Gudenian got to his feet. He swung the torch-beam over a line of packs and sleeping-bags. The beam travelled on to a remote section of bare floor. "You can put your sleeping-bag there, Bruce."

He scrambled to his feet, trying to stay in the light of the torch. "I don't think you people understand—Sasso will be here in the morning! We've got to decide—"

"What've they got—rifles, pistols?" Chernitz asked casually.

"No, bows and arrows," he snapped. "Listen, Gudenian—"

The torch-beam shone in his face. "Get into your sleeping bag, Bruce, we'll let you know what we decide."

A hand steered him toward the rear wall. Somebody threw down his pack. He started to plead and argue with the faces behind the blinding light but nobody answered and he heard himself sounding like a querulous old man and he stopped talking. Not knowing how many people were watching, he sat down with as much dignity as was possible and pulled off his boots . . .

Gudenian let the torch-beam rest on the resin-cocoon. They formed a circle round the upward glow of soft, yellow light.

"Well?" he said. Nobody spoke. "Do you believe him?"

"We've got his radio," Manuel said, "he can't communicate with anybody."

"We've got two things to settle," Gudenian said. "One, what do we do about Sasso's bunch. Two, what do we do about Bruce. Let's hear from everybody." He looked at Manuel Gento, who was on his immediate left.

"As far as we're concerned their intentions are

hostile. However, if we stay to fight we will be outnumbered. We must vanish before they reach us."

"And Bruce . . . ?"

"He is older than any of us but he came a long way on his own. We could use his experience of surviving in the wilds."

Gudenian looked next at Peta.

"Manuel's right—Sasso's interested in only one thing—taking over the Colony. I say we hide—if we fight them somebody's bound to be killed." She looked over her shoulder into the darkness. "I don't trust *him*. Power's a habit—he'll want to take over. Give him some food and let him find his own way back."

"Magda?"

She hesitated, feeling uncomfortable at the center of attention. "I don't want to go back . . . I suppose we should hide . . ."

"What about Bruce?" Gudenian's voice was reassuringly gentle. She stared at his bruised, stubbled face, trying to remember what he'd looked like when they'd first made love. "I don't think he's a bad man," she said. "I mean . . . you wouldn't kill him or anything, would you?"

Gudenian's face gave no clue to his thoughts.

"Abram?"

"I don't want to go back—not ever! But we could use all the equipment and weapons he says they're carrying. I think we should ambush 'em, take whatever they got. We could jump 'em somewhere along the line—"

"Bruce?"

Chernitz shrugged. "He's giving us a lot of crap now but he's the guy who signed a detention order for every one of us. We don't need him—in fact, I got to say this, I mean I don't want to . . ." He shifted his weight, glancing at the other faces and then finding it easier if he stared down at the glistening fur of the dead mouse. "He's an extra man and we've already got a problem in that direction . . . if you follow . . ."

"Raoul?"

"I like the idea of trapping them for their weapons and ammunition," said the big man. "We could use the radio—"

Gudenian shook his head. "Uh uh—I gave it to Lindop."

"Why?" Chernitz demanded.

"As long as it was here somebody would be tempted to use it. We're finished with the Colony—right? Anyway—" his hand fumbled in his jacket pouch—"I don't think it would be much use to Lindop." He opened his first, showing them the flat circuit-chip.

They stared at each other, coming to grips with the brutal logic of the man who was their leader. "I'll tell you this as well," Gudenian went on, "I went out there tonight to cut Lindop's throat only it wasn't Lindop. Whatever we do from here on is for one purpose only—to stay alive. Nadine?"

"I haven't finished," Delmer interjected. "We can't avoid it any longer so I might as well bring it out in the open. We will live in harmony together only if there is no jealousy. It is how we were meant to live—one man for one woman. Bruce would be useful as a hostage to exchange for another woman from the Colony."

They all stared down at the glowing mound of resin. Gudenian met Nadine's eyes and nodded.

"An ambush would be dangerous—they won't just lay down their weapons and go away. I say we should hide. As for Bruce . . . I dabbled in anthropology at one time. Kindness is an evolutionary asset for humans. Primitive groups that kept their old people alive had a data-bank of experience to draw on. Bruce has had more experience of staying alive at this level than almost anyone else." She looked at Delmer. "As for the question of pairing up—"

"Not now," Gudenian said brusquely. "Is that all?"

"You haven't said anything," Peta murmured.

He nodded. "Bruce can stay—just let him know he has to forget he was Controller. As for this Sasso —we're going to ambush them."

Gento frowned. "With only three rifles?"

Gudenian reached down to touch the hard, smooth resin, shaking his head. "No, not with guns —with a nice big feast of welcome . . ."

Left alone in darkness, Bruce listened to the low murmurs of their voices, knowing they were discussing his fate. When he raised his head from the sleeping bag he saw their dark silhouettes standing against a glow of strange amber light.

He lay back, staring into a black void. He should have expected suspicion and hostility—they all resented him as a figure of authority and Gudenian saw him as a threat to his own position. "Old man," somebody had called him!

He frowned, gradually seeing a way to ensure his own survival. Nobody was afraid of old men!

John Lindop spent that night cowering in a narrow space under a trunk of vicious thorns, consoling himself with vicious thoughts of revenge on the bastard Gudenian who had sent him off with a useless radio.

He had worked his way all through the bramble forest before he discovered why he could not raise Bruce's patrol on the transceiver. Gudenian had sent him off into the jungle of the great park to *die!*

Sheer hatred kept him from panicking. Not knowing what route the patrol was taking to reach the house, he had retreated into the dead forest, shivering through the endless night in his narrow trench.

At first gray light filtering down through the high canopy of green leaves, he started back the way he'd come, darting from cover to cover, pistol drawn; to reach the house Bruce's patrol would have to cross the thistle-lawn—and he would be there to guide them straight to the hive!

The thought of revenge gave him courage to keep going when he felt the vibrations of running feet and saw the movements of large furry bodies.

When he reached green leaves, he eased cautiously toward daylight. In a soft, misty dawn black and brown rabbits were grazing on dew-heavy grass. Beyond the giant thistles he saw the dark shapes of the hives. He touched his swollen cheek. The inflamed wound was turning itchy—a good sign.

"I'm going to enjoy seeing your face, Gudenian you bastard," he muttered grimly.

It came to him as a brainwave. They were still sleeping. From the nearest thistle he could cover the hive with his pistol, pin them inside until Bruce arrived, earn the Controller's gratitude!

He checked the pistol and started out across the wet grass . . .

Vulpes Vulpes lay nose to ground in thick nettles, every muscle and nerve tensed to spring.

The young black doe, heavy with her first litter, moved with little hops, grazing methodically, each hop taking her a few inches farther from the huge brambles which covered the warren's widely spread entrances.

Robbed of his sense of smell by the membrane-searing acid, Vulpes Vulpes could still hear the faint impact of furry paws on grass. His one eye, unable to focus on stationary objects, could still detect the slightest movement that might mean prey. He could outrun any rabbit, provided he could get between it and the nearest bolt-hole.

He moved his head imperceptibly, keeping the doe in sight by constant scanning. His hind legs were poised to spring forward.

Then something alerted the rabbits.

The doe's ears pricked up.

Vulpes Vulpes launched himself out of the nettles in a snarling rush.

The doe sprang for the brambles. An urgent

drumming of a buck's hind feet sent all the other rabbits darting for the huge bank of greenery.

Vulpes Vulpes hit green leaves a few inches behind the doe. He crashed among the brambles, losing her. His ears were confused by the drumming of feet on all sides. He raced back into the open, looking for any rabbit caught out on the lawn.

He registered a movement, a small creature, running.

His burned nose-membranes gave no warning of Man.

Sight and hearing directed his streaking dash into the middle of the lawn.

The little creature screamed and ran toward a huge thistle. He skidded round, black paw-pads slewing up sprays of dew.

John Lindop's arms hugged the thorny trunk, clinging desperately to spikes that cut open his hands and face.

The huge yellow canines crushed through the small, struggling body. There was a cracking of bones.

The scent of Man flooded the taste-buds in the mouth of the giant fox.

But the flesh was sweet.

In that moment Vulpes Vulpes had become a maneater.

25

"*Something* scared those rabbits," Delmer said, crouching inside the entrance. "Didn't you hear the scream?"

Gudenian looked out on a gray, misty dawn. "Rabbits panic easily—that's how they stay alive. Abram? Manuel?"

The four men emerged onto the ledge. Nothing moved on the big lawn.

Gudenian, then Gento, then Chernitz dropped onto wet grass. Delmer stood above them, rifle across his chest.

"Build the fire out in the open—we want them to see it from a long way off," Gudenian said. Delmer nodded. "Biggest fire you can make, Raoul!"

Delmer surveyed the dew-covered lawn. "What if they turn up while you're gone?"

"Stall 'em—we'll be as quick as it takes Abram to prove he's not bullshitting about his marksmanship."

They moved under the ledge, heading toward the garden wall . . .

Bruce could smell burning wood. He blinked in a dim light from a gap in the wooden wall. He scrambled stiffly to his feet, kicking off his sleeping-bag. "Anybody there?"

A figure appeared in the light from a low opening at the front of the hive.

"So you're awake at last," said Nadine Boden. "Gudenian said you had to work but we took pity on you. Hungry?"

He rubbed his eyes. "I'll do my share, you know." He peered into the shadows. "Last night—what was that light coming from?"

"Our lucky mascot!"

He followed her round a gaping hole in the floor. She touched the hard cocoon, smiling at him. He came near enough to see the dead mouse.

"If the other hives swarm they may pick on this one," he said. "You'd be lucky then not to find yourself sealed up in propolis."

He watched her lift green leaves off a partially dismembered rabbit carcass. Stretched from splinters on the wall were two rabbit pelts. She cut into the cold roasted meat. "You know anything about drying animal skins? Somebody said we should spread them on the roof—"

"The sun would crack them—they'd also attract crows. Where's Gudenian?"

"They've gone to shoot a cavy. You think your friends will be here soon?"

"*My friends?*" He shook his head indignantly. "I explained last night—by the way, what did you decide about me?"

She gave him a thick slice of cold roast impaled on her knife. "Our cooking is still pretty crude—burned on the outside and raw on the inside."

He tore off a sliver and chewed on it slowly. "Lindop said you were at the house."

"I'm afraid Gudenian played a dirty trick on John—his radio won't work. Still, he was betraying us, wasn't he?"

"What's Gudenian going to do about Sasso? I found you easily enough—I could hear your voices right across that big stretch of grass."

"All he told us was to start a fire—there's some old rotten seed-boxes beside the garden wall, if you want to help. Oh yes, we did make a decision—you can stay with us for the moment."

"I didn't realize you were running such an exclusive club, Doctor."

"I'm not Doctor Boden now, I'm Nadine."

He smiled. "A delicate way to remind me I'm no longer Controller Bruce."

She looked at him for a moment. "We've had some traumatic experiences since we escaped. Don't expect delicate treatment. I'll give you some advice, Bruce. We wouldn't be alive but for Gudenian—"

"Sooner I get on terms with him the better—that the message?"

She nodded. Her voice was clipped and terse. "Yes—*his* terms. You'd better understand about Gudenian. He went out last night thinking you were John Lindop—and he would've cut John's throat. He killed three guards back in Glasshouse—we had to watch him smashing Markstein's head to a pulp! He isn't ever going back—and if he even *suspected* you of any trickery he wouldn't hesitate." She drew her hand across her throat. "And none of us would help you. Do you want to stay with us?"

He sighed ruefully. "Nadine—I'm an old man who doesn't belong anywhere. I don't blame you people for not trusting me. I wouldn't even blame you if you pushed me out that—"

"They're coming!" Peta shouted from the ledge, where she had taken Delmer's place with the rifle while he carried wood. Nadine hurried to the entrance. Bruce followed her quickly.

By the time Gudenian and Gento and Chernitz came in sight, dragging a dead wood pigeon by its feet, Bruce was staggering toward the fire under an armful of wet, rotting wood, taking care to stay well in the background.

Chernitz put his foot on the pigeon's white neck-ring, inviting them all to admire him.

"Two shots—right in the eye," he said proudly.

"Anybody know how the hell to pluck the god-damn thing?" Gudenian growled cheerfully. Bruce was careful not to catch his eye as he threw the bits of broken plank onto the smoking fire. Delmer sank his hands into the smooth gray feathers of the bird's bulging chest. His neck veins throbbed as he pulled on tight feathers.

"Why don't we just roast it as it is?" Peta said.

"We could make mattresses out of the feathers," Magda protested. Delmer finally managed to pluck out one large wing-feather. Bruce threw another armful of wood onto the fire.

"There's one thing you might try," he said diffidently. Gudenian eyed him warily. Bruce shrugged. "Just a suggestion—but if you pour boiling water on a bird the feathers come out quite easily."

"Get a tin," Gudenian said quietly . . .

The naked bird was sizzling in the heart of the big fire when Chernitz saw the first black and red uniform out in the middle of the lawn. He turned his back, facing the fire.

"They're here," he said.

Gudenian showed no reaction that would have been visible to anybody watching from the thistles. "You'd better get inside, Bruce," he said calmly.

He nodded and climbed onto piled planks to pull himself onto the ledge. Inside he found Gento lying prone in the shadow, one rifle at his shoulder, the other two propped against the wall. Around him lay the last ammunition clips. He motioned for Bruce to get down beside him. Together they watched black and red uniforms flitting from thistle to thistle.

"They're surrounding us!"

Gento nodded. "We could not fight them anyway," he muttered. "You point out this man Sasso—if it goes wrong he will be the first to die. Are there other leaders?"

Bruce blinked. "No," he said quietly, "Sasso is the boss."

Sasso and Empie stood together behind the tall thistle.

"I don't see how it could be a trap," Empie said, "we know there are only eight of them and we can see six—"

"Where is this man Lindop?" Sasso demanded. "He was to contact us by radio. And where is Bruce?"

"Bruce is probably lost back there somewhere. Could be they found out Lindop was using the radio. I don't see what's to be nervous about."

The small, swarthy man grunted. "If they know Lindop was betraying them why are they not in hiding? Gudenian is a man who escaped from Interrogation—would you have said that was possible?"

"We have sixteen armed men—"

"But we can't risk any shooting in case the girl gets hurt!" He sniffed. "They are cooking something ... all right, we're wasting time, Empie. Tell the others to stay out of sight. If anything goes wrong they will just have to attack."

"Two of them," Chernitz muttered.

Gudenian looked over his shoulder. A pale sunlight was beginning to dissipate the morning mist. Crossing the open lawn between them and the thistles were two figures in black and red OD suits. By now the bees were zooming off into the park. There was no wind and white smoke from the fire of rotting wood climbed greasily into the sky in a spiralling column.

He saw the dumpy little man Bruce had described. As they drew nearer he recognized Empie, an SG area-captain whose quick promotion had caused a lot of gossip. He thrust his knife into the charred skin of the roasting wood pigeon. Succulent juices bubbled out of the gash.

"Okay," he muttered, "here we go." He turned and pretended to see Sasso and Empie for the first time.

He raised his hand and strode towards them, a big smile on his face.

"You're just in time," he shouted. "Bruce told us you were coming." He held out his hand. "Only two of you? I'm David Gudenian."

Empie shook his hand. Sasso merely nodded. He looked at the people standing round the fire. He recognized Nadine Boden and Peta Sandor but none of the others. The dark-haired girl must be Hoessner. She became uneasy at his steady appraisal.

"Where is Bruce?" he demanded.

Gudenian smiled. "Well, he was a little nervous about meeting you. Where are the rest of your people? We're just going to cut this bird up and—"

"And where is John Lindop?" Sasso demanded.

"I thought you'd know that, Sasso," Gudenian grinned.

The small, swarthy man walked round the fire toward Magda. He looked at her and shrugged. "You are Nurse Hoessner?"

She nodded. Gudenian slashed at the crisp brown skin of the sizzling wood pigeon. "Yeah, that's Magda," he said. "Bruce says you've got some idea of taking her back to the Colony, Sasso?"

"You are a very important young woman," Sasso said, "things will be very different for you, I promise you that." He turned, looking through smoke at Gudenian. "You have no future out here. Bruce has told you what our plan is?"

Gudenian nodded. "Sure. Let's eat first, and we'll talk about it."

Screwing up his eyes against the smoke, he cut out a long sliver of firm, dry flesh. Chernitz rammed his knife into the crackling skin.

"Boy, does that smell good!"

Sasso frowned, his hand hovering near his pistol.

"We might as well enjoy it while we can," Empie muttered. "You're just naturally suspicious, Sasso." He walked out in front of the hive and cupped his hands round his mouth. "You can come out now," he shouted.

From the shadowy interior of the hive, Bruce

and Gento saw them appear from behind the big thistles, a widely spaced ring of men and women, packs on their shoulders, each one of them carrying a rifle. Empie waved at them and the circle began to converge toward the hive. "I hope there is some left for us," Gento muttered.

Bruce watched the faces breaking into smiles as the tantalizing aroma of roasted flesh reached their nostrils. He saw Annette Rosa—and poor old Bogaert, looking near to exhaustion. He felt responsible for every one of them—but it was out of his hands now...

Gudenian waited until they had eaten as much roasted meat as they could hold. The last trace of mist had gone. People were sprawled on the grass, some with their eyes closed, some bare to the waist, letting pale sun-starved skin enjoy a luxury they had been denied in the fortress-colony. He strolled out into the sunshine in front of the hive, glancing quickly at the ledge and then flopping down on the grass.

"So what's your plan now, Sasso?" he asked in a loud cheerful voice, making sure they could all hear. For half an hour Nadine and Chernitz and the others had moved among the newcomers, answering their questions, sowing the seeds.

Sasso came toward him, eyes nervously scanning the blue sky. "I think you and I should discuss it between ourselves," he said quietly.

Gudenian squinted up at him, licking charred fragments off his lips and beard. "What've we got to discuss that everybody can't hear?" he drawled. "Don't you feel warm in that goddamn suit? Take it off, man, the bees don't eat people!"

Sasso wiped his face. He blinked in the strong sunlight, searching out the girl Hoessner in the crowd of sprawled bodies. "We will talk in private," he muttered.

Gudenian yawned, showing his teeth and stretching his powerful bare arms. "I thought you Chalk Circle people were hot on democracy and all that jazz. You want to go back to the Colony, right? You think Khomich's going to forgive and forget, right? I don't know, Sasso—the moment he gets his hands on Magda what's to stop him banging the whole bunch of you in the Diggings?" He looked round a circle of pale faces. "That's if he doesn't shove you up against a wall and—"

"My people know the plan," Sasso said curtly.

Gudenian grinned up at him. "Mine don't."

"At this moment the prisoners in the Diggings have seized their guards. This afternoon there will be a strike of field workers. Khomich will have no option but to negotiate with us."

"And Magda's the ace in the hole?" Sasso made a slight shrugging gesture. Gudenian licked his tongue round his teeth and slowly stood up. "I suppose you all know that Magda there—" he gestured toward her —"well, she's pregnant." He smiled. "She and I have decided we want our child to live out here—we don't have guards to protect us, of course, but the food's better!"

"You're right about that," growled one of Sasso's men.

Sasso's face tightened angrily. "Listen to me, Gudenian—"

"No, you listen. All of you listen," Gudenian said calmly. "I am not going to that stinking Colony and neither is Magda and neither are the rest of us. You people can make up your own minds—we'll be happy to take anybody who wants to join us provided—"

Sasso beckoned urgently at Empie, who started to get up. Sasso's hand went for his pistol.

"I wouldn't do that, man," Chernitz said, pointing up at the hive entrance. "There's a guy called Manuel up there with a rifle aimed right at your belly-button."

Gudenian moved away from Sasso. "That's right, mister," he said, "you just stand there and let your people as you call them make up their own minds. I'm not promising you a feast like this every day but there's plenty of food out here. We've got enough hardware to keep us going until we learn other ways to hunt. Anyway you look at it, Glasshouse is a prison—"

"We are going to take over the Colony and change the whole system," Sasso barked. Gudenian raised his hand, warning him to stay exactly where he was.

"I guess we just prefer it out here," he went on. "I'm not promising you paradise—I'm not threatening you, either." He stopped quickly, picking up a rifle. "You're free to go back or to stay here. There's only one condition—we want an equal number of men and women." He rested the rifle across the back of his neck. "Tell you what—if you're joining us stand over there beside the fire . . ."

Bruce held his breath.

Gento tightened his grip on the rifle.

People looked at each other.

"Take his rifle, Empie," Sasso snapped.

Nobody moved.

The man whom Bruce remembered from the panic at the time of the floods, a burly field worker with a broken nose, raised his hand. Gudenian turned to look at him, arms draped on the rifle across his neck.

"Is it true there is a fox loose in the park as we have been told?" the burly man asked.

Gudenian nodded. "Yup. He paid us a visit last night. He's half-blind and right now he's suffering from a shot of acid up his nose. We'll have to kill him sooner or later because he's competing with us for food but—"

Through a rising murmur, Bruce heard Nadine's voice. She stood up, turning this way and that to address the people sprawled on the grass. "I was a founder-member of the Chalk Circle, I had the same ideas as Sasso about changing the Colony. I can only tell you that in the last few days I've felt like a human being again and not a numbered unit of personnel. Ask Magda. Ask Peta. We've all been scared to death but we're not going back to the Colony, not under any circumstances. Do any of you remember what it was like to be *free*?"

Bruce closed his eyes.

When he looked again, one of the pale-skinned men from Sasso's party had risen to his knees, looking at a fair-haired woman.

She hesitated, then they both got to their feet and moved together through the sprawled bodies, passing Sasso and Gudenian and walking together toward the smoldering fire. More people began to get up.

Sasso snarled something.

Gudenian shook his head. "It's called free choice, mister!"

Men and women hurried to get up. They moved toward the growing crowd round the fire, avoiding Sasso, who stood alone in a circle of grass.

Gento smiled at Bruce and clambered to his knees, holding the rifle in front of him as he crawled out onto the open ledge. Gudenian pointed up at him. "Just in case you thought I was bluffing. Sasso." He turned to the five men standing alone. "Any time you have a woman who wants to break out of that place with you—we'll be here. Take all the meat you want and—"

Out of the steady buzzing from the bee flight-paths came a louder, metallic roar as the black and yellow helicopter zoomed down past the dark shape of the house and skimmed over the hive, turning in a sharp semicircle to drop on the grass.

Gudenian waved at them to run for the hive.

Out of the SG wasp spilled a line of black-uniformed men carrying submachine guns.

Standing in bright sunshine on the high ledge, Bruce recognized the square, ramrod figure of Khomich. The black-uniformed guards formed themselves into a widely spaced line, training their ugly, prototype weapons on the jostling crowd of people trying to hide behind the big wooden legs of the hive.

Khomich raised his hand. At that distance his voice was chillingly impersonal.

"Stay where you are. Anyone who moves will be shot."

Chernitz shoved people out of the way to reach Gudenian in the shadow under the wooden floor. "We could get round behind them," he yelled in Gudenian's ear to make himself heard above the screams of the terrified people.

Bruce recognized Lindsay's red hair as the former deputy-commandant emerged from the line of black guards and raised one of the new weapons. There was a light chattering noise. When it stopped one of the giant thistles slowly began to topple.

Small flies and moths fluttered into bright sunlight as it crashed to the ground.

Khomich stood with his legs apart, hands clasped behind his back. He shouted across open grass at the confusion of frightened people under the black wooden box,

"I want Magda Hoessner and David Gudenian."

The eye could detect only movement.

There had been a noise of Man, a harsh metal noise that memory and instinct told him meant danger. His leg muscles went taut, poised to turn and run for deep cover.

The scanning eye saw only the movements of the small creatures that his mouth taste-buds associated with the recent satisfaction of sweet flesh.

The scanning eye saw no looming figure of Man. The flicking ears felt no vibration of Man's heavy feet.

The scanning eye saw the small sweet creatures moving on green grass.

Vulpes Vulpes broke through green leaves in a low, bounding dash, his long, grinning jaws stretched forward to snatch and kill.

26

Screams.

Bruce saw it all from the ledge . . . and did not believe what he saw.

Screams and bullets.

People fought each other to reach the ledge.

The huge red fox was a blurred streak.

The line of black-uniformed guards broke in a dozen different directions. The lucky ones kicked and fought each other to get inside the helicopter.

One man dropped to his knee, firing at the long jaws.

Vulpes Vulpes felt a stinging sensation on his nose and gums. Pain meant nothing at the moment of kill. His yellow teeth crunched on the small, screaming creature. He dropped the broken body and ran in short, snarling bursts, snapping at everything that moved.

His momentum brought him nearer to the hive. Hunger was the driving force—but the lust to kill knew no logic.

In his panic, Bruce hurled himself through the narrow opening. The fox saw a surging movement of the small sweet creatures. He ran toward the wooden box, red fur glistening in the sun.

Manuel Gento closed his eyes. His lips trembled with the words of a prayer he had last spoken in childhood.

The people ran from under the hive, spreading out in a mad dash for the garden wall.

Manuel Gento took one deep breath. He clamped his mouth shut. His hands trembled on the rifle barrel.

The red giant snapped low at a running man.

Manuel Gento's heart thumped in the iron cage of his chest. A glinting orb came into his sights. He squeezed the trigger.

The glistening eye exploded inward like a punctured watermelon.

The animal scream transcended all other noise. In that moment of ultimate agony, blinded by searing red waves, Vulpes Vulpes crashed against the wooden box. A stilt leg tore away from the plank wall with a gentle splintering noise. This wooden structure lurched, sagged forward, then crashed over onto the grass.

Vulpes Vulpes ran in a demented circle, snapping at his own body, head jerking back until his long jaws were pointing skyward. In the obscene madness of unbearable agony, he was trying to bite at his own face.

The two small red and black figures ran out into brilliant sunshine. The towering giant snapped on his own bushy tail, whirling in a circle of red fur. They stopped, not knowing which way to run.

Vulpes Vulpes stumbled and fell. They changed direction and ran farther out onto the open green plain. Its engine drowned by the fox's snarls and yelps, the black and yellow helicopter rose at an angle, rotor blades blurring into a glinting arc.

Vulpes Vulpes clawed himself upright, head swaying low from side to side.

Gudenian and Chernitz reached the first broken body of a black-uniformed guard. Gudenian kicked lifeless hands away from the ugly black weapon.

Vulpes Vulpes ran at one noise. The searing red

waves throbbed across his sightless eyes. The long jaws snapped at empty air.

Chernitz saw a darker black line in the shadow beside a body so mangled and bloody it might have been headless. He pulled the submachine gun free with his boot.

Gudenian waved at him. They ran together, circling the huge red fox. Gudenian pointed. The fox turned away from them, its long thick tail whipping warm air against their faces.

Vulpes Vulpes heard another noise.

He turned blindly.

They aimed together at the blood-wet socket.

Bruce crawled out from under wooden wreckage and dragged himself toward a jagged patch of sunlight.

He clambered through the hole head first, big splinters tearing at his clothes. His dazed eyes recoiled from the brilliant light. He heard a staccato, chattering noise.

He came round the wooden wall, vaguely realizing that the hive no longer stood on stilt-legs. There were silent people all round him, shocked faces staring out across the lawn.

"What happened?" he asked but it was as if he had become invisible.

He blinked, following the direction of the unbelieving eyes.

Vulpes Vulpes, the red intruder, staggered in a drunken semicircle. Two small figures followed his swaying head, raising the black guns again.

Vulpes Vulpes collapsed hind legs first, the pale fur on his belly crushing down on grass. His long, killer's jaws made slow biting motions and then his forelegs buckled and he slumped, muzzle resting on grass. His tail twitched. His huge red body convulsed and then sagged sideways.

They stood in two lines, facing inward.

Khomich looked neither to the left nor to the right as he passed between the silent, staring faces.

He reached the helicopter, then turned round. His small blue eyes flicked across the rows of faces. He saw Bruce but he gave no sign of recognition. He ignored the machine guns in the hands of Abram Chernitz and Manuel Gento and Raoul Delmer. He addressed the big blond man with the bearded Viking face.

His voice was precise and without emotion.

"I will say it once again—any of you willing to accept the Colony's laws without question has exactly two days in which to return. After that, the doors will be closed against you for all time. The Colony will go on without you. No individual is more important than our collective future. There will be changes but only to make us stronger and more secure."

He nodded curtly and stepped into the helicopter.

They moved back as it rose into the blue sky.

Gudenian caught Nadine Boden's eye. She smiled. He stared at her for a moment then he put his hand on Magda's shoulder. She was unique, a valuable prize for whom men had died. She was the future and only the leader deserved to own her.

The helicopter disappeared into the sun.

"We were lucky this time," he said loudly, "but Khomich will be back, make no mistake about it. We're a threat to everything he stands for. He's given you two days—I'm giving you two minutes. Make up your minds now—but if you stay with us you're going to do it my way."

He waited. Nobody moved.

"All right. First, we find a place to live. I also want two volunteers to skin that goddamn animal—from now on we don't waste *anything* we can use . . ."

They moved slowly back across the lawn, falling silent in awe as they circled the lifeless body of Vulpes Vulpes, the red intruder.

A Special Preview of
a dramatic opening section of

THE MICRONAUTS

The first novel in this series by

Gordon Williams

sprays—those were the very things he was escaping from. . . . Man's guilts on the battlefields.

Keeping just below the skyline, he set off on his long, lonely trek to reach Gudenfels, his legs falling into a striding rhythm that he could keep up all day.

They came in over the treetops, circling the big house once, seeing only walled gardens and greenhouses and a small pond beside some trees before they came down.

As soon as the old twin-prop troop carrier touched the gravel drive in front of the mansion, Khomich and Robinson ducked out under the scything blades. Bruce pushed in front of the black-uniformed soldiers, his gray hair flying about his face as he straightened up beside Khomich. If nothing else, he might stop them from killing anybody.

As they approached the porch columns, the door opened and three men stepped out, two of them in white laboratory coats. Bruce recognized the other one immediately, a small, slightly-built man with a few strands of white hair and a small beard.

"Doctor Jany, isn't it?" he said.

"Yes—what is the explanation for this intrusion?" demanded the small Frenchman. "Who are you?"

"My name's Bruce—I used to run the Biology Institute in Brussels."

"Oh yes—Professor Bruce. You sat on the Enquiry Board which vetoed my project. What are you doing here with these soldiers? This is a Rest and Recuperation Clinic, we cannot have—"

"Major Wollaston—take control of all communications," said Khomich, pushing past Jany into the paneled hallway. Jany ran after him, face red with anger. "You have no authority, I forbid you—"

Bruce put his hand on Jany's shoulder. "Staff-Commander Khomich has all the authority he needs, Doctor. I wouldn't try to obstruct him."

"What authority? Why are you here?"

"Project Arcadia, of course."

"What project? What are these soldiers doing?"

"Taking charge of your communications," Khomich said, watching two black-uniformed SD men disconnecting an old-fashioned PBX switchboard while two more SD men manhandled its elderly operator against the oak-paneled wall. "Now," Khomich said, "show us this Project Arcadia."

"This is a Rest and Recuperation Center! I must insist—"

"According to personnel records in Paris, you're looking after thirty-eight rest cases here," Bruce said briskly. "You keep them all indoors on a fine morning like this?"

"They are under medical care; they must not be disturbed. I order you out of this building—I will make the strongest complaints to my superiors."

"Who are your superiors?"

"I refuse to answer any more questions!"

Khomich nodded. He strolled across to a large carved stand on which stood a bell-shaped glass case. Inside the case, artistically mounted against a background of ferns and flowers, were scores of stuffed hummingbirds in flight. He nodded appreciatively at the brilliant plumages of the tiny birds.

"Look, Jany," Bruce said quickly, "you can either show us everything or Staff-Commander Khomich will conduct his own guided tour—and he rarely bothers to knock."

Jany shook his head.

"Is George Richards here?" Khomich asked.

Jany's mouth tightened.

Khomich hooked his right boot round the foot of the carved plinth, then gave it a vicious jerk.

The bell-shaped case tottered at an angle, then hit the tiled floor. The glass shattered. Dried leaves and stuffed hummingbirds spewed across the tiles.

Jany stared at him in horror. Then his shoulders fell. He looked at Bruce. "I appeal to you as a scientist—these soldiers have no place in a research establishment—send them back to their helicopter and I will discuss this with you—"

Khomich shoved between them. "There will be no discussion. On the authority of the Commissioner I will search this building."

Jany closed his eyes and sighed. With a little shrug he said. "Oh well, it had to come sooner or later."

Bruce and Khomich followed him into a dimly-lit corridor. Khomich using his elbows to make sure he was never more than one pace behind Jany. They entered an old-fashioned library. The sight of so many leather-bound books, on shelves that went all the way up to the plaster moldings of the ceiling, made Bruce gasp. In a world where books were considered at best to be irrelevancies, a collection like this was surely reason enough for the secrecy surrounding Arcadia. But he was given no time to inspect the shelves.

Jany pressed a button under the light-switch.

A concealed door slid soundlessly open and they were looking into a huge, split-level studio full of cameras and laboratory equipment. People in white coats stared as Jany led them across the floor. Jany led them up a short flight of stairs to an upper-level platform facing out over the rear gardens of the mansion. Immediately below was the domed glass roof of what appeared to be a small conservatory extension. On the raised platform several technicians were at work, one using what looked like a periscope scanner, others speaking to faces on video-screens.

"Still no contact, Doctor," a woman said without looking up from her console.

"Thank you, Jeanette."

Jany gestured at the view beyond the huge plateglass windows. Bruce saw a wide, uncut lawn and then a sloping rockery or rock garden. Beyond that were shrubs and ferns and then trees in a large overgrown garden surrounded by a red brick wall.

"Well—there is Project Arcadia," said Jany.

Khomich looked down at the mass of equipment on the floor beneath them. "Does this look like the stuff on the list, Professor Bruce?"

"Could be." Bruce peered out over the garden. "*That's* Project Arcadia?"

Jany grimaced. "I will have to explain—"

"Getting him now," exclaimed the woman he had called Jeanette, pulling down an RDF wheel.

Jany picked up a hand-mike. "Control to Richards. We are hearing you faintly. What is your position, over?"

Through a dull roar of static, they heard a small, urgent voice.

"Richards to Control, Richards to Control, Mayday, Mayday, Mayday . . ."

Into another speaker, the woman operator said, "Control to Recovery, take a bearing on this transmission, Professor Richards on Channel B. Status Red Alarm, over."

"Control to Richards, what is your current position?" Jany said into the hand-mike. He was frowning. "Why isn't he using the pack-set? Try Carrere on Channel A, Camisa."

"Tell Recovery to scatter-drop LS capsules in the general area of Crossing Two," Jany said to the woman operator.

"Was that Professor Richards?" Khomich demanded, peering through the huge plate-glass windows. "I cannot see him."

Jany used the hand-mike again. "Control to

Richards. Capsules now being scattered around Crossing Two—transmit for fix, over."

"Richards to Control, I am hearing you now. I am roughly south of Crossing Two. We were heading for Station Three to be lifted out. I have lost contact with the others. They may have crossed to the north side of the stream. You must scatter-drop LS capsules. Get somebody with a rifle to—"

For a brief moment, they heard an upsurge in the static—then a dull, acoustical silence.

"Recovery couldn't get a bearing, sir," said the woman operator. "He's probably too low for them—our Grid bearing is south-line five-two. Capsules have been dropped."

"We were lucky to pick him up on a personal communicator at that range."

"Is Richards taking part in some kind of simulated stress experiment?" Bruce asked patiently. Jany shook his head.

"Ask Recovery if they've seen any big birds—they must be shot immediately."

"They're looking now. It must have come in from the south, through the trees at the pond."

"We must speak to Professor Richards immediately," Khomich said. "Where is the door to the garden?"

"Nobody is allowed out in the garden, it is too dangerous," said Jany.

"*Dangerous?* What have you got out there—tigers?"

"I will explain in one moment. Camisa—be ready to take cross-bearings if he transmits again. Keep constant surveillance of both channels."

"Yes, Doctor. You think Professor Richards is testing the emergency procedure we were discussing at the last planning committee?"

"I hope so, but we will presume it is for real." He turned to Khomich and Bruce. "If you will come with me."

They followed him down the steps to the ground-level. He stopped at a brightly-lit model garden on a stand. His finger hovered above tiny replicas of grass and stones and trees and shrubs. "Richards is on an acclimitization exercise," he said. "His route took him across this lawn, down this short rockery slope—across this open ground—his party was heading originally for Station Four—" He pressed a button on a small panel. A light came on under a tiny glass canopy in one corner of the model garden. "But now he seems to be in this section—" His finger indicated an area close to a small stream running into a miniature glass pond among some model trees.

Bruce saw that Khomich was ready to explode. He took Jany's arm. "We don't know what the hell you're talking about, Doctor."

"I want Professor Richards here immediately or my men will go out there to find him," Khomich snapped, "I don't care what stupid scientists' games you are playing."

"I will take you to Richards," Jany said calmly.

They followed him through the big house. Through half open doors they saw people working in laboratories and workshops. Jany stopped at a steel door. Above it was an illuminated sign: CRYOGENIC ROOM—NO ADMITTANCE. Jany pushed a serrated plastic card into a slot on a control panel. A green light came on above the door, which slid open. They stepped into a brightly-lit room with a low ceiling. The air was cold. The door closed behind them. Jany went to a large instrument console and started pressing switches. The room's lighting dimmed, to be replaced by a low, pinkish glow. He punched a series of numbered buttons.

From a bank of what looked like large filing drawers began slowly to emerge a long, metal cabinet.

The room seemed to become even chillier.

They looked down into the cabinet.

"You wanted to see George Richards," Jany said with a little sweep of his hand.

"He's dead!" Khomich exclaimed.

Bruce frowned. George Richards's eyes were shut. The interior of the cabinet was lined with a shiny metal. The naked body was submerged in a thick, opaque liquid—only the face above the surface. Clamped to every part of the head and body were thin gold wires. The face was deathly pale. There was no sign of breathing.

"You will understand cryogenic techniques, Bruce," said Jany. To Khomich he said, "He is not dead. He is in suspended animation—on ice you might say."

"But if that's Richards—who did we hear on the radio?"

"That was George as well."

"I am putting you under arrest," Khomich said firmly. "All operations will cease immediately—we will radio for doctors—"

"Why don't you see all of Project Arcadia before you do anything stupid?" Jany snapped.

"I have seen enough—"

Bruce shook his head. "The Commissioner's instructions were to evaluate the entire project—we want to see everything." He followed Jany back to the instrument panels. Jany pressed two switches. The metal cabinet slid back into the wall. The lighting returned to normal.

"Life support systems?" Bruce asked, looking at the dials and electrographs.

"Yes—we have seventeen guests in deep-freeze at the moment. All bodily functions are monitored and controlled by this analog computer—it can react automatically to a very wide variety of input variables. The technique was evolved at Houston for the Stellar Probe project. Our longest resident has been here for three months. As far as we know, there is no reason why suspended life could not be maintained indefinitely—even past the normal life span."

For the first time, Khomich looked doubtful. "You have *seventeen* people—in these cabinets?" Bruce asked.

"You will understand when you see what else we can do."

"Is that titanium lining the cabinets? I wondered why you needed two tons of it."

"So that's how you got onto us? We always knew there was a risk of somebody checking on the missing materials."

"It came out in a routine stock audit. How long has all this been going on, Jany?"

"About two years. We went operational six months ago. Now, if you will come this way."

"When I sat on that Board you were working on genetic engineering. Has it anything to do with that?"

"You will see. As a scientist, you know how obsessive we can be."

"So when we vetoed your pet project, you simply carried on illegally? And Richards backed you because he'll do anything to prove he's bigger than the WFC administration. Who else is involved?"

"All of us here are deeply involved."

"I mean at top level."

Jany shrugged. "I do not know if George told any of his senior colleagues—everyone here took a vow of secrecy. Here we are—the clinic, as we call it."

Several people in white coats looked at them with unmistakable hostility. "Mary—can you operate the projector for us?" Jany said to a dark-haired girl who was working what Bruce recognized as an infrared spectrograph. They went into a small room. Jany pulled out chairs in front of a screen. "We'll go through the whole sequence, Mary."

The lights dimmed. The first slide came up.

"Recognize that, Bruce?"

"It's a single cell—human?"

"Right. From the liver of an adult male." The second slide was of two identical blobs. "The single cell has replicated—these photomicrographs are all of the same culture. You know anything about cell-cloning, Bruce?"

"I know it was banned."

"All scientists are branded as heretics at some stage—if they are any good. This is known as cell-cloning, Staff-Commander. I'll try to explain in layman's terms. We have about fifty million million cells in our bodies. Each contains the twenty-three pairs of chromosomes which carry the full genetical blueprint for our physical entities. Normally, reproduction starts at a half-cell—meiosis—when the male sperm and female ovum fuse to form a single cell carrying hereditary material from both parents. That first cell then starts dividing equally—mitosis. For cloning, we use the process called anucleation. We remove the nucleus from a single cell and replace it with the nucleus of a sex-cell from the same donor, making sure it is of the donor's sex. The fertilized cell is then induced to replicate itself—as in the womb. All the hereditary material comes from the original donor of the cell.

We induce replication by putting the cell in a culture media made from twenty different amino acids—these make the necessary proteins for the cell to develop and divide. Proteins form the structure of the body and they also make enzymes, which control the body's chemical reactions. Once the original cell has started to divide in the culture, it is merely a case of providing an artificial womb environment. Although we have special sex cells, the fact is that *all* our cells contain the twenty-three pairs of chromosomes that make us the individuals we are. So we can produce an identical twin to the person we took the original cell from—only, with Project Arcadia, there is one very important difference—which you should find fascinating, Bruce."

"You were specifically forbidden to experiment with cloning, Jany. God knows, I detest the WFC bureaucracy, but I agreed with them on that."

"Galileo was also forbidden to challenge the ruling assumptions of his time. Keep showing the sequence, Mary."

At the next slide, Bruce drew in a sharp breath. Khomich frowned, glancing uneasily at Bruce.

"That's right," said Jany, a slight note of triumph coming into his voice. "Beginning to look like a foetus now. Of course, we have cheated—by now we are adding a variety of growth hormones—this sequence is from one of our earliest attempts. As we became more sophisticated, we hurried the process along by adding cells from different parts of the body. Look—see the heart beginning to beat?"

"You mean you have actually replicated a living human embryo?"

"*That* is simple. Even before I was disciplined, people were making tissue cultures and incubating cell colonies." Jany laughed. "They thought that transferring me to plant biology would keep me out of mischief! Now—here is Stage Two. We are now using ordinary photography—notice that our little man is wearing an oxygen mask. In normal terms he has been born—and I want you to note that these photographs are still from the same sequence, still from that first single cell . . ."

They were looking at a perfectly normal, naked, well-proportioned adult male!

The lights went on. Jany thanked the girl. She put the boxes of slides into a cabinet and left the projection room. Jany smiled at their suspicious faces. "Yes—the sequence was shown in correct order and everything came from one cell."

"That was a fully-developed man! Even if you

could do it, a sequence like that would have taken eighteen years at least—"

"So how could I have shown you slides of such an advanced cloning technique from eighteen years ago?" Jany stood up, his face glowing with triumph. "Bruce—those slides were all taken between September and November of last year. From single cell to fully-developed adult male in forty-three days! And believe me—we have become a lot more sophisticated since last year!"

Khomich looked impatiently from Bruce to Jany and then at Bruce again. Bruce stared at the Frenchman, who seemed delighted at his bewilderment.

"And that is not even half of it, Bruce," he said enthusiastically. "Do you realize that the final sequence of photographs were all life-size?"

"Life-size? But they were—"

"Exactly! Why do you think we had to work in total secrecy? That fully-developed male you saw—his name is Carrere, a radio-operator. He is out in the garden at this moment."

"It's the wrong time for jokes, Jany."

"Bruce—did you ever hear about my mini-wheat fiasco in New Mexico? We were using polyploidy and growth hormones to produce a bigger wheat—but what did I do? Quite accidentally I grew ears of wheat about twenty times *smaller* than normal. Instead of a Growth Stimulating Factor, I'd come up with a Growth Inhibiting Factor. Naturally, it was not considered a great triumph to produce micro-wheat with a world food shortage but—" he smiled modestly "—well, I'm well-known as a maverick, although I prefer to regard it as devotion to pure science. I isolated the hormones which produced the Growth Inhibiting Factor, then I evolved the chemical formula for synthesizing the GIF. The miniaturizer you might call it. That was when I got in touch with George Richards—he has always been on the side of pure science against the dictates of bureaucracy. It worked with individual organs—we could produce a functional human liver to any size we wished. We tried it on fish and mice—and then pigs—on a trial and error basis, of course. We had our fair share of monsters at the start—but even I was surprised by what we could produce—micro-fish—complete in every detail! Then mice and pigs. And finally—human beings!"

"Are you serious, Jany?"

"Of course! Why else did we have to steal the equipment? Genetical engineering is the single most emotive issue of recent history—but imagine the outcry if we combined identical-twin cloning with miniaturization! We had to go on with it, of course, we had no choice—it is going to be the salvation of the human race!"

"What is?" Khomich demanded. "Making us all dead bodies in freezing cabinets?"

Jany was amused by Khomich's stupidity. "You understand what I have been trying to explain, Professor. Believe me, it works. Once we have a single cell, we can clone identical twin replicas of any person alive on earth. A hybrid computer with an optical monitoring capability is programmed to control the replication—we can't simply produce a perfectly proportioned micro-man because volume and weight increase or decrease at a ratio of eight times to each doubling or halving of the size. Adjustments have to be made or the muscles would be so strong you would rip your arm off if you lifted something heavy. The smaller organism also needs a much higher metabolism rate to make up for the extra heat loss caused by the proportionally large increase in the body's surface area. So the computer stimulates cell division with one set of hormones and controls the size to which the organs and muscles and bones grow with the GIF hormones."

Khomich looked at Bruce. "Is he telling us that they have produced—small people?"

Jany threw up his arms in triumphant excitement. "You've got it! People thirty-five times smaller than life-size! Micro-people—some of our lab technicians have nicknamed them *micronauts!* That is what Project Arcadia is all about—that is why your soldiers cannot go into the garden. There are six people out there somewhere—micro-people! Before you saw them, you might have crushed them to death under your boots!"

And so Man's last hope, Project Arcadia, begins. In this bizarre experiment the six scientists probe the ultimate frontier, risking their lives in the strangest land that ever existed.